TWICE BRIGHTLY

Harry Secombe

Robson Books

This paperback edition published in Great Britain in 1999 by
Robson Books, 10 Blenheim Court, Brewery Road, London
N7 9NT

British Library Cataloguing in Publication Data
A catalogue record for this title is available from the British
Library

ISBN 1 86105 264 2

Printed and bound in Great Britain by Creative Print and Design
(Wales), Ebbw Vale.

For Spike, Peter and Mike — who were there

My thanks to Jennifer
who badgered me to finish this book,
to Jane
who badgered Jennifer to badger me,
and to Myra
who was all set from the start.

This is essentially a work of fiction although, naturally, I have drawn on my own experiences in the variety theatre for its creation. It is not intended to be autobiographical, nor are any of the characters other than imaginary. Any real names I have mentioned are synonymous with the world of variety at that time. Any resemblance to actual persons living or dead is purely coincidental.

H.S.

Sunday Night

He stood uncertainly outside the station, clutching his suitcase with the rope tied around it in his right hand and the battered brief-case containing his pyjamas and band parts in his left. The clock in a nearby church boomed eleven times, sounding sombre and reproachful in the rain-soaked night.

The journey up from London had been dreary and uncomfortable and the cardboard sandwich he had washed down with a pint of tepid bitter at Crewe lay watchfully in his stomach, ready to make a reappearance.

Because he had elected to carry his own luggage, the only porter in the huge echoing station had refused him information about buses and trams to his destination, dismissing him with a sarcastic 'Chap like thee can afford taxi.'

He looked across at the lone taxi gleaming in the rain and then at the driver lounging inside the open door of the cabman's canteen with a steaming mug of tea in his hand. The money in his pocket would not last long if he indulged in luxuries like taxis—it might mean that he'd have to do without a meal later on in the week. Anyway Wally had told him that the digs were not very far from the station, and the directions he had given were clear enough.

Squaring his shoulders, Larry Gower set off to find 3, Windmill Terrace. He had gone about two hundred yards along the main road when he saw the Royalty Theatre poster. His heart quickened, and putting down the cases he wiped his spectacles with his sleeve, the better to read it. This was what he had always dreamed of—his name on a theatre bill. He focused his eyes, expecting his name to leap out at him, but it didn't.

9

Julie Tempest was the top name in bold black letters, with the legend 'nude but nice' in smaller red type underneath. Then came 'Long and Short—witty wheezes'; 'Simba, born in the jungle'; 'Henri Lamarr—novelty juggler'; 'Wally Winston, a laugh a minute'; 'April and June—happy feet'; and right at the bottom, in very small print, 'Barry Bower, first time here'.

Larry straightened up, shocked and angry. They had not even got his name right. All his pent up frustration burst out. Lifting his foot he gave a hefty kick at the poster, forgetting that it was stuck on a wall. The pain in his toes brought him back to his senses, and moaning softly to himself he picked up his cases again and limped on into the night.

An hour and five different sets of directions later, soaked to the skin, his feet squelching in his shoes and his hands blistered from the worn handles of the cases, he arrived at a small terrace of back-to-back houses, black and unfriendly in the dim light cast by the street lamps at each end.

He rang the bell of No. 3, apprehensive about his reception and the lateness of his arrival. Wally had fixed the digs for both of them, but he was not arriving himself until Monday morning from Sunderland.

A light went on in the window above him, and a few minutes later he heard footsteps descending the stairs and then a scuffling of slippers along the passage. A chain rattled, a bolt slipped, and the door opened about three inches.

'Who's that?' snapped a hard, suspicious voice.

'It's me,' mumbled Larry insanely, then, remembering himself, 'Larry Gower—Wally Winston wrote to fix for me and himself.'

The door opened wider, revealing a vast bulk in a dressing-gown. The light from the hall spilled over Larry's sodden form. He was aware of being scrutinized as he stood hunched against the driving rain. His fair hair was now plastered over his forehead, and his round face with the black-rimmed spectacles wore an anxious, owlish look.

'Come in, then,' said the flat nasal voice, devoid of sympathy. Thankfully Larry picked up his cases and stepped damply into the house.

He was in a narrow hallway, lined with framed photographs, which led to a flight of red linoleum-covered stairs. The door slammed behind him and he turned to face his first landlady. Mrs. Rogers was huge, absolutely huge. Her hennaed hair was crimped in curlers, and with her arms folded over her tremendous bosom, and her woollen dressing-gown reaching to feet that were surprisingly dainty in fancy fur-trimmed slippers, she looked like Boadicea about to order her chariots into the attack. Her fleshy face was undistinguished except for a large, hairy wart just under her lower lip, and as she spoke it writhed as though it had a separate, sinister existence of its own.

'You're late', she accused him. 'There's no supper for you, but there's a bottle of milk in the kitchen. Got your ration book?'

Larry nodded, vaguely frightened. After much fumbling he drew from his inside pocket a tattered ration book. She took it disdainfully, holding it with two fingers.

'This is your room,' she said, flinging open the first of three doors which led off the passage. 'Breakfast is at nine o'clock, in the kitchen.' Gathering her dressing-gown around her she swept up the stairs with all the dignity of a circus elephant.

Larry watched her go, open-mouthed, and then picking up his cases again he entered his room. When he had finally managed to locate the light switch, he stood in open dismay at what he saw.

It was a fair-sized room containing a brass bedstead in one corner covered with a greasy quilt, a wardrobe whose door swung open, a rickety bamboo table, and an armchair from the arms of which grey stuffing protruded obscenely. Apart from a raffia bedside mat, the floor was covered with the same red linoleum he had seen on the stairs. Here and there it curled up like the sandwich he had eaten at Crewe station. On the walls, shaggy Highland cattle browsed in ornamental frames and over the mantelpiece Landseer's 'Monarch of the Glen' peered uncertainly through dusty, broken glass. On the mantelpiece itself stood a framed photograph of a Junoesque lady wearing tights and feathers and a wide false smile. This, on closer inspection, proved to be Mrs. Rogers.

Larry grinned to himself. So she was an old pro then, he thought. Those majestic hams must have given many a stage-door Johnny ideas. He thought of them now, how they must look, and shuddered involuntarily.

He undressed, shivering in the cold damp air. There was a gas fire in the room, but he couldn't get it to work, and he crept under the sheets, his skin shrinking from the icy contact. Blast! He hadn't put the light out. The bulb swung nakedly above the bed, taunting him, and then, as he swung reluctantly out of bed, he felt the urge to empty his bladder.

Wonder where the toilet is, he thought. Should have asked the old bag before she nipped upstairs. He went into the hallway and switched on the light, his stockinged feet sliding on the over-polished lino. The photographs on the wall trained a whole battery of theatrical smiles upon him. They were all photos of pros, all inscribed to Ma Rogers. 'Thanks for a wonderful week, Ma, Yours ever, Randolph Sutton,' 'Ma, I love your apple pie. Lots of luck, Fred Emney.' Double acts, who in real life never spoke to each other, posed with arms entwined; singers sang top notes in tail coats, and cross-eyed comics leered at each other across the walls, all welded together into one happy company—'Ma Rogers' lodgers'.

Larry's need became more urgent as the cold began to seep through his thin socks and he gave up his inspection of the photos and concentrated on finding the toilet. He tried the door which led to the kitchen. The knob clattered under his hand and the door creaked open four inches—and stopped against an obstruction. He pushed harder and was rewarded with a low animal growl that chilled him to the marrow. In the half light from the passage he saw a huge tawny body lying across the door on the inside. An Alsatian dog looked up at him, teeth bared in a snarl.

'Good dog,' Larry croaked, offering a tentative hand. The dog moved its head sideways, watching him like a cobra about to strike. Larry wasn't very good with dogs; they had always had a cat at home, and even that used to bite him sometimes. The situation was desperate, his need was great, but he wasn't going to risk his manhood by stepping over this great lout of an animal. And, almost as important, he didn't want to come face to face with Mrs. Rogers again. He mustn't make a noise, but somehow he must make water.

Shutting the door as quietly as possible he eyed the stairs. Perhaps there was a toilet up there? But that was where Mrs. Rogers slept—he couldn't risk opening the wrong door. Those beefy arms could kill a man. Back in his own room again he searched frantically for a vase, a tin, a waste paper basket—anything. There was nothing.

One solution remained. Open the front door and nip outside to the bushes. That's it, that's it, he repeated to himself as he padded up to the door. With trembling fingers, his face taut with anguish, he slipped the bolt, drew back the chain and opened the Yale lock. The rain hit him in the face through the half-opened door. He should go back for his coat, really, but hell, he'd never make it. I've got to go, I've got to go. He slid round the door and turning his back began to rid himself of his agonizing burden.

The door blew shut behind him, the catch locking firmly into position.

With a light-headed feeling of inevitability he rang the bell again. The previous procedure of the light going on and the footsteps descending was repeated, only this time Mrs. Rogers stood aside and motioned him inside wordlessly.

Larry forced a wet smile. 'Thought I'd have some fresh air.'

Mrs. Rogers humphed and began to walk up the stairs again. On the fifth step she turned and in a grim monotone said, 'The toilet is the first door on the right at the top of the stairs.'

Larry slopped back into his room, frozen to the bone. Clawing off his soaking pyjamas he wrapped himself in the top blanket and crept miserably into bed. Mercifully, sleep came quickly to him. On the pillow his face without the spectacles looked strangely helpless and bereft.

Monday

He awoke to the sound of violent banging on the door and a shrill voice calling, 'It's eight o'clock, no breakfast after nine.'

The grey light filtering through the grubby lace curtains made the room look even worse than it had the previous night. Above Larry's head a large discoloured crack ran half way across the ceiling, stopping abruptly at the light fitting, and a stain the shape of Italy decorated the wallpaper by the side of 'The Monarch of the Glen'.

Larry lay looking at the stain, sleepily tracing the Naples coastline. Could do with a bit of that sunshine now, he mused. Wonder what Concetta is doing? He smiled secretly, remembering the warmth of her generous bosom, the slight suspicion of a moustache on her upper lip which always used to bead with perspiration when they made love, the way she used to look up at him, her dark eyes afloat with tenderness. Warmth began to creep back into his body and he sighed regretfully. That line of thought would not do him any good. Naples and the army were a hell of a way off. Still, Wally might have some news.

He grinned, thinking of Lance Corporal Wally Winston, his mate, his old army china—the lad himself. He would see him at the theatre at eleven o'clock band call, thank God. Wally had the knack of making others as happy as himself, of catching them up in his net of good humour and bludgeoning them into laughter. Short, wiry and with quick bird-like movements, he was a superb mimic and found humour in any situation. It was Wally who had fixed him this first variety date through his own agent.

They had been together in a 'Stars in Battledress' show in Italy and Wally, who had been a professional comedian before being called up, had encouraged Larry to take up show business after the war. Larry's eccentric humour had appealed to him and he had sensed the untapped source of talent which lay beneath the shy, bespectacled exterior.

When they were demobbed together, only four months ago, Wally had taken Larry along to the Nuffield Centre where entertainers performed for the boys from the services. He had also persuaded his own agent to see the act, which went extremely well with the audience. The agent had promised to put Larry in a variety bill as soon as possible and this was it. The opportunity had come just when Larry was beginning to think of trying another job outside the business.

'Are you up yet?' came from outside the door.

'Shan't be a moment,' shouted Larry guiltily and swung his legs over the side of the bed. Steeling himself for the encounter with the icy lino he launched himself off the mattress and climbed, shivering, into his damp trousers. He found the toilet at the top of the stairs, and after an unsuccessful attempt at using the gas water heater he shaved miserably in cold water.

By the time he had dressed he felt refreshed and ready for his breakfast. Remembering the previous night's experience he opened the kitchen door very carefully, watching for the Alsatian.

The kitchen was warm and cheerful and surprisingly spotless. A table was laid for four in front of a roaring fire and a little man was frying bacon at a gas stove. He turned as Larry entered.

'Locked yourself out last night, eh?' The voice was high-pitched and came from a toothless mouth, slashed in a sharp-nosed face which was salvaged by a pair of twinkling blue eyes.

'I'm Jack Rogers,' he said. 'I'm married to her.' He stabbed his finger at the ceiling. 'The old cow. We used to be an act you know—Jack Rogers and Jill, Knife Throwers Extraordinaire.' He threw the table knife he was using into the air and tried to catch it by the handle. It clattered to the floor. As he stooped to pick it up a low growl came from under the table.

'Get out, you bastard!' he shouted, and the Alsatian emerged, snarling, from its hiding place. Cursing wildly, Rogers kicked the dog towards the back door and aimed a slipper at it as it vanished, tail between its legs, into the yard.

He shuffled back in, red-faced, one slipper missing. 'Can't stand that bloody dog. It's hers. Here's *my* pal.' He moved towards a high-backed chair by the fire and picked up a huge marmalade cat which purred sensuously as Rogers smoothed its silky fur.

'You don't like Rex either do you, Cynthia?' he crooned. Cynthia yawned sleepily and flexed her claws in his old woollen cardigan.

Larry stood with his back to the fire, amused by Rogers's affection for the cat.

'Why did you pack up the business?' he asked, savouring the new word.

Rogers put the cat down, and returning to the stove he lifted off the frying pan. 'Got her in the thigh with a burning hatchet during my blindfold bit,' he said, heaping bacon and egg on a plate for Larry. 'Pity I didn't make a good job of it while I was at it. She's never forgiven me, and that was fifteen years ago, at the Alhambra, Bradford.' He cackled suddenly, causing the cat to look up sharply from her toilet in front of the fire.

'A bit further up and I might have lost me hatchet.' Rogers demonstrated coarsely.

Larry reddened and bent over his plate. 'Nice bacon,' he said, forking some into his mouth, wishing to change the subject. To hear an older man talking about his wife in this way was embarrassing to him; and he thought of his own parents' soft-spoken affection for each other.

'Do all the cooking here myself,' said Rogers proudly. 'That's the only reason she puts up with me. She can't boil a bloody egg herself. I'm the guv'nor in the kitchen—the rest of the house is hers, but I'm in charge here.' He slapped his chest with a tattooed hand, and immediately burst into a fit of coughing which was so prolonged that Larry became alarmed.

'First World War,' wheezed Rogers when he began to get his breath back.

'Mustard gas?' enquired Larry solicitously.

'Manchester,' gasped Rogers. 'Fell in the canal coming from the sergeants' mess one night. Had a weak chest ever since.'

Further reminiscence was cut short by the arrival of a young lady in curlers and a torn dressing-gown. She plumped herself down in a chair, took a half-smoked cigarette from her pocket, and resting her elbows on the table motioned Larry to light it. He lit a match, and taking his hand she applied the light to her cigarette, eyeing him boldly.

'Ta.'

She blew a cloud of smoke in the air and began to cough, the sound reaching deep into her chest. Larry couldn't help himself.

'Fall in the canal, too?' he asked.

This set Rogers off and the two of them barked a bronchial duet while Larry sat uncomfortably waiting for them to finish. When they had both recovered Larry was relieved to see that Rogers had not taken exception to his remark. The girl, however, said 'What canal? I'm bronchial and that's nothing to laugh at.'

'Just a gag Mr. Rogers and I were sharing,' Larry said hastily. 'No offence meant. I'm Larry Gower. I'm working at the Royalty this week.'

'So am I,' replied the girl, smiling for the first time. It changed the character of her face completely and compensated for the smudged lipstick and black-rooted blonde hair. 'My name's April, of April and June. We're on the bill too. You a friend of Wally's?'

Larry nodded.

April giggled. 'He's a boy isn't he? June's looking forward to seeing him again. We had a marvellous time with him and Ron Rollett at Blackburn. June's here too, she should be down in a minute.'

Just then Rogers placed her plate in front of her. She reached up and kissed him noisily on the cheek. 'How's my lover this morning?'

Rogers hooted delightedly. 'There's life in the old dog yet,' he said putting his hand on her knee and squeezing.

'You dirty old swine! Get on with the breakfast.' Mrs. Rogers stood in the doorway, her mouth set firm. The cat arched its back and spat angrily before disappearing under the table. Rogers turned back to the stove, mumbling. His wife looked stonily at April, who tossed her head defiantly then picked up her knife and fork and began eating her breakfast. Mrs. Rogers stared at the plates. She pointed an accusing finger at her husband. 'You're giving them too much bacon again. I hope it's *your* rations you're dishing out.'

Rogers muttered an old army expression which startled Larry and produced a smothered titter from April.

'And I don't want any trouble from you lot. If I find any nonsense going on I'll have you out in the street, lock, stock and barrel.' She looked at the clock on the mantelpiece. 'Where's that other girl? It's five to nine and she'll get no breakfast after nine, I'm telling you!'

As if on cue the missing guest stumbled over the threshold, her face blank with sleep. She was taller than April and had none of the other girl's coarseness. Her dark hair was cut short and framed her heart-shaped face with an abundance of soft, tumbled curls. Even beneath the shapeless wrap her figure was obviously well formed and she walked towards her place at the table with a fluidity of movement which had Larry breathing sharply through his nose.

' 'Morning, all,' she said, a Northern accent discernible in a voice still husky from sleep.

'Only just in time,' declared Mrs. Rogers, frustrated, and with one more glare round the kitchen she left, slamming the door.

Jack Rogers blew a toothless raspberry over his shoulder, and April stuck out a white-coated tongue at the closed door.

'Old bag,' she exclaimed, pushing her empty plate away. 'By the way, this is June,' she said to Larry. 'This is Barry Bower, a friend of Wal's, he's on the bill with us this week.'

'Larry Gower,' said Larry with a touch of asperity. Would they never get his name right?

June nodded sleepily. 'Delighted,' she said, not really meaning it.

Larry smiled uncertainly and lapsed into silence, content just to watch the newcomer. There was nothing symmetrical about her features, yet their very irregularity was attractive in itself. A slight scar cut into her upper lip giving it a sweet upward curve on the right side, and her eyes, though large and brown, had a fullness of the lower lids which gave them the appearance of twin setting suns.

So this was Wally's girl. Pity. He took off his spectacles and polished them, hoping she would notice that without them he didn't look too bad himself. Funny thing, he always felt more sure of himself and less self-conscious when he could not see other people. That was why, even later on, he never wore his spectacles on the stage; his short-sightedness was a shield against the world. Unable to see individual faces in the audience, he could imagine them as a big pink mass of clay to be worked on and shaped to his own design. Without glasses, everybody was smiling, the auditorium was full of happy faces. To see them as they really were, fidgeting in their seats, fussing with their programmes, sometimes scowling, sometimes indifferent, would have terrified him. It was not his spectacles that were rose-tinted, but his eyeballs.

He put his glasses back on, and looked at June to see what effect he had made. She burped absent-mindedly.

'Pardon me,' she said. Larry pushed back his chair and made his excuses.

'See you at the theatre,' called April giving him a saucy wink.

Jack Rogers ran after him. 'Good luck for tonight, son,' he said. 'It's your first date, ain't it? They're a bit sticky Monday first house, but they'll be fine by the end of the week. Do any juggling?' Larry shook his head.

'Pity, that,' said Rogers. 'They like a bit of juggling here. Never mind, son—you'll be all right.'

Larry thanked him and returned thoughtfully to his room to pack his stuff for the theatre. Already his stomach was beginning to churn at the prospect of the ordeal ahead. It was all right entertaining the service lads, where any sort of rough and ready comedy would do, but he was now in a different class altogether. Competition was keen among comedians these days. So many budding Max Millers and Tommy Trinders were leaving the services, determined to try their luck in the variety theatre after their concert party experiences. Only a few could possibly survive. A lot of them were first generation show business like himself, with no previous professional experience, but there were quite a few who were picking up the threads of stage careers interrupted by the war. They at least had contacts in the theatre, and the agents gave them preference over the amateurs. Wally was one of them, though he had been big-hearted enough to use his influence to help his old army mate to get on. It was to be the survival of the fittest.

Larry put his suitcase on the bed and opened it. Well, the double-breasted dinner jacket didn't look too bad, and the fine patina of grease on the lapels would shine like silk in the stage lighting. The trousers were a little frayed at the bottom, but not all that much, and the patent shoes were as good as new. Not a bad bargain at all, he told himself. Eight quid the lot, and the bow tie thrown in free by the generous proprietor of the used clothes shop he had gone to in Brixton. It would do until he hit the big time, anyway. He began to whistle as he closed the lid and retied the rope round his case.

A watery sun nudged its way shyly through the grey clouds, as, filled with a mixture of excitement and apprehension, he walked out of the front door in search of the theatre.

The Royalty Theatre was an old variety house which had seen better days, but was now a murky shadow of its former self. It was situated in a part of the city that was no longer fashionable, and the stone cherubs, which had long ago been turned into little urchins by soot and grime, looked sadly down from their perches over the entrance hall onto a street which contained four pubs, a rupture appliance and rubber goods shop, and a glue factory. The cracked glass show-cases which had once contained pictures of Mr. Dan Leno, Florence Ford, Marie Lloyd and George Robey, now displayed Miss Julie Tempest in a provocative pose behind a potted palm, and pictures of the rest of the current week's company, including one of Larry himself. It was one of a half dozen 10 × 8 prints taken by an amateur photographer friend in Cardiff especially for the occasion, as his contract stipulated that he had to supply six front-of-house photographs, to be sent on the week before. It showed Larry in a pop-eyed, open-mouthed pose, with his right finger placed stiffly against his nose, and appeared to have been taken underwater with a box Brownie; but at least it was recognizable as Larry.

He walked round the side of the theatre looking for the stage door, and found it half-way up a debris-littered alley. The door was open and he eased himself and his cases into the narrow passage. In a little cubby-hole surrounded by theatre display cards, a wizened old man in a cloth cap sat smoking a pipe. Larry put down his cases and cleared his throat.

The old man took the pipe out of his mouth. 'You Barry Bower?'

'No. *Larry Gower*—they spelled my name wrong on the bills,' babbled Larry, almost hysterically.

'Nowt to do with me, lad, I didn't write 'em,' said the door-keeper complacently. 'You're in number twelve dressing-room with Wally Winston and Tom Tillson from the lion act. Sorry I can't help with your bags.' The old man patted an empty sleeve.

'First World War?' asked Larry.

'Fell under a train in Sheffield,' he replied, handing Larry a key from the rack behind him. 'There's a letter here for yer, too.'

It was in his mother's handwriting, so he pocketed it to read later when he had sorted himself out, and picked up his cases.

The dressing-room was on the second floor and as he unlocked the door he reflected painfully that if he didn't succeed in show business he could always get a job as a porter—he was getting plenty of practice. Inside the room three rickety chairs stood in front of a cracked mirror which ran the whole length of the far wall. There was a sink in the corner, which no one had bothered to clean up after the last occupants. A half-open window looked out over the glue factory.

Larry put his case on the shelf in front of the right-hand side of the mirror and began to unpack. He had just hung his dress suit on one of the rusty hooks on the green-painted wall near the door, when he heard Wally's voice. 'Hello! Hello! Hello! How's the old Welsh wizard, then?' Larry flung open the door, eager to see his friend again.

'Give us a hand with this perishing trunk, mate!' Wally was struggling with a huge cabin trunk at the foot of the second flight of stairs. Leaping down the steps two at a time, Larry seized Wally's hand and pumped it vigorously, slapping him on the back.

'Am I glad to see you, you old devil,' he yelled.

Wally staggered back under the onslaught. 'If this is how you treat your friends, I'm glad I'm not your enemy,' he laughed breathlessly. 'Let's get this ruddy thing upstairs and I'll give you all the news.'

Together they humped the trunk into the dressing-room, chipping the wall here and there as they did so.

'About time they gave the place a coat of paint anyway,' said Wally, straightening his back. He was wearing a well-cut black Crombie overcoat with a yellow scarf and a dashing grey trilby. Larry felt a twinge of envy at his friend's affluence, but dismissed it immediately. Good luck to him, he thought.

Wally sat in a chair and smilingly looked Larry up and down, pushing back his trilby with a gloved hand. 'You look a bit umpty, Larry me old amico,' he said. 'Old Ma Rogers frighten you, did she?' Larry nodded, grinning.

'A bit,' he confessed, and went on to recount his experience of the previous night. Wally shouted with laughter when he had finished.

'Lucky you didn't get pneumonia. By the way, is June at the digs?'

'Yes, she is,' Larry replied, flickering his eyebrows.

'You lay off her, you Celtic Casanova. The other one's yours —no trouble there, boy.' He winked lecherously.

'Well, how did you go in Sunderland?' asked Larry hastily, not wishing to get involved in a conversation about the girls, aware that he was attracted to June.

'I paralyzed them Saturday second house, but the rest of the week was murder. I was second spot and they only gave me eight minutes.' He spread his hands wide. 'After all, how can you establish yourself in that time? They were still looking for their seats when I came on. The girls did a quick four-minute routine, and then, stand by for blasting, it's your uncle Wally. They eat their young alive up there. I tried a new bit Saturday, though, and it went like a bomb.' He stood up, tucking back the chair. 'Remember that officer routine you used to do in the concert party?' Larry nodded. 'Well, I did the old funny walk with my hands in my pockets, and the salute bit.' He proceeded to demonstrate, walking to and fro across the room.

Larry watched, stunned, forcing himself to smile. 'Funny thing, Wal, but I was thinking of doing it myself in the act. You know, I've been working on it since the Nuffield Centre show, when your agent came to see me, and I—'

Wally cut him short. 'Larry boy,' he said, throwing his arm round his friend's shoulder. 'I didn't think you'd want to use it again. Blimey, I'm sorry, china—come to think of it, you'd do well with it here. Where in the act were you thinking of doing it?'

'Just before the duet with myself—you know, the Jeanette MacDonald and Nelson Eddy bit.' Larry was eager to talk about his act. His uncertainty about its success had been haunting him ever since he'd received news of this first variety date.

Wally shook his head doubtfully. 'It's rather tricky there. You want to open with it, and get the drummer to give you the temple blocks on the funny walk. By the way, what are you doing for on and off music—you know—to bring you on stage and take you off?'

'I thought of using "Happy Days Are Here Again"—it's the only orchestration I've got, except for "Sweethearts" and that's mostly piano,' said Larry.

Wally clapped a hand to his head. 'That's what I'm using! The management won't allow us both to use it—and fair's fair, Larry, it's been my signature tune for years.'

Larry's heart sank. He couldn't possibly get another orchestration done in time for the show, and yet he saw Wally's point. In variety a signature tune was very important, almost sacred. A successful performer could get applause as soon as his particular tune was played—even before he made an appearance on stage. He cursed himself for not remembering that Wally had always used it.

'I'll have to try and think of something else,' he said apologetically.

'Old Dan will get his lads to busk something for you,' said Wally, glad that Larry had put up no resistance. 'Come on down and see if they've started the band call yet. Put your books down?'

'What books, where?' asked Larry, puzzled. He was learning a lot of new theatrical terms on his first day.

'Your band books—your music.'

'Oh!' said Larry, reaching into his case for his music, 'It's here.'

Wally explained as they walked down the stone steps to the stage. 'It's an old unwritten law in variety that the first books down on the stage, starting from the centre mike, are the first ones to be rehearsed. Doesn't matter if you're the star of the show, it's first come first served. That's democracy, mate.'

They walked onto the stage, where half a dozen stage hands were working under the supervision of a large man whose greasy flannel trousers, belted over his pot belly, revealed an overlap of six inches of grubby woollen underpants.

' 'Ullo, young Wally,' he said in a gruff, kindly voice. ' 'Aven't seen you since you were called up. Learned any new jokes in the army?'

Wally laughed. 'Plenty, but none I can tell on here.' He turned to Larry. 'This is my ex-army pal, Larry Gower. Larry —Joe Armsworth, the best stage manager in the business.'

Joe rumbled a laugh which shook his huge belly, and gripped Larry's hand with his own callused one.

24

'You want to watch him, son, he'll nick all your material,' he said, jerking his thumb at Wally. 'Did he ever tell you about the time when Max Wall had a go at him?'

Wally flushed, and grinning uneasily took Larry down to the front of the stage where the piles of band books were already stretching away from the microphone in the centre of the footlights. 'Put your books down quick before anybody else gets in. You'll have a long wait as it is. There's only the lion act and the girls from the digs to come, from the look of this lot. I put mine down when I came in.' He indicated his own leather-bound books with his foot. They were only three in from the beginning of the line. Embarrassed, Larry dropped his single sheets of music at the end, conscious of their nakedness beside the opulent, gold-lettered, maroon and black leather covers of their neighbours.

Wally excused himself and went over to talk to the growing group of pros assembling in the stalls. Larry was glad to be alone for a while to assimilate the strangeness and excitement of this new atmosphere. Behind him Joe Armsworth was manoeuvring into position a faded back-cloth upon which was painted a gross misrepresentation of a garden in full bloom. Hollyhocks and roses grew in tired profusion round a lop-sided sundial. A number of shamefaced trees of no recognizable species sprawled in the background, and the picture was completed by a bird—half seagull, half swan—which appeared to be flying backwards into a tree top.

'Up on your long a bit, Charlie,' Joe shouted to an unseen character operating the ropes from the flies above the stage. The garden tilted crazily. 'No, no, not that much! The bloody cloth will tear in a minute. Come on now, pull your finger out. That's better. Now—up on your short. Right, tie off.' The backcloth settled dustily into position. 'All right, now drop in the street cloth.'

Larry looked out towards the red plush auditorium. At the back of the stalls two turbaned cleaners shrilled a popular tune as they pushed up the seats and searched out the debris of Saturday's audiences. Another cleaner leaned out of one of the boxes at the side of the stage and shouted to her colleagues below.

'You'll never guess what I've found up here. The dirty devils! I wonder when they found the time.' She shook her mop out into the stalls and disappeared singing through the box door. The pros chatting in the front seats roared with laughter.

The circle rail was being assaulted by a wax-moustached man in commissionaire's trousers, his wide braces scarlet against a striped flannel shirt. He rubbed the rail vigorously with a yellow cloth, making the brass gleam in the light from the stage. Above the circle the balcony looked bare and lifeless, the wooden benches giving it an air of desolation. It must only be full at weekends, when all the other seats have gone, Larry mused. Wonder how much they can see from up there? He remembered the wonderful evenings he had spent sitting on similar benches in the gods at the Swansea Empire, discomfort forgotten in the magic of the stage performance.

There's not much magic here, he thought, looking at the drab auditorium and the noseless cupids chasing each other in weary plaster pursuit round the front of the circle. And yet there was something he could feel—an excitement, a latent energy lying beneath the surface grime, needing only the lights and the music to bring it pulsing to the surface. He felt it in himself, this force, and he knew then with more certainty than ever before that this was his destiny. Whether he proved to be a good, bad or indifferent performer, the theatre had him trapped in its dusty coils and he was a willing and eager victim.

The activity in the theatre was beginning to increase. From somewhere beneath the stage a trumpeter blared a phrase from 'The Chocolate Soldier', melting disastrously on the top note, and a tall, stoop-shouldered man appeared at the conductor's stand in the orchestra pit. He was wearing a heavy overcoat and scarf, and opening a brown paper carrier bag he took out a conductor's baton and a pair of mittens.

Realizing that the band call was about to start, Larry found the door at the side of the stage which Wally had used and took a seat in the stalls a few rows behind the other, still chattering, performers The feeling of not yet belonging was strong in him.

The conductor tapped irritably on the stand with his baton. 'Come on, lads, 'urry up. There's a lot to go through this morning.'

At this cue six gentlemen made their appearance carrying a variety of battered instruments. They were all clad in overcoats and were complaining bitterly about the cold.

'I can't feel me finger ends,' said the grey-haired violinist seating himself reluctantly in front of his music stand.

'The way you play, it might be a bloody improvement,' remarked the conductor sarcastically.

'Watch it, Dan,' said the drummer, 'he's our shop steward.'

The conductor started to say something, then changing his mind declared, 'We'll do the overture first, lads. "Chocolate Soldier"—the parts are all out. Right, in four with me.' He raised his baton, his spectacles bright in the light of his stand, the beaky nose with its dew-drop eagerly alert.

'Just a moment.' It was the saxophonist, a bald-headed man, who was obviously not ready. 'I'll have to change me reed.'

The conductor dropped his arms in disgust, shaking his head but not saying anything. Hands on hips, he stood in an elaborate attitude of waiting until the fumbling saxophonist was ready.

'Right?' The bald man nodded.

'Right then, off we go.' Up went the baton again and the six-piece orchestra crashed into life. Regardless of split notes from the trumpet and a complete lack of rhythm from the pianist, the conductor swayed with the music, humming loudly and only stopping when the bass player, who was not quite as tall as his instrument, dropped his bow.

Three times they played the selection from 'The Chocolate Soldier', each time getting a little further from the composer's original intention, until at last the conductor brought down his stick on a welter of wrong notes and declared himself satisfied. Even to Larry's untrained ear, it sounded dreadful, and he wondered fearfully what they would say when he asked them to busk his music.

'Who's first?' Dan turned round to the performers behind him.

'It's us, dear, Long and Short, comedy with a difference.' A tall figure detached itself from the group in the stalls and walked languidly up the steps at the side of the stage, followed by a very short man wearing a teddy bear coat.

'Nice to see you, Jimmy,' said the conductor as the languid figure handed him the band books.

'Wish I could say the same for you, darling,' said Jimmy Long, smiling to take away the sting. 'Same act as before. We open with "Happy Days Are Here Again".'

Larry stiffened and looked across at Wally, who shrugged his shoulders. He came over to Larry.

'That's done it, mate,' he laughed. 'Now neither of us can do it. Whoever uses the tune first at band call has the right to do it for the rest of the week. That's why it's always best to get in first with your music.'

Up on the stage the two female impersonators were giving instructions to Dan on how to play their music.

'When Georgina here comes on in the tight gold lamé,' said Jimmy Long, indicating his partner, 'we want "St. Louis Blues", as sexy as your lads can make it.'

Dan looked at his 'lads' and then back at Jimmy, 'It's going to be a bit of a struggle,' he said.

'Play it anyway, and let's see how it sounds,' replied Jimmy hopefully.

The conductor nodded, and raised his stick. 'Sexy as you can then, lads, in four with me.'

The band quavered uncertainly into action. When they had finished Jimmy Long shook his head slowly, and passed his hand over his face. 'You've got a band of ruddy virgins down there, darling.'

The violinist stood up and shook his bow at Jimmy. 'We'll have none of them insults here, you old pouf,' he shouted indignantly.

'See, now you've upset the shop steward,' said Dan, not without malice.

'Sorry, dear,' answered Jimmy, unperturbed. 'Keep your

hair on your G string. Well, let's get on with the rest of the opera, don't want to keep the others waiting, do we?'

Wally nudged Larry. 'They're very funny, those two. Dead queer, of course, but they keep it to themselves. They've been going for years. Done some good work in their day, too, but George has been ill for a long time and Jimmy has passed up a lot of solo offers just to look after him. Wish I could get a wife who'd be as faithful.'

Larry could not make up his mind whether to feel sorry for the two men or revolted by their relationship. He hadn't encountered many homosexuals in his life, and those he had met in the army had always been figures of fun. Yet, watching the pair as they finished their band call and walked off the stage with linked arms, he felt a stirring of compassion for them.

The rehearsal dragged on. The female impersonators were followed by a woman wearing severe black-rimmed spectacles, a shapeless mackintosh and a coloured headscarf, who received a very hearty welcome from the conductor. She commenced her run-through in a brisk, no-nonsense manner, beating out the rhythm firmly with her flat-heeled shoes as she explained over the music to the drummer how she wanted the tempo.

Larry was surprised to learn that this was Julie Tempest, the striptease artiste, and the week's top of the bill. There was nothing remotely glamorous about her appearance and Larry felt vaguely disappointed.

Wally laughed, seeing his expression. 'She's a proper tartar. That's her old man over in the corner talking to Joe Armsworth.' A small man in a large American-type trilby was talking animatedly with the stage manager. 'He's her manager and by God she doesn't half lead him a dance.'

At that moment the band ground to a halt and Julie Tempest said, 'Right, I suppose that's as near as you'll ever get it. Now let's try the music for the tableaux.'

Dan shuffled the music on his stand then looked up. 'That's all there is here, Julie. We've played all we've got.'

'You mean you haven't got the "Rustle of Spring" down there?' Dan shook his head.

'Tommy!' Julie Tempest's voice screamed. The little man in

the American hat started violently and came scurrying across the stage.

'What's up, love?' he asked, his voice almost a whine.

'Where's the "Rustle of Spring" music?' demanded his wife, thrusting her face into his. 'I'll bet you left it behind last week in Huddersfield. Did you? *Did you?*' Her voice reached a crescendo, causing all other sounds in the theatre to cease, and bringing stage hands from their corners to listen in morbid fascination.

'No, love, honest. I brought all the music out of the pit myself on Saturday night. It must be in one of the cases upstairs. I'll go and look.'

He was off like a scared rabbit before his wife could say any more. She stared after him, her face ugly with contempt.

'Useless bastard,' she declared to the world at large.

Dan looked down at his music and the pros in the stalls all began talking loudly at once.

Larry felt sick at this exhibition of rudeness, identifying himself with the incompetent, down-trodden husband.

'I've found it, love. It was in your trunk with the fans.' The whole theatre breathed a sigh of relief as Tommy ran down-stage waving a bundle of music. She snatched it from him and handed it herself to the conductor with a false laugh.

'You wait till I get him home,' she said, and Tommy permitted himself a wan smile at the company in front before rejoining the stage manager in his corner.

'Watch out for her,' whispered Wally. 'If she takes a fancy to you, she'll drag you into bed before you can say Jack Robinson.'

Larry felt the hair prickle at the back of his neck.

'If she tries anything with me I'll run a mile,' he said.

'I don't know so much,' Wally replied. 'She's got a smashing figure underneath that machintosh, mate. There's plenty there to get hold of.'

Larry shook his head. 'Not for me. I like to do my own chasing anyway. Remember Concetta? Now there was a girl.' His eyes glazed with remembrance, and he felt the old familiar warmth again.

Wally smiled cynically. 'You'd better forget her. I'll bet she's got herself another bedmate by this time. Old Dusty Miller was all lined up there when you left, he was just waiting his chance.'

Larry turned on him indignantly, but before he could say anything, Wally was out of his seat and heading for the stage for his band call.

Larry settled back in his seat, still flushed with anger. The thought of Miller with his thin pencil moustache and patent leather hair pawing Concetta was distasteful in the extreme. Yet he knew in his heart that Wally was right, and the knowledge distressed him. It's about time I grew up, he thought. I always get romantically involved with the girls I take out. Why can't I take my fun where I find it and forget them afterwards, like Wally?

Love 'em and leave 'em, that's me in the future. Harden the old heart, boy. He felt comforted by this resolution and concentrated on Wally, who was going over the music with Dan. He couldn't help admiring his friend's jaunty, professional approach.

'Do you think we could sit next to you, sir?' April and June were standing in the aisle at his side. It was April who had spoken, but he had eyes only for June, who nodded vaguely to him with the same sleepy expression she had worn at breakfast. Here we go again, he thought.

The girls sat one on each side of him. April was wearing a headscarf over her curlers, but June had let her hair blow in the breeze on her walk to the theatre and it was endearingly windswept.

'Done your band call yet?' asked April, fussy and friendly on his left.

'Not yet, but it won't be long now,' said Larry, feeling suddenly nervous.

Wally had finished his call, and the next act, a juggler, had begun. He was a squat, neckless man whose enormous shoulders seemed to grow level with his ears. He addressed the conductor in fast broken English, banging the stage hard with his foot to emphasize the tempo he wanted.

April nudged Larry. 'That's Henri Lamarr. We call him "Droppo" because he's always dropping his clubs.' She giggled. 'He fancies his chance with the girls, too. All that garlic puts me off, though. What are you doing in your act?'

The sudden question threw Larry. 'I haven't decided properly yet,' he stammered, bringing to the surface the fear which had been lurking in his mind all morning.

April's eyes opened wide. 'Hey! You've left it a bit late, haven't you? You must have some idea of what you're going to do.'

'Oh, I've got a pretty good idea, but I don't know how to put it into the best order. Anyway, I shan't use the orchestra much because frankly I haven't got much music.'

Throughout this conversation June had sat dreamily in her seat, taking no part in it. Now she nudged Larry with her elbow. 'I think it's your turn now—you'd better think of something fast.'

Larry turned, startled, towards the stage, and sure enough the conductor was calling for the next act.

'Coming,' he shouted, and stumbling past April's knees he made for the stage, his heart thumping madly and a sick feeling in the pit of his stomach.

He could feel the eyes of the other pros on him as he mounted the steps and picked up his music. He handed the meagre bundle to the conductor in an agony of embarrassment.

Dan turned it over in his hands. 'Is this all?' he asked, incredulously.

Larry nodded. 'Could you play some music for me to come on to, please?' he asked, his voice croaking with nervousness.

Dan looked up, his nostrils twitching. 'What's that? Haven't you got any tab music then?'

Larry's head shook in concert with his knees. He could hear a snort of amusement from the stalls but could not lift his head to look.

Dan's musicians shifted restlessly in their seats, already scenting the beer they would shortly be drinking in the pub next door.

' "Crazy People",' suggested the bass player.

Dan turned on him. 'What did you say?'

'I said "Crazy People". We can busk that.'

'All right then,' agreed Dan, raising his stick. 'Let's have it.'

The sound was awful, but once again Dan seemed satisfied. He looked up at Larry.

'There. You're a lucky young lad. Not many bands could play that without music. Now what else do you want?'

Larry indicated the music which Dan had taken from him, and explained that all he wanted was a few chords in C from the orchestra and the rest could be played on piano only. Dan handed the piano copy to the pianist. ' "Sweethearts" in C,' he said.

'I do it in two voices,' explained Larry, wishing he were dead.

The pianist played a florid introduction, using the full length of the keyboard and making it impossible for Larry to find the note he had to start on.

'Could I just have a C please,' he asked, desperately. The pianist looked pained but Dan, leaning back against the rail, called, 'He doesn't want a bloody solo from you. Give the lad his note.'

Larry thanked him with his eyes and Dan, smiling slightly, winked back at him.

Somehow he managed to get through the song without breaking down, but Larry was conscious of amused looks from the pros when he sang the soprano part. It was supposed to be comedy but he lacked the courage to put the gags in, and just sang the song through without stopping, the quality of his tenor voice showing in spite of his extreme nervousness.

When he had finished Dan nodded approvingly. 'You Welsh?' he asked.

'From Llangyfelach, near Swansea,' Larry replied, a little surer of himself now.

'Thought so. Right, next act.' Dan winked again, and as he went thankfully to his dressing-room, Larry felt he had made a friend.

The two girls in the stalls watched Larry's stocky, retreating figure.

'I think he's lovely,' said April. 'He'll be a star one day, you wait and see.'

June said nothing, but her eyes followed Larry with an awakened interest.

Back in the dressing-room Wally was preparing his place on the table. He had spread a clean square of chintz material in front of the mirror and was now arranging his make-up and toilet requisities. A silver-backed hairbrush gleamed brightly, strangely incongruous in the drab room. He looked up as Larry entered.

'Bet you're glad that's over,' he said.

Larry nodded wordlessly, and straddling one of the rickety chairs he rested his chin on the back, watching his friend.

'You've certainly got all the gear, mate,' he remarked admiringly as Wally flicked traces of powder from his sleeve with a spotless white handkerchief. 'All I've got is two sticks of five and nine and a soap and towel.'

Wally surveyed his belongings with unconcealed pride. 'A pro spends most of his life in dressing-rooms, lad, and nearly all of them are crummy, so I believe in having as much comfort as possible wherever I go.' So saying, Wally reached into his trunk and brought out a brightly-coloured satin cushion which he placed on his chair. With an elaborate display of sensuous pleasure, he slowly lowered himself on to it. The leg of the chair gave way and Wally sprawled on the floor, cushion and all. Larry roared with laughter as his friend struggled to his feet.

'Next time I'll tour my own bleeding chair as well,' he said ruefully before joining in Larry's laughter.

'What's all the row about, then?' A tall, lugubrious individual stood in the doorway.

'Come in, Tom,' called Wally. 'The leg of this chair gave way. It must be the one you train that lion of yours with. This is Tom Tillson, dare-devil lion-tamer.'

Larry shook Tillson's hand, introducing himself as he did so. The other accepted the introduction with no change of expression on his long clown's face, and shuffled forward to the dressing-table with his burden of two carrier bags.

34

'Meat for my animal,' he explained, placing one of the blood-stained bags perilously close to Wally's immaculate display.

'Watch it, Tom,' cried Wally, moving quickly, 'Don't mess up my place.'

Tillson grumbled to himself as he pushed the meat into the corner by the window.

'You've taken the best spot again, I see,' he said. 'All self, some bloody people.' He wiped his hands on his long blue over-coat and flat-footed out of the room.

'He seems a jolly sort of bloke,' said Larry, half amused.

'Oh, never mind him. I've shared with him a few times and he's always like that. That lion of his—you wait till you see it. It's only got two teeth at the front and it's scared of everything. Forest-bred it's supposed to be—Epping Forest, I reckon. Last time we were together on the same bill the lion wouldn't budge from its cage because Bob Napier's performing terrier Susie was barking at it. They nearly had a fight over it, him and Bob.' Wally chuckled at the memory. 'The only thing you've to watch with old Tillson is the booze. He gets a bit of a nuisance when he's on the bottle, but I should think we ought to be able to manage him between us. How about lunch? We can't go back to the digs, we only get breakfast and supper there. Let's have some fish and chips round the corner. It's pretty clean and they're always generous with the chips for the pros.'

Larry agreed wholeheartedly, not wishing to eat alone, and taking his clean towel from his case he folded it in half on the dressing-table. Then, in conscious imitation of Wally, he placed both his brand new sticks of make-up on it and indicated with a flourish what he had done. 'How's that? I've got a long way to go to catch you up, Wal, but I've made a start.'

They looked at each other, smiling, but Larry knew that Wally had caught the implication in his words.

'Nothing better than a bit of healthy competition, Larry,' said Wally, slapping him lightly on the shoulder—but Larry felt a slight drop in the temperature of their friendship and was saddened by its inevitability.

Lunch-time passed quickly enough, with each man, in the embarrassing consciousness of his new-found rivalry, going to great lengths to please the other in the evocation of shared experiences. Afterwards Wally insisted on paying for their lunch and Larry jingled the unspent silver in his trouser pocket, conscious of having lost the first skirmish in their undeclared war.

He made his excuses to Wally as soon as he could, and spent a miserable hour wandering through the mean streets near the theatre, finally coming to rest in a windswept recreation ground where a party of schoolboys was being instructed in the rudiments of Rugby football. The sight of the blue-shorted lads chasing each other about brought back memories of Larry's own childhood in Wales. The tension left his body and he relaxed, grinning, on the hard bench seat. The ball was kicked in his direction and he reached it about three paces ahead of a red-cheeked boy whose agonized panting suggested many an illicit fag smoked in the school lavatory. Larry swept up the ball easily and drop-kicked it back to the teacher.

The master trapped the ball against his chest, falling over his long woollen scarf in the effort. Larry ran forward and helped the red-faced, swearing young man to his feet.

'Stop that bloody sniggering,' he growled at the boys, who were enjoying the scene.

'You're a long way from home,' said Larry, emphasizing his own Welsh accent.

'Good God, man—a fellow Welshman.' Larry's hand was pumped bloodless. 'Wait a minute, let me get these idiots doing something, then we can have a natter. Cockcroft!' A gangling youth in a torn jersey and shorts reaching below his knees came running up. 'Get the boys to practise making a scrum like I showed you and see that they keep their knees down.' He fumbled under his scarf and took from his neck a whistle tied to a piece of string. 'Take this with you.'

The boy gave a snaggle-toothed grin of delight at the sight of the whistle and bounded away in long, hopping strides, blowing with all his might.

36

The master watched him go, shaking his head. 'Look at him. Like a kangaroo, same brain capacity too, mun. Dull as hell—and he's the brightest boy in the class. Thank God I'm only temporary.'

He turned to Larry, smiling, passing a hand through his short sandy hair. He was an inch or two taller than Larry but with less breadth of shoulder, and the short stubby moustache he affected did not disguise his youth.

'My name's Elwyn Thomas. From Tredegar I am, boy. What brings you to this part of the world?'

'I'm at the theatre here this week,' Larry replied, feeling rather important.

'Oh, aye. Actor then, are you?'

'Well, not exactly. I suppose you'd call me a comedian—do a bit of singing as well at the end.' Larry found it suddenly difficult to explain what he did, realizing he wasn't very sure himself.

'I'm an entertainer, like, you know. Larry Gower's my name, only they've spelled it wrong on the bills.' He felt a momentary flash of frustration again.

Thomas looked at Larry with respect. 'Duw,' he said. 'I've never met anybody on the stage. Nearest I ever got to an actor was when Bransby Williams opened our miners' Welfare Hall, and then I only saw the back of his head. I was surprised to see that he gets dandruff like the rest of us. Have you been at it long, then?'

Larry shuffled his feet, unwilling to relinquish his pose as an experienced performer. Then with a laugh he said, 'It's my first week, really. Though I did a lot of entertaining in the army.'

'I used to do a bit of writing for squadron shows when I was in the RAF,' said Thomas, thrusting his hands deep in his duffle coat pockets. 'Used to write sketches and parodies, like. I'd have liked to do some writing for the stage when I came out, but it's a hell of a job to get in. Still, teaching's not too bad as long as you've got your health and strength.'

He turned and looked towards the yelling boys who had

abandoned the ball and were now fighting among themselves. The leaping Cockcroft was agitatedly trying to restore order. 'There's my ruddy audience every day—there, that lot. At least I've got one advantage over you, I can get in amongst 'em and belt 'em round the earhole; which is what I am about to do now. Excuse me.'

Thomas strode quickly to the struggling mass and laying about him, managed to get the boys lined up.

'Right,' he said, 'you'll all be kept in after school for this. Cockcroft!'

The lad came forward hesitantly. His face and jersey were plastered with mud, and he held his hands over a large tear in the front of his shorts. 'T'weren't my fault, sir, they all ganged up on me, sir. And I got mud in me whistle.'

'You'll catch a cold in it as well if you don't get some trousers on.'

Thomas stifled the giggles with a warning finger. 'Put this on and march these idiots back to the school.'

He took off his duffle coat and draped it over the lad's shivering shoulders. Cockcroft was transformed. Shouting orders, he springheeled off across the recreation ground, shepherding his grumbling flock towards the red brick school down the road.

'Well, I'd better follow them,' said Elwyn Thomas.

Larry grinned at the retreating figure of Cockcroft. 'He'd make a marvellous character for the stage,' he said, jumping up and down in imitation of the boy's strange gait.

Thomas laughed. 'You can have him any time. By the way, how about meeting one day for a noggin? Better still—I know quite a crowd of Welsh lads here, so how about me bringing them to the theatre on, say Tuesday night, that's tomorrow? We'll give you some real good Welsh support, boy. Don't worry— we'll buy our own tickets.'

Larry was overjoyed. The prospect of having people out front who were going to be on his side was most reassuring.

'Delighted,' he said. 'And we'll get together after the show then, shall we? If you come round to the stage door and ask for me at the end of the performance—better make it second house—we'll all have a drink together.' Larry made a mental note to go easy with his money and hoped that they would all be beer drinkers.

'So long then, Larry,' called Thomas, trotting off after the boys. 'See you tomorrow night.'

Larry waved, and looking ruefully at his muddied shoes he made his way back in the gathering dusk to the theatre. Now and then he practised the leaping stride of Cockcroft, giggling to himself and drawing strange, sometimes hostile, glances from passers-by.

He obtained the dressing-room key from the stage door-keeper and glanced at the clock. It was now half past four, an hour and three quarters before the first performance—time he sorted out in his mind what he was going to do in his act.

He walked slowly onto the stage, wanting to absorb a bit more atmosphere. The stage hands had all gone, and apart from the light in the stage manager's corner, the only illumination came from two blue pilot lights above the stage. Larry could make out the shadowy outline of an animal cage at the back where the scenery was stacked. Prompted by curiosity he went over to it. His eyes gradually became accustomed to the gloom and he could see clearly the shape of a lion, lying full length on its stomach with its nose pressed against the bars. There was a switch on the wall near the cage. Larry pressed it and a dusty bulb on a long flex came to life in a corner. He stopped about three feet away and peered through his glasses at the animal. This is a *lion*, he thought; the Lord of the Jungle, a legendary creature; the symbol of nobility, the king of beasts. Now here he is, poor sod, cramped in a cage; condemned to twice nightly performances—at least in the Colosseum in Roman times they only did one show a day, with a nice juicy Christian at the end of it. Wonder how tame he is? He clicked his tongue. 'Here, boy,' he said, not knowing how to address a lion.

The animal lifted its head and fixed Larry with a mournful amber stare. Then, opening its jaws wide, it yawned, revealing a mouth lined with blackened tooth stumps, only the large fangs at the front still intact. The jaws shut and the large head slumped forward onto paws which bore no sign of claws. The eyes looked dolefully up at Larry for a second, then closed, and the lion uttered a great shuddering sigh.

'Poor old feller.' Larry felt an immediate affinity with the beast, and was sufficiently moved to walk towards it and pat its head. 'There, boy,' he murmured, fondling the lion's mane. He stopped suddenly, appalled at his own daring, remembering his fear of the Alsatian the previous night. The lion had moved its head sideways, obviously liking the attention it had received. Amazed at the reaction, Larry tickled it behind the left ear. It turned over on its back and rumbled quietly in appreciation, the flea-bitten flanks heaving gently.

Larry murmured soothingly. 'Fed up, aren't you, mate? You should be out stalking a gazelle, or whatever it is you fellows stalk.' He went on smoothing and tickling.

'Seems to 'ave taken a fancy to you, does old Simba.' Joe Armsworth, the stage manager, had come in unnoticed and now stood, hands clasped over his paunch, watching the pair of them.

Larry turned and smiled. 'He's very tame, isn't he? Not very well fed, though, from the look of him.'

Joe scratched his grizzled head. 'Old Tom Tillson 'asn't been doing too well with the act lately, the big halls won't book it any more. After all, he's been working the same routine now for donkey's years. That's the trouble with these old performers—never change their acts. Old Simba there could almost do the act on his own. All he does is jump through a hoop, dance a waltz on his hind legs and eat a joint of raw meat off Tom's face. Though how he can stand the smell of Tom's beery breath beats me. That's the finale of the act, the meat bit—and you should see old Tom wrestling with Simba after first house performances.'

'What for?' asked Larry.

'To get the joint back for second house, lad—Tom can't afford two lots of meat.'

40

Joe Armsworth winked at Larry and lumbered downstage towards his corner.

'By the way,' he called, 'don't let old Tillson see you near the lion. He doesn't like people getting too friendly with it, says it's hard enough as it is getting the thing to growl during the act. He likes to pretend it's fierce.'

Larry thanked him for the information and with a farewell pat left the stage. The lion lay on its back for a while, paws limp in the air, until, realizing that its friend had gone, it turned stiffly on its side and stared with rheumy eyes into the gloom, the sawdust from the floor of the cage speckling its mane like lunatic confetti. Then it put its head against the bars, sighed again and fell into a tail-twitching doze.

'Beginners, please!' A raucous voice echoed along the corridor.

Larry stood up. 'I suppose that means me.'

'You're second—after the girls—aren't you?' asked Wally, who was sitting in his vest at his place before the mirror, applying an elaborate make-up.

Tillson had not yet appeared. Conversation between the two friends had been a little forced, mainly because of Larry's nervousness about his act. Wally was by nature a kind man, and sensing the tenseness of his friend had tried to make his ordeal easier by recalling the old days in Italy. Larry had been an unresponsive listener, realizing what Wally was trying to do and at the same time resenting him for doing it.

Larry looked at himself for the last time in the cracked mirror. His make-up was too heavy, he thought, but with Wally watching he decided against altering it. The suit did not look as good as he thought it might. He looked down at his trousers. They sagged rather badly at the knees.

'Never sit down in the props, me old lad,' said Wally, following his friend's glance and understanding the reason.

'The bloke who had this suit before me must have been a pianist. You can see where his blasted knees have been.' Larry bent his legs slightly. 'If I walk on like this I won't look too bad.'

Wally laughed, and rising from his chair took Larry's hand in his. 'Good luck, old flower,' he said. 'I won't come down in the wings and watch you this house, it isn't fair. Hope they're good to you. Don't expect too much, first house Monday; they can be real bastards—especially to the early turns. Remember you're a pro now—you're getting paid to make 'em laugh. It works out about a tanner a titter.'

Larry gripped his friend's hand. 'Thanks for the chance, Wal. Sorry I've been a bit edgy today. It's all so new to me, and I feel as nervous as hell.'

He straightened his drooping bow-tie, and opened the door. 'Those about to die salute you,' he intoned and descended the stone steps with a quaking heart.

The sound of the overture drifted up the stairs to meet him. The band had not improved since rehearsal and the air was tortured with split notes from the trumpeter and quaint Chinese chords from the pianist.

April and June were standing in the wings. He hardly recognized them in their costumes. They were dressed as toy soldiers with little wooden rifles and cheeks bright with circular red patches of rouge. Both girls wore tights and Larry noticed that June's legs were remarkably lovely.

April, fussily pulling at her skirt, smiled cheerfully at Larry. 'Best of luck, love,' she said. 'We'll break 'em down for you.'

June nodded in his direction as she adjusted the strap of the pill box hat perched on the side of her curls.

'Tiddle om pom-pom, tiddle om pom-pom.' The band went into the 'March of the Toy Drum Major', and shouldering their rifles the two girls stepped smartly out of step onto the stage, April leading, the steel taps on their shoes clicking madly on the bare boards.

Joe Armsworth looked at the clock in his corner, and noted down the time of the girls' entrance in the time-sheet on his little desk.

'Six eighteen,' he said to Larry. 'You go on at six twenty-four. You're down for eight minutes, so don't go running over your time. They play hell at Head Office if the show's late. People miss their buses and they complain to their friends the show finishes late and we lose their custom.'

Larry wondered whether he would be able to keep going as long as eight minutes, let alone run over time. He fidgeted nervously, wiping his sweaty palms on his handkerchief as he watched the stage hands working.

When the girls moved forward into their last routine, the once gold curtains moved jerkily across the stage behind them and the garden backcloth he had seen at rehearsal came wearily down into position.

'Take your blues out, Don,' called Armsworth to an overalled figure at the switchboard above him.

'Bower's next, Barry Bower. We'll want a full up for him.'

Larry felt sick, too sick even to notice that they'd got his name wrong again. The girls were working up to a climax, their scuffed white tap-shoes a blur as they fought a losing battle with the orchestra in a jazzed-up version of 'Colonel Bogey'.

'Please God make it go all right. Please God.' His mouth was dry and he began to tremble violently. Sweat stood out in great beads on his forehead and his fists clenched and unclenched as he fought to take control of his shaking limbs. Why do I want to do this? Why should I torture myself? He put his hands to his face and leaned his head against the wall. Joe watched him sympathetically.

'Come on, son—they'll not bloody well eat you. The girls are nearly off.'

April and June finished their routine with three bars of music to spare, and, after a fixed smile and a bow to the audience and a glare and a whispered threat to the conductor, they left the stage at the opposite side.

'Did you hear that bleeding band?' April's voice was clearly audible over the first quavering notes of 'Crazy People'. The lightboards on either side of the proscenium arch changed to two.

Larry's feet refused to obey him. He stood transfixed, unable to move an inch. He looked round desperately at Joe Armsworth. 'I can't do it,' he croaked.

' 'Course you bloody well can,' said Joe and pushed him out onto the stage.

The spot from the back of the circle picked him up as he stumbled on, and for a second he stood transfixed, a small Welsh zeppelin trapped in the beam of a searchlight. Then he walked on leaden soles to the centre of the stage, his upper lip sticking to his teeth in a death's-head grin.

'Hello, folks!' he said in a high-pitched, hysterical voice.

The scattered audience of landladies and other recipients of the free seats for the Monday first house glared at him over folded arms, mouths already pursed in sour dislike. 'If you please 'em here, you'll please 'em anywhere,' was the proud boast of the regular patrons, and they settled back in their faded plush chairs, preparing for eight minutes of harsh scrutiny.

Larry blinked stupidly at them, his brain turned to jelly. Fortunately he was unable to see his inquisitors, having removed his glasses in the wings, but he was acutely aware of their hostility. No warmth reached out to him from the sparsely-populated auditorium. Dan, the conductor, vaguely visible below him, nodded at him to begin, suddenly afraid of the silence.

'I'd like to start off with an impression of an army officer on guard duty doing his rounds of the sentries.' The words came out with a rush and Larry was launched into his first routine.

'He's working much too fast.' Jimmy Long, in female make-up, looking grotesque without his wig, drew his dressing-gown tightly around him as he stood at the side of the stage.

Joe Armsworth nodded. 'Better get the next act down quick in case he finishes too bloody early.' He turned to a stage hand. 'Tell Henri Lamarr to come on down straight away.'

Jimmy Long shook his head slowly as Larry continued his act. 'He looks absolutely terrified out there.'

'Should have seen the poor bastard before he went on,' said

44

Joe. ' 'ad to push him out. Thought he was going to bloody well faint or something.' He stood back and called up to the electrician. 'Stand by for a black-out. This lad may not finish his turn.'

On stage Larry was living in a nightmare. The pieces of business where the laughs should have come meant nothing to the audience. They greeted each sally with cold, stony silence, daring him to continue. He wanted to run off and hide from the glare of the lights, to bury his head in his mother's lap. *Please* like me, he tried to say to them. Laugh just once—at me or with me, but please *laugh*. And all the time he could hear himself stumbling hurriedly, frantically, through half-remembered routines, wanting only to get to the end.

At last he got to the song, the duet with himself. 'Jeanette MacDonald and Nelson Eddy singing "Sweethearts". I do the two voices, the high one is Jeanette MacDonald. The note, please.'

The pianist started a run up the piano, but was halted by a crack on the head from Dan's baton. 'He's got enough trouble—the *note*—just the bloody *note*,' he hissed.

Larry regained some control over himself as he began to sing. 'When we were sweethearts in June—May—June,' he alternated between soprano and tenor. He managed to finish the last few bars strongly, the chord from the orchestra making him sound more out of tune than he actually was. Then it was all over, and for a moment he was strangely calm as he bowed to the audience.

There was no answering burst of applause and the few perfunctory hand claps he did receive died abruptly before he had left the stage.

Dick Lovegrove, the theatre manager, puffed his way from the auditorium through the pass door and called for Joe Armsworth.

'I've never seen anythin' in my life as bad as that last bloke. What was he supposed to be doing then? He finished three minutes early as well. Who booked him?' His voice shook with indignation.

'He's a mate of Wally Winston's so I suppose he's booked by the same agent. Better go and ask him yourself.' Joe had little time for the manager. They had been feuding for years, each jealous of his own authority. 'Excuse me.' He turned away pointedly and looked towards the stage where the juggler was stooping to pick up a fallen club from the footlights.

Dick Lovegrove eyed his back uncertainly. He always felt at a disadvantage backstage, knowing it was Armsworth's domain. In his own office, surrounded by photographs and posters, he reigned supreme, his fat bottom snug in the swivel chair behind the battered desk, and a bottle of gin handy in the drawer by his right knee. He stood nervously fingering his greasy bow-tie, blinking his watery blue eyes, then he stumped off towards Larry's dressing-room, his shiny patent shoes squeaking in protest. During the pantomime season this sound always sent the chorus girls scurrying to put their tender little rumps against the nearest wall. The usherettes were immune to his rear offensives. They were mostly middle-aged and there was little purchase for his stubby fingers on their withered flanks.

He knocked on the door of the dressing-room and without waiting for a reply waddled importantly inside. Larry was on his own. Wally, sensing what had happened as soon as he saw Larry's face, had made a hurried excuse and gone along to the girls' room. Simba's lord and master had not yet appeared. Being in the second half of the bill, he had plenty of time to get ready.

'What was all that about, then?' asked Lovegrove, rocking to and fro on his heels, his leather uppers screeching for mercy, his hands forced into the pockets of his dinner jacket.

Larry looked up at him, still bemused by his experience. 'Pardon?' he said emptily, his face expressionless.

'This act of yours, if you can call it that. What's it all about? Are you supposed to be a comedian, then? My patrons—' he rolled the words round his tongue, liked their taste and repeated them, 'my patrons won't have it.'

46

'I'm trying to create something—do something different. After all, they laughed when Stephenson built the Rocket.'

'Not Monday night first house they didn't,' said Lovegrove.

This conversation is developing into a very bad cross-patter act, thought Larry idiotically.

'You've not got a bad voice,' Lovegrove grudgingly admitted, 'but where are the jokes? All that army stuff's no bloody good here, you know. You'll need to buck your ideas up second house or I'll have to take you off the bill, me lad.'

That possibility had not occurred to Larry, and the realization filled him with dread. To be taken out of the bill was the worst thing that could happen to anybody in the business. It would make future bookings very hard to get and more than likely ruin his career before it had begun.

He felt he must make some excuse for his failure. This bloke was obviously the manager, he could tell that by his dinner jacket. It was the uniform of authority, a badge of office—that much he had learned from Wally.

Lovegrove stood watching Larry's reaction to his words, feeling the power surging through his gin-soaked veins. He revelled in the situation. Larry, in spite of his newness to the profession, was to receive fifteen pounds for his act, provided he lasted the week out, and that was exactly two pounds ten more than Lovegrove would be taking home to his long-suffering wife on Friday. There were, of course, the 'perks' of his job. A few tickets marked 'complimentary' on the house plan could be sold, the money finding its way into his own pocket, and there was always the programme fiddle and a bob or two from the ice-cream money. But in spite of all these extras, it always came hard when he had to pay out the performers on a Saturday night. He would plonk down the packets of notes on the dressing-room tables and breathe enviously through his strawberry nose as the money was carefully counted. With the tops of the bill it was different. With them he was jolly, especially if the business had been reasonably good—it was never wonderful. He would hand them their salaries as though he were Father Christmas, addressing them by their first names with a gruesome familiarity which bred an easy contempt in the recipients. Some managers had many genuine friends among the stars. Lovegrove had none.

Larry stood up. 'It's my first week.'

'I can well believe it.' Lovegrove's tone was one of heavy sarcasm.

'I'll try and adjust myself,' said Larry lamely.

'You couldn't adjust your bloody braces.'

This shaft of wit delivered, the manager headed for the door. 'Don't forget, now—I shall be watching second house.'

He slammed the door behind him and then remembered that he had not asked who Larry's agent was. He hesitated outside the door.

'Hello, Mr. Lovegrove. Not paying out already, are you?' Wally approached him along the corridor.

'I'll be paying that lad out tonight if he doesn't improve by second house.' He inclined his head towards Larry's door. 'Is your agent booking him?'

'Yes,' said Wally, frowning. 'Lou Hyman. You don't mean he went that badly do you?'

'He damned well did, and I've just told him so an' all. I'll be ringing Hyman in the morning; so will Head Office when they see my report.'

The Head Office of the Brotherton Circuit of Theatres, of which the Royalty Theatre was one, and the Rotunda, Bingley, the other, consisted of three scruffy rooms above a kosher butcher's shop in Barnsley, where old Fred Brotherton sat sipping cups of strong tea, spending most of the day picking losers on the race track with one hand, and his nose with the other. But it was Head Office to Lovegrove. It was the rock upon which his authority was built, and because he did not have to visit the place more than once a year it remained in his mind a tall, shining, twenty-storey marble building, staffed by briskly efficient secretaries, run by God himself, and he endeavoured to impress this conception upon those under him. Naturally, no one ever believed him.

'I'll have a word with him,' said Wally, wondering what he could say to his old friend.

'Jokes, he wants. Some good jokes. All that army stuff's no good.' Lovegrove caught sight of April leaving her dressing-room and tugged at his bow-tie. 'Yes, you tell him then,' he said, walking quickly down the corridor after the girl.

As Wally opened the door he heard a squeal from April followed by a loud smack and a grunt from Lovegrove.

'You leave me alone, you filthy old swine. Next time I'll kick you where it hurts.'

Wally stopped and turned, his hand still on the door knob. 'Good for you, April,' he called.

The manager passed him, rubbing his face angrily. 'You mind your own bloody business, and tell that mate of yours to do better second house or I'll pay him off.'

Lovegrove stumped down the stairs, his shoes shrilling indignantly. April gave him a V sign and continued on her way to the Ladies.

Wally laughed and went into the dressing-room. Larry looked up from his position at the dressing-table. 'What was all that about?' he demanded of Wally's reflection in the mirror.

'That was Lovegrove getting his come-uppance from April. He's got the charming habit of pinching ladies' bums, and that was one he'll remember. You could see April's finger-marks right across his cheek.'

Larry managed a feeble grin. 'Serves him right. He was just in here giving me a right old bollocking for not doing too well in my act. Threatened to pay me off, too.'

Wally began to prepare for his own appearance. Taking a smartly-cut suit from its hanger, he brushed it carefully before putting it on.

Larry watched him dress, marvelling at the care he took and making a mental note to take more pride in his own stage appearance.

'Is my collar down properly at the back?' Wally stood looking in the mirror, turning his head from side to side as he adjusted his tie. Larry got to his feet and patted his friend's collar into position. 'Lovely bit of material, isn't it? Cost me thirty guineas from Sidney Fisher's. But it's worth every penny, mate.'

'Don't you wear a dinner jacket on stage any more, then?' asked Larry.

'They're out for comics today, me old son. The smart day suit with a bright tie, and a trilby with the brim turned up in front—that's what all the top boys are wearing.'

Wally reached up and took from a peg a wide-brimmed Borsalino-type trilby. He set it carefully on his head and turned the brim upwards, juggling with it until he had placed it at the correct jaunty angle.

'Stand by, Mr. Winston.' The call came drifting up from below. The theatre did not employ a call boy as such; instead Joe Armsworth or his assistant Arthur stood at the bottom of the stairs and shouted up to the dressing-rooms when an act was due on. Strangely enough they were always heard, principally because the performers could sense when they were due to go on without even looking at their watches, and were unconsciously waiting for the call.

'Best of luck, mate,' said Larry, admiring Wally's composure. 'Not that you'll need it.'

'Thanks. I'll need it all right, but I'm not going to let that lot out there think I do.' Wally gave one last pat to the handkerchief in his breast pocket and giving Larry the thumbs-up he bustled out of the room.

When he had gone Larry thought of going down to the side of the stage to watch, but decided against it. He would find it hard to bear if his friend went too well, and at the same time he would be ashamed of his secret delight if he did badly.

He sat for a while wondering what he could do to improve his act second house, when the door suddenly opened and a strong smell of whisky entered the room, followed by the lion-tamer.

Larry ventured a 'Good evening,' but was ignored as the half-drunken Tillson began to divest himself of his clothes, muttering to himself as he did so through rotting teeth. At last Tillson stood revealed in his dirty underwear, his legs a mass of blue varicose veins, a ripe body odour rising to join the spirit fumes. For the first time he noticed Larry and, scratching his left armpit, he addressed him. 'Where's fancy bloody pants, then?'

'If you mean Wally, he's gone on stage.' Larry's nose wrinkled with disgust.

'Don't turn your nose up at me. From what I heard on the way in, you smell a bloody sight worse to them out there than I do to you in here.'

Tillson laughed and sat down at his place before the mirror, pleased with his wit.

Larry found himself without words. Tears of humiliation and rage pricked his eyes and he walked blindly out of the door.

'Hello! I was just coming to have a chat with you, dear.' Jimmy Long adjusted the sash of his dressing-gown as he looked shrewdly at Larry's obvious distress. 'Has our brave lion-tamer upset you, then? He has a delicious aroma about him, too, hasn't he?'

Larry hesitated, not wanting to get involved with Jimmy, yet feeling the need to talk to someone.

'I suppose it's my own fault, really. My act didn't do too well and I don't know what to do about it.'

'Come on down to our dressing-room,' said Jimmy, taking his arm. Larry blushed furiously and tried to disengage himself. 'It's all right, love, I'm not after your honour, all I want to give you is a cup of tea. George has got the kettle on.'

They walked together down the steps to the next floor, Larry still apprehensive, not knowing quite what to do in the circumstances.

'In here, dear.' Jimmy opened the door of his dressing-room and ushered Larry in. He was taken aback at what he saw. Bright chintz curtains disguised the window and a length of the same material ran along the wall behind a row of sequined gowns. The table in front of the mirror was similarly covered, and two small rugs lay on the floor. In one corner an electric kettle was whistling merrily and the bulb in the ceiling was decorated with a gay shade.

George Short rose painfully from his chair to greet him.

'Delighted to meet you,' he said in a surprisingly deep voice. Larry looked startled.

'I suppose you expected a lisp at least,' intoned the little man, amused.

Larry stammered in confusion. 'Well, not exactly—I—'

'Get the cups out, George. I'll make the tea.' Jimmy was already pouring the contents of the kettle into a silver teapot. George reached under the table and, after much unwrapping of newspaper, produced three cups and saucers of fine quality china. 'Always carry an extra cup and saucer for visitors,' he rumbled, giving them a rub with a clean cloth. Sugar and milk were already on the table, and Larry was told to help himself to both as he was handed his tea.

'Sit down, dear, we're not going to eat you,' said Jimmy kindly. 'I just thought you'd want a bit of cheering up after your performance. I saw it all from the wings, you see.'

'Oh,' said Larry, waiting for the dagger to strike.

'Plenty of good ideas there. I like the way you refuse to use a routine of gags. All the comics nowadays seem to be Max Millers and Tommy Trinders. It's time somebody came along with something different.'

Larry warmed to Jimmy. 'I'm glad you think so. I know my act is a mess at the moment, but I've always tried to get away from just telling a string of jokes. I usually get the pay-offs mixed up.'

All three laughed and Larry relaxed completely.

'I know how you feel,' said Jimmy. 'We first met in the army in the First World War.' He patted George's hand affectionately and for a moment they looked into each other's eyes. Larry looked at the ceiling.

'It was in a prisoner of war camp and between us we put on all the camp concerts—and believe me, some of them were really camp. So we decided when we got out that we would try our luck on the halls as a double act. We had a terrible time getting into the business because, of course, we were so different.'

You can say that again, thought Larry, taking another sip of tea.

'Anyway we persevered until we were at the top of our

profession in the 'thirties. We'd be there still if it weren't for the War.'

'Were you in the army, then?' asked Larry.

'No, dear, we were too old. So we joined ENSA. It was lots of fun at first—you know, meeting all those young fellows, but we got torpedoed.'

'In a convoy, were you?' enquired Larry.

'No, on a battleship in Southampton Water—we were doing a concert on board at the time. George was hit in the stomach by a piece of shrapnel and I never thought he'd live. He was in hospital for nearly a year, then I nursed him in our flat for a long time. We lost a lot of work through it, especially in the months after the end of the war. Still, we're together again and that's all that really matters, isn't it, dear?' George nodded.

'That's right, love,' he said, squeezing Jimmy's knee. 'We've still got each other.'

Larry resumed his survey of the ceiling. I don't know how much more of this I can stand, he thought.

'Your trouble is that you speak too quickly for the audience to follow what you're saying,' said Jimmy.

This brought Larry's head down with a jerk.

'Try breaking up your sentences a bit. Take more time explaining to the people what you're going to do. An audience is like a child, it has to be told clearly and distinctly how to behave. If they are supposed to laugh at a certain point, tell them so beforehand. They might not laugh, of course, but at least give them the opportunity. That first performance of yours—you rushed through it like a mad thing. Try and learn a little repose. It takes a long time to acquire, but now is the time to start. And use your singing voice more—don't throw it away, it's a gold mine if you use it properly. Every comic has to sing a song to get himself off, but how many of them can really sing? And above all, don't lose your nerve on there. Don't let on to them that you're terrified, because nothing communicates itself quicker to an audience than fear. They become embarrassed themselves and then they get restless and someone shouts "get off" and that, darling, is your lot.'

Larry had been sitting on the edge of his chair while Jimmy

was talking. He blinked rapidly and cleared his throat. 'Never thought of it like that, Jimmy. I felt that I had to get on quick and get into the funny bits of business before they lost interest. Still, I'll try and slow up second house. Thanks for the tea.' He put his cup and saucer down and made for the door.

'What is more important, my lad,' said George, 'don't be stampeded into changing your act too much—work on it, polish it, add to it, but don't lose your faith in it.'

'Thanks a lot.' Larry opened the door. 'Try and watch me next time and see if you notice any improvement,' he said.

'I'll be there, dear,' replied Jimmy, with a smile.

As Larry mounted the steps towards his dressing-room Tillson brushed past on his way to the stage. He was wearing a threadbare chocolate-coloured uniform with gold epaulettes, and Larry was wickedly pleased to see that the trousers were as baggy as his own. Under his arm he carried the brown paper parcel containing the meat which was to feature in the finale of his act. He went by without looking at Larry, and Larry found himself hoping that when Simba ate the meat off the tamer's face he would keep right on going. Even though he had no teeth to bite with, he might give Tillson a nasty suck.

Larry had only been in the dressing-room for a few minutes when Wally burst in, beaming, a film of sweat streaking his make-up.

'I paralyzed them,' he said, his voice shaking. 'I really knocked 'em cold. Imagine—first house Monday, and they were eating out of my hand.' He began to take off his stage suit, handling it very carefully in spite of his excitement. 'They were marvellous—never known anything like it, mate. If I can get my agent to bring up the big boys to see the act this week it'll be Palladium next stop—or Finsbury Park Empire, at least.'

He paced up and down, making plans for the future. 'If Hyman can persuade Morrie Green to come up, I'll be in.

After all, if I can make these bastards laugh I'll have no trouble in town. You know what they say—"if you can please 'em here, you'll please 'em anywhere".'

He stopped his pacing and dug Larry in the ribs. 'Blimey, *you* know how hard they can be. You couldn't get 'em going at all, could you?'

Larry shook his head, trying to keep his grin from fraying at the edges.

'Got any change? I'll phone Lou Hyman now; I've got his home number.'

Larry nodded towards his meagre collection of silver on the dressing-table. 'Help yourself,' he said.

'Wally darling, you were wonderful,' June called from the doorway. She came forward and threw her arms round his neck, nuzzling him. Wally drew her to him and gave her a big smacking kiss.

'How about that, then?' he said, gaily. 'First house Monday at the Royalty and they're shouting for more.'

'I was at the side when you were on,' June told him, looking deep into his eyes.

Larry noticed with some small satisfaction that she had to bend her head to do so.

'I must phone my agent,' Wally said, giving June's bottom a tender pat. 'Look after her till I get back, Larry. And no funny business, mind.' Playfully wagging a warning finger, he swept up some of Larry's change and whistled his way out.

June's face, which had suddenly come alive when speaking to Wally, now reverted to its usual almost withdrawn expression. She sat down on the chair with the wonky leg, which promptly gave way and threw her onto the floor in a delicious flurry of bare legs and half-revealed bosom.

Larry's eyes were still wide as he helped her to her feet.

'You knew that bloody thing were broken. You deliberately let me sit on it.' June's accent was now full-hlown Yorkshire as she wrapped her dressing-gown round herself, her eyes no longer twin setting suns but narrow oriental slits.

Larry stood open-mouthed. 'Just a minute, mun,' he said,

his own Welsh lilt very prominent. 'You didn't give me a blooming chance to—'

'You Welsh are all the same,' she spat and turned on her her heel in time to bump into Wally who had just arrived back.

'No reply,' he said. He looked from June to Larry, and his happy grin faded. 'What's all this about, then?'

'Ask *him*,' retorted June with a toss of her head as she left the room.

'The chair broke again. She sat on it and it broke,' said Larry, eyeing Wally carefully.

'Oh?' Wally raised a disbelieving eyebrow. 'Now watch it, Larry boy, I've got that one lined up for myself.'

'I didn't lay a finger on her!' Larry was angry now. 'If you don't believe me, look at the bloody chair.'

Wally looked down at the collapsed chair, then, his excitement over his success returning, he clapped Larry on the shoulder.

'Sorry, mate—I believe you. Blimey! What an audience!' He went across to his place at the dressing-table and began combing his hair, talking to Larry in the mirror.

'This could be the start of the big time for me. The Palladium, a smart West End revue, perhaps—I can do it.'

Larry nodded at Wally's reflection, stifling the emotions welling up inside him. Was it jealousy he felt, or rage at his own inability to win over the audience? Perhaps a mixture of both, he thought, forcing himself to look interested.

'We'll celebrate tonight, my old son,' said Wally. 'I'll get a bottle of vino and we'll share it with the girls at supper.'

'What about Mrs. Rogers?' asked Larry. 'She's not going to like any high spirits at that time of night.'

'You leave that old cow to me—I'll charm her into it, even if it costs me a glass of wine.'

'She'll take some charming, that one,' smiled Larry. 'She reminds me of old Sergeant Major Tomlinson in Milan.'

'God, yes.' Wally turned from the mirror and laughed. 'They'd have made a fine pair. Remember that night when you did your impersonation of him in the sergeants' mess concert?'

56

'I thought he'd kill me.' Larry's good humour reasserted itself in the warmth of their revived memories and he stuck out his chest in imitation of their old sergeant major.

'Is that supposed to be me, eh? Eh? *Eh?*' His voice rose to a nasal crescendo as he strutted round the dressing-room to the accompaniment of Wally's laughter. 'Rise and shine! Come along there, the sun's burning your bleedin' eyes out. Hands off cocks and on your socks.'

'Very nice language in front of a lady, I must say.' April stood in the doorway, wearing a Red Indian outfit that consisted of a single lop-sided feather fixed to a wide, beaded headband—completely obliterating her eyebrows—and a leather-fringed leotard which allowed little room either for her ample bosom or the imagination.

'Anybody got a fag?'

Wally, still laughing, tossed her one. Larry stood awkwardly, a little abashed at being overheard. April motioned to the cigarette in her mouth, and Larry, remembering her gesture at breakfast-time, hastily struck a match for her.

'Thanks, cheeky,' she said, and throwing her head back inhaled deeply. 'I'll bet you two had a hell of a time in the army.'

Words and tobacco smoke poured out together as she exhaled, resulting in a sharp burst of coughing, during which Wally made his excuses and went off to phone his agent again. As he shut the door, he winked heavily at Larry and gave the thumbs-up sign.

'I'm a martyr to it,' wheezed April, her plump shoulders quivering as she fought for breath.

One shoulder strap fell and a heavy breast threatened to reveal itself completely.

'Oops! Me dumplings are boiling over.' April thrust a thumb under her shoulder strap and wriggled back into respectability.

Larry licked his lips nervously, his palms sweating a little. April was no Venus de Milo but she was very well built. Though her legs had none of the classic beauty of June's—they were too heavy in the thigh for that—they were shapely, nonetheless. The tan make-up covering her shoulders and arms softened the contours, he thought. Hold on, mate, you're beginning to work yourself up. It's June you really fancy. Still, a bird in the hand . . .

'That happened to me once on stage, you know.' April had her back turned, and was talking to him in the mirror as she straightened her eagle feather, which now looked even worse for wear after her coughing bout.

'What did?' asked Larry of her reflection.

'My bosom fell out in "The Toy Drum Major". It was at Catterick when I was working for ENSA. My bra strap broke. I did feel a fool but I kept going and all the lads clapped and cheered when we finished. Me and my partner took four calls. The comic was furious, they wouldn't let him begin his act, kept on stamping and shouting for more.' She turned and faced Larry, her eyes teasing as she adopted a cover-girl pose, lifting one shoulder so that the strap fell down again.

'Encore,' breathed Larry, taking a tentative step forward.

'Ooooh! Naughty, naughty,' giggled April in mock concern. Larry closed in on her, and pressed her back against the table.

'You'll get make-up all over your shirt, and you'll ruin me feather.' April wriggled delightedly against him as Larry pressed his lips in the hollow of her throat. 'We've got to open the second half in a minute.' She held Larry tightly to her as she spoke. Then suddenly she released her grip and broke away.

'What's up, love?' protested Larry huskily, the blood throbbing wildly in his ears. He was able to see only dimly through his steamed-up glasses.

'Go on, lover boy. Don't mind me—I like watching.' Tillson had come in and was leering at April. She shuddered, and without a word ran out, her feather bobbing precariously.

'Don't waste any time, do you, son?' There was a slight note of respect in Tillson's voice. He lumbered towards the dressing-table and proceeded to brush his thinning scalp with Wally's silver-backed brush.

'If you get anything there, let us in on it.' He winked almost benignly at Larry's reflection. 'There's life in the old dog yet, you know,' he said with the air of one making an original remark, as he removed his tunic and dropped it carelessly over the back of his chair.

Larry was rooted to the spot with indignation. 'Of all the bloody nerve,' he began, his voice choked with rage. He stopped, unable to go on.

Tillson had begun to take off his boots, unaware of Larry's reaction, and was contemplating a large hole in his left sock.

'I wonder if she'd do a bit of darning for me?' mused Tillson, wiggling a large and very dirty big toe.

Larry put his fingers to his nose and left the room hurriedly, slamming the door hard behind him.

Not knowing quite what to do, he found himself heading down the stone steps towards the stage. As he stood uncertainly by the door bearing the legend 'Stage—Quiet' he recognized Long and Short's music filtering through. He was not really sure whether he would be allowed to stand at the side when the other acts were performing, but taking a chance he pushed through the door.

Apart from the shafts of light slicing through the side drapes, it was quite dark and he edged his way cautiously towards the light shining from the prompt corner where Joe Armsworth was giving instructions to the electrician.

'Take your blues out, Don. Right. Now tell that chump on the spot to pick up George Short. Come on, for Christ's sake, he's in the bloody dark.'

Jimmy Long appeared suddenly at the side.

'That lad on the front spot thinks he's an usherette. He's shown two old ladies to the toilet since we started the act.' He wore a tight, blue sequined evening dress which curved in and out in a surprisingly seductive manner. A blonde page boy wig lessened the grotesqueness of his full female make-up, and standing side stage in the half light he looked like an attractive woman. He caught Larry looking at him.

'When did you first take a fancy to me, dear?' he drawled, swinging his hips.

Larry gulped.

'Only kidding,' said Jimmy laughing. He jerked his thumb

over his shoulder at the audience. 'They're a right lot of Chinese bastards out there tonight. Mind you, the band aren't helping much. Listen to them crucifying Georgina.' He winced as a quavering chord followed by a cymbal crash announced the end of his partner's solo.

'Well, here we go again, duckie,' he said, and picking up the train of his dress with one hand, he minced back on to the stage.

Joe Armsworth turned to Larry. 'He won't hurt you, son—keeps himself for George. And by the way, if you're going to stand in the wings go round to the O.P. side and you won't get in anybody's way. Julie Tempest is next on and she doesn't like to be watched from the side. You'd better nip round now while Tommy's setting up her act.'

He turned away and hauled the number one runners into position behind Long and Short. 'Drop the screen in, Charlie,' he called to a man in the flies, and a large projection screen jerked perilously down from above.

Larry walked round the back of the stage, unnoticed by Tommy, Julie's husband and manager, who was agitatedly supervising the setting-up of a slide projector. His wife, in a wrap, was imperiously ordering a stage hand to place her props on a table in the wings.

On the far side of the stage Larry found himself wedged in a corner with two stage hands, one of whom was adjusting a large pageant lamp on an iron stand. The other held a pile of coloured filters. 'Don't get them filters mixed now, Sammy,' said the smaller and elder of the two. 'If the wrong one goes in she'll have your guts for garters when she comes off.'

The lad grinned nervously, and scratched a crop of fresh blackheads on his chin. 'Eeh! I've heard she's got a grand figure.' He licked his lips and nodded at Larry. 'Oh, hello,' he said. 'Hey, you didn't do very well, did yer? Ah thought you were going to get the bird.'

Larry coughed and flushed red, unable to reply.

'Mind your own bloody business, Sammy, and keep your mind on the job,' snapped the older man, making a final

60

adjustment to the lamp. 'Don't pay any attention to this idiot,' he said to Larry. 'He wouldn't know a good act if he saw one. All he thinks about is crumpet, and he's never had any of that either.'

Sammy shuffled the gelative filters in his hands. 'Give over, Arthur,' he protested, looking sideways at Larry.

'Get ready,' ordered Arthur.

Long and Short had finished and the spatter of applause died quickly as Dan hurled himself into action, baton waving madly. The band followed, wrestling manfully with the opening bars of 'Tannhäuser', dominated by the trombone player who had a passion for Wagner and for the first time that evening felt on safe ground.

The curtains opened fitfully, revealing Tommy in a dinner jacket, perspiring visibly.

'Ladies and gentlemen,' he began to announce into the microphone, which he gripped in front of his mouth, 'we come to the star of the show, the lovely Julie Tempest.' He paused, expecting applause and getting none.

'Contain yourselves, folks,' he laughed, raising his hands to still the non-existent ovation. 'In just one moment you shall see the lovely Julie Tempest in the flesh.'

Tommy winked roguishly at the assorted collection of hatchet-faced landladies and they stared stonily back, clutching their shopping bags to their bosoms. In the front row two furtive men in cloth caps settled their raincoats more firmly into their laps.

'First, the gorgeous Julie will give you her interpretations of famous women in history, from Cleopatra to Nurse Edith Cavell.'

Tommy turned his head and looked into the wings for the signal from Joe Armsworth that the projector and slides were ready. Joe nodded briefly. With a sigh of relief Tommy turned back to the audience, and in his best 'March of Time' voice began his introduction to the act.

The lights went down and a second set of curtains opened in the darkness. Larry could see the dim ivory shape of Julie

Tempest making last-minute adjustments to her props as she stood on a built-up platform before the screen.

'Cleopatra, Queen of the Nile,' declaimed Tommy into his microphone, and the spotlight flickered into life.

'Stand by with the surprise pink,' whispered Arthur to Sammy.

The lights revealed the luscious figure of Julie as Cleopatra, wearing only a circlet of gold over a short black wig, one hand strategically placed on her groin, the other holding a mummified snake which she flicked from side to side in a semblance of life. Behind her, the Pyramids, though sharply in focus and in beautiful colour, were upside down.

'Ooh! Look at her,' slavered Sammy in awe. Arthur clipped him smartly across his left-ear.

'Give us that gelly,' he hissed angrily.

Larry felt vaguely embarrassed at the sight of an undraped female body at such close quarters. From this distance he could see the slight sag in the bosom and the scar of an appendectomy, and no amount of body make-up could disguise the goose pimples which now covered the over-ripe figure of Miss Tempest. She stood fixed in position, waiting for the lights to go out again. They went off suddenly, and as Tommy intoned, 'Boadicea, Mother of British freedom', Larry decided to make his way back to his dressing-room.

He tip-toed quietly round Arthur and fell headlong over Sammy who had bent down to find his next filter. Throwing out an arm to save himself, Larry sent the pageant lamp and Arthur flying onto the stage.

At that moment the lights went up again to reveal a furious Julie, clad only in a helmet, restraining herself with the greatest difficulty from hurling her spear at Arthur, who, mumbling apologies, was now scrabbling about with his broken lamp in the centre of the stage. To make matters worse, Sammy had come on to help his mate and was standing transfixed, mouth open, staring at the majestic Boadicea.

'Cor!' he said.

Julie lost her restraint and flung the spear, which fortunately for Sammy was made of painted wood. In the background, Stonehenge hung upside down.

Out in the audience there was a ripple of laughter which Tommy seized on desperately, and tried to turn to his advantage.

'Everybody's trying to get into the act, folks. These lads just can't resist her.'

Meanwhile, aware that he had created this chaos on stage, Larry moved swiftly across the back of the tabs, unnoticed in the confusion by everyone except Joe Armsworth, who jerked his head in the direction of the exit to the dressing-rooms.

'Get up there quick before she finds out who did it. She'll kill you, boy.'

Larry nodded gratefully, and without attempting to explain what had happened made hurriedly for his room.

Joe Armsworth met Julie Tempest as she came storming off stage at the conclusion of her act.

'I want those bastards fired,' she fumed.

'Go easy, love,' said Tommy, patting her arm.

'It was an accident, Miss Tempest,' said Joe Armsworth, trying not to look at the breasts which swung freely to and fro beneath the half-open dressing-gown.

'Sack the buggers,' she raged, 'or I'll get *you* fired as well!'

'Go ahead,' replied Joe calmly. 'Send for the manager. He'll do you a lot of bloody good for a start. There's not a stage manager in the business who'd do the job at the salary they're paying me.'

'Balls!' shrieked Miss Tempest, sweeping furiously from the stage. Tommy shrugged his shoulders hopelessly at Joe before following on her heels.

Joe grinned as Arthur and Sammy came hesitantly forward.

'Don't worry, lads,' he said. 'It couldn't be helped. I'm a match for that old cow any time. I saw young Larry coming round the back after the crash. Now, don't let on that he was over the other side of the stage with you, or she'll take it out on him. I can protect you two, but that poor little so-and-so is on his own.'

Back in the dressing-room Larry walked straight into a flaming row between Tillson and Wally. They both shut up as he came in.

'Sorry,' he stammered, backing out again.

'It's all right, mate,' said Wally with an effort. 'This scruffy individual has been using my hairbrush.'

Tillson swore and shouldered his way past Larry.

'You should see what I've just done,' confessed Larry when the door had closed. 'I've just ruined Julie Tempest's act.'

'Good God—no!' Wally laughed. 'What happened?'

When Larry had explained, Wally sat back in his chair and whistled.

'If she finds out you did it, she'll make it pretty difficult for you. Still, Joe Armsworth's a good sport and he'll cover up. You'd better watch yourself, though.'

Wally sounded a little smug and Larry once again felt like the new boy in class.

He started removing his jacket. 'Better get ready for second house.' His stomach lurched again at the thought of it.

'Damned cheek,' grumbled Wally, briskly rubbing away with a bar of soap at the bristles of his silver-backed hairbrush. 'He'll be using this on that blasted lion next.'

The second performance was not quite as bad as the first. The orchestra was now more familiar with Larry's music and he even raised one or two laughs. Though it was less of a disaster, Joe Armsworth's pat on the back as he came off, sweating and miserable, did little to alleviate Larry's feelings of failure.

'You'll get 'em yet,' said Joe, at the same time signalling to the electrician. 'Full up for Henri Lamarr, and if he drops as many clubs this house as last give him a ruddy black-out.'

Turning back to Larry, he said, 'I've cleared that business

with Miss Tempest. She's got no idea you were watching from the O.P. side—so say nothing about it. The lads won't let on, either—I've threatened 'em.'

Larry thanked him wholeheartedly, and felt better as he mounted the stairs. He was glad it was all over, and though he knew that in bed that night he would relive the day's experiences in all their nightmarish horror, he was now suddenly and pleasantly numb.

It's like beating your head against a wall, he thought. So nice when you leave off.

Wally rubbed his hands together with great satisfaction as he came back into the room after his act. Larry had been waiting for him so that he would not have to face Ma Rogers on his own.

'They were fabulous this house—really fabulous.' Wally carefully undressed and brushed his stage suit vigorously before putting it on the hanger. He started getting into his street clothes.

'I'm looking forward to that bottle of vino with supper tonight. Might get the girls in the right mood.' Wally chuckled at himself in the mirror. Behind him Larry forced a smile of appreciation.

'Yeah,' he said.

The door opened and June came in wearing her Indian costume.

'Wait for us to finish our second spot and we'll come back with you to the digs.' She gave Wally a squeeze.

'Aye, aye,' said Wally, quickly brushing at his lapel. 'You'll get make-up on the old jacket, love.'

June pouted and Wally pinched her cheek. 'Got to look smart for old Ma Rogers.'

June smiled again and twitched her hips.

'Hurry up—we're nearly on,' called April from the door. She gave Larry a friendly grin. 'Are you going to wait for us?'

Larry nodded uncertainly, wanting only to get home and get his head down. His first day in variety had been a long one and he was thinking that the best way to celebrate it would be by committing suicide.

On the way back to the digs, Wally stopped at an off-licence and bought a bottle of wine, borrowing half-a-crown from Larry's fast-dwindling small change to make up the price.

'We're in condition tonight,' exulted Wally, waving the bottle at the girls.

'Ooh!' said June, clutching his arm. 'Are you going to get us tight?'

'Yes, my dear—then it's every man for himself.' He gave a maniacal laugh, and twirled invisible moustachios.

Larry, unable to enter into the spirit of things, grinned feebly.

April put her cold lips to his ear and whispered 'Buck up, love. Forget your act and enjoy yourself.' She tucked her arm under his and snuggled her head into his shoulder, her head-scarf blowing in the chilly wind. Wally and June were walking ahead of them, every now and then breaking into a little jig.

Larry made a great effort to recapture a little of the elation he had felt on meeting Wally that morning, but the sense of failure would not leave him, and he remained silent. April seemed not to mind and left her arm under his. A feeling of unreality came over him. Here he was, walking along an unfamiliar road with a girl he'd only met that day clinging to him as though they had just celebrated their first wedding anniversary. You certainly make friends quickly in show business, he thought. And enemies, too, he added to himself, thinking of the theatre manager and Tillson.

With a sudden movement, almost as though in a dream, he detached his arm from April's, put it round her waist and gave her breast a squeeze. She gasped, then giggled. 'Naughty, naughty—and we haven't even had the wine yet.'

'Cold spam and tomatoes, that's all I can manage for tonight.' Ma Rogers, magnificently intimidating in black, greeted them at the door of the kitchen.

His enthusiasm a little dampened, Wally revealed the bottle of wine.

66

'This'll help it down, Mrs. Rogers,' he smiled at her with all the charm he had used to soften two audiences.

'I don't usually allow liquor in the house,' she said, relaxing the tightness round her mouth. 'But as it's you, Wally, I won't say anything this time.' Larry was amazed at the change in the old battleaxe. 'Your room's ready for you—you're in the blue one.'

'Thanks, love,' said Wally, kissing her hand with an exaggerated flourish. 'Were you out front tonight?'

'I was indeed—first house. Jack and I always go first house on a Monday.'

Behind her in the kitchen, Jack Rogers derisively thumbed his nose.

'We thought you were grand, Wally. Easily the best on the bill.' Mrs. Rogers looked balefully at Larry as she said this. He blushed, and ducked his head. 'Come from Wales, don't you?' Larry nodded. 'Well, you'd be better occupied down the mines, judging from what you served us up tonight.' Mrs. Rogers's wart quivered indignantly.

'You should have been at the second house,' said Larry, pushing past her into the kitchen. 'I paralyzed them.'

She snorted and turned back to Wally, who shrugged his shoulders and said, 'Give him a chance—it's his first variety date. We were together in the army, and I've seen him do wonders with an audience.'

At that moment the girls came clattering downstairs, slowing up at the sight of Mrs. Rogers.

'*You* could do with some dancing lessons, too. What happened in the Toy Drum Major routine?'

In the kitchen Larry sat down at the table, seething with frustration. Jack Rogers patted him on the shoulder as he handed him his supper.

'Don't take any notice of that old bitch,' he said. 'She wouldn't recognize good talent if she saw it. I think you've got something, lad, honest. It needs working on, but there's plenty of talent there. Pity you don't do any juggling, though—I like a bit of juggling myself.' Jack set the plates before the others.

'Sorry it's only spam, but the butcher's shut today and the

corner shop's out of potatoes. Want that bottle opened?' He smacked his lips and rolled his eyes.

'Go on then—open it,' laughed Wally. 'Get some glasses out for all of us. Care for a drop, Mrs. Rogers?' He looked over his shoulder at the landlady.

'No thank you, Wally. I only take wine very occasionally. I'm practically T.T.—and it might have been better for the act if my husband had been the same.'

Jack blew a raspberry again and after glaring at him she bade Wally goodnight, pointedly ignoring Larry and the girls.

'Come on, folks, drink up.' Wally raised a full glass to the others and said, 'Let's drink to success.'

'Success!' cried the girls.

'Success?' muttered Larry, and drained his glass at one gulp.

Wally was too caught up in the occasion to notice Larry's reluctance to join in the general conversation and when Larry excused himself, he hardly looked up.

'Good night, mate,' he called over his shoulder, and the others joined in, turning their heads back quickly to Wally so as not to miss a word of his experiences in summer season at Ramsgate before the war. Their laughter followed Larry into his bedroom.

He undressed miserably in the light of the swinging bulb, and as he hung his jacket over the armchair he remembered the letter from his mother which he'd picked up from the stage door-keeper. He took it from his pocket and clutching it between his teeth he shivered his way between the clammy sheets. Then he opened the letter and began to read.

'My dear Son,
Well, I hope you are having a big success up there in the frozen north (ha ha). We are all thinking about you and praying that you are being well looked after in your lodgings. I'll bet you could do with some of your old Mam's cooking. Your Dad says he knows that area, he was there in the first War and if you have time to get round to Rudley Lane perhaps you might ask if Mrs.

Talbot still lives there. He stayed with her family for about six months when he was stationed up there in 1916. He says they looked after him very well and he would like you to remember him to them. That is, if you have time, what with rehearsing and everything.

We haven't heard from Glyn lately, but I suppose he must be busy too. Last time we heard he was in Palestine but was expecting a posting to a camp in Egypt somewhere. He's been made Captain, too. Fancy our Glyn a Captain and him only five foot three! Still, he's the same old boy by his letters, full of old fun and nonsense. Pity you and him didn't get up an act together for the stage, you used to have such fun as boys, him playing the piano and you fooling around with my hat on.

We were only talking last week to Mrs. Thomas the rent woman about the fun we used to have when you two boys did turns at the Church socials. She's got to look much better since her father died. You remember Mr. Morgan the milk who was always sniffing? Well he sniffed for the last time about six weeks ago—he was a strange old fellow though really, and it's a blessing for her not to have to look after him. They say that he couldn't do anything for himself at the finish. She's looking quite smart these days, and I caught her making eyes at your father when she came for the rent last Friday. I'll have to keep an eye on them two (ha ha).

Well, Son, I don't know what I'm telling you all this nonsense for. It gets very lonely here without you two boys and with your father working nights most weeks at the old steel-works. I was thinking of asking your Auntie Doris to come and live with us. We've got the two spare rooms and we could put all you boys' things together in your room and let her have Glyn's. Besides, I could do with a bit of extra coming in. She's on her own, poor dab, and she's always been good to you boys when you were little, after all she is your Dad's sister. Mind you, I won't do anything until I hear from you boys.

I must go now. Young Elspeth Parsons is expecting her first baby. She's only eighteen and it was touch and go whether her and that Frank Watson would get married in time. He was stationed in Germany and they had to apply for compassionate leave for him. I'd give him compassionate leave, the dirty young devil. She wants me to hold her hand, so I mustn't let her down. You were sweet on her when you first came back from Italy on leave, weren't you?

Do look after your old self, Larry, and don't get too upset if things don't go too well at first. You're young and you've got plenty of time to learn the job and it doesn't matter what anybody else says—we all know that you are going to be famous. Wouldn't it be lovely if you could come here to the Empire and have your name plastered all over town? That would shake a few know-alls around here, I'll tell you.

And even if you don't become famous there's always a place here for you at number seven with your old Mam and Dad.

God bless you always and don't forget to go to Church when you can, there's nothing to be ashamed of about asking for a bit of help from upstairs now and again.

Your loving Mam and Dad.

P.S. Your Uncle Arthur passed away yesterday with bronchitis. Happy release. Don't forget to air your underclothes before you put them on—you know you've always had a weak chest.'

Larry let his thoughts wander tenderly over his years spent at home. They had been very happy years and he smiled as he thought of his mother sitting at the kitchen table, her tongue sticking out of the side of her mouth in concentration as she wrote.

He could see her, rushing off like a bullet to Elspeth Parsons, her little fat bottom jiggling as she scuttled down the hill to the green gate of number twelve. She wouldn't want to miss any of the gossip. She'd come back and tell Dad what the baby looked like, how she had held the baby whilst the midwife cut the cord and how much the baby resembled Elspeth's father's side of the family.

He suppressed a little shiver as he remembered how easily he might have been the father. Elspeth had been very free with her favours in the district and when he came home on leave from Italy he had nearly fallen into the trap. Only her mother arriving home unexpectedly early from Saturday night shopping in the market had saved him from being Elspeth's fourth victim that week. He had only gone there to mend a fuse and before he had even sipped the cup of tea she made him, Elspeth had him on the settee, panting and groaning, and tugging at his braces.

Poor Frank Watson—he never had a chance. Fancy being married to a piece like that, thought Larry. Wonder if Glyn ever got seduced by her? He'd have laughed all the way through it. It's a wonder that he stopped laughing long enough to get his commission. Larry felt a little pang of envy as he remembered how smart his elder brother had looked when he came back home for the first time with his new shiny stars and the gleaming Sam Brown.

Glyn was three years older than Larry and had joined the Territorial Army a year before war broke out. By the time Larry had volunteered, in 1940, Glyn was already training to be an officer in the R.A.S.C., his experience as a Terrier coming in very handy. They had had hysterics saluting each other—the three of them—his father in his Home Guard uniform giving Larry the order, 'Longest way up, shortest way down.'

Glyn had inherited his father's temperament, always quick to laughter, but with a quiet authority which had made him a good officer, and which aroused resentment in Larry on occasions. Larry was more introverted and was his mother's favourite, chiefly because as a child he had had more than his share of illnesses, one of which, scarlet fever, had left him short-sighted.

His father, who worked in the steel-works, was a short, round man with more than a hint of strength in his tubby little frame.

He had brought the boys up to respect him and their mother, not by physical force but by the strength of his authority. He would look sternly at them over the top of his glasses, quietly warning them to behave. If this had no effect he would rise and with no apparent effort separate the squabbling boys, take them upstairs, one under each arm, and shut them in their respective rooms.

'Now, Ernest, be careful with young Larry, you know he's not strong,' his mother would cluck anxiously from the bottom of the stairs.

'I'm not hurting the little bugger,' his father would laugh. 'Let me handle them now, Maggie.'

Later the lads would creep downstairs and apologize and their mother would cry a little over them. Then she'd put the kettle on the hob and they'd all have a cup of sweet comforting tea, and Glyn would slip onto this father's lap, and Larry would bury his head in his mother's generous bosom and she would croon him to sleep.

Larry closed his eyes and sank deep into a self-pitying oblivion.

Some time later, April, feeling a little guilty at not taking much notice of Larry at supper, saw the light under his door. She was on her way upstairs, having left June and Wally in the kitchen with Mr. Rogers, who had long outstayed his welcome but was blissfully unaware of the fact. Larry's door was not shut. She pushed it open gently and put her head inside the room. Larry lay fast asleep, the letter still in his hand.

April tip-toed across to the bed, took the letter from him and looked down at his sleeping form.

'Goodnight, lad,' she whispered, and kissed his forehead with a genuine tenderness.

Larry smiled in his sleep and turned his head on the pillow.

'Goodnight, Mam,' he murmured.

'Good God, he thinks I'm his mother,' gasped April, truly shocked, and she left the room, switching off the light as she went.

Tuesday

Larry awoke promptly at half past six, a left-over reflex from his army days. He was instantly awake, without experiencing the gradual rising through layers of consciousness of a normal sleeper. Instinctively he reached for his glasses—without them he was useless. He put them on and looked around.

He compared the seediness of the bedroom with some of the other places he'd awoken in over the past few years. There had been times when a roof over his head would have been an unthinkable luxury, when sheets and even a mattress were the stuff of dreams. The contrast between his present situation and his past army experiences diminished his feeling of depression. At least the audiences don't fire back, he thought.

He contemplated the day ahead. There were at least twelve hours to go before he faced the enemy again, and the thought comforted him. Tonight he would have them hanging on his every word. If Wally could do it, so could he. He remembered the times in the army shows when he had manipulated his audience with a greater skill and success than his friend. He had been able to communicate with a mass of people of his own age in a way that Wally had never been able to. It might have been that Wally's professionalism was too slick for an audience which was largely unused to theatregoing. The majority of servicemen to whom they had played in Italy had never been to a theatre. Some of the smart revues sent out by ENSA met with nothing but embarrassed incomprehension from the troops out front. They were polite and clapped dutifully, but there was little rapport between performer and public. Some of the shows were given a wary reception, except for those featuring the big radio stars whose names and catch-phrases everyone knew. And even then, the troops didn't like to hear very blue jokes from the famous comics. Although they used all the four-letter words themselves in normal barrack-room conversation, they found it shocking to hear them even hinted at by performers whom they had heard on radio in the sanctity of their own family circles. It was like coming across the padre defecating.

Larry closed his eyes for a moment and dropped off to sleep again. He awoke with a start for the second time and looked at his watch. 'Mama mia—eight thirty!' He tensed himself for the encounter with the cold lino and dressed hurriedly. Grabbing his shaving gear from his case he opened the door and climbed the stairs to the bathroom. From within came the sound of Wally singing.

'Hurry up, mate!' Larry banged on the door.

'Shan't be long, old son,' shouted Wally in reply.

The door opposite the bathroom opened and Ma Rogers stood framed in it in her now familiar dressing-gown, her hair a frenzy of curlers.

'Less noise, please,' she snapped.

'Yes, Sergeant Major,' said Larry, whipping up a salute.

'And I'll have no bloody cheek from you. You ought to be back in the army where you belong—not trying to take the bread out of the mouths of the real pros.'

Larry flushed as she slammed the door, his confidence shattered, feeling once again that perhaps he was making a mistake.

Wally came out of the bathroom, whistling, 'It's all yours, china.' He bowed deeply to Larry, presenting a head of hair perfectly groomed and brilliantined.

'About bloody time,' scowled Larry, still smarting from Ma Rogers's remark and feeling the resentment rising once more against his old friend.

'Bit touchy, aren't we?' Wally's voice hardened, and he went into his bedroom shutting his door with a bang.

Larry shaved angrily, cutting himself as he did so. I shouldn't take it out on Wally, he thought. After all, he got me the job

74

this week. Better apologize. He dipped his brush in the wash-basin and started re-lathering his face. Suddenly, idiotically, he began lathering over his glasses, making the soap fly everywhere.

A throaty laugh brought him back to earth. April had come into the bathroom and was leaning against the wall in her dressing-gown, the inevitable cigarette in the corner of her mouth.

'That's very funny,' she gasped. 'Do you always do matinées this early?'

Larry stopped his frantic lathering in mid-stroke and began chuckling too.

'Anything for a laugh,' he said. 'Hey! What a fabulous idea for an act—the way people shave. I can see the caption on the bills—"He fills the stage with soap".'

' "He fills the stage with blood" is more like it.' April took his towel and dabbed at his face. 'You've cut yourself all over the place. Here, let me put something on those cuts.' She took some toilet paper off the roll, and without removing her cigarette, licked some little pieces to make them stick, then put them on his wounds.

Larry meekly submitted to the treatment. He was just warming nicely to April's proximity and wondering how he could grab her for a kiss without burning his lips, when Ma Rogers interrupted them.

'I won't have mixed bathing,' she thundered. 'I keep a respectable boarding-house.'

'I was only stopping him bleeding over your lino.' April was unperturbed. She took the cigarette from her mouth and tapped the ash into the pocket of her dressing-gown. 'There, see how tidy I am?'

Feeling very foolish, Larry stood stock-still, his glasses white with soap and his face covered with bits of toilet paper. Ma Rogers stared at him grimly. 'I've finished anyway,' he said, gathering up his toilet things.

'You'll both be finished in this house if there's any more hanky-panky.'

'Come off it, Ma,' said April, calmly setting out her tooth-brush and paste on the shelf over the basin. 'Nothing's happened, and anyway there's a few bloody stories going round the business about you and the giant from *Jack and the Beanstalk* a few pantos back.'

Ma Rogers took a step forward, her wart waggling menacingly. As she did so Larry was startled to see June slip cautiously out of Wally's room and into the one she shared with April.

'You listen to me, you little cow!' Ma Rogers was quivering with a mixture of rage and embarrassment. Larry quickly sidled past her while her attention was fixed on April, and made for the stairs.

'No! You listen to me, you *big* cow,' he heard April saying, still without raising her voice. 'If I told your old man what you'd been up to he'd get his hatchets out again and he wouldn't be blindfolded this time. He might hate the sight of you but I don't think he'd fancy hearing what I've got to tell him.'

Larry was back in his room before Ma Rogers could reply. He thought of leaving the house without breakfast and coming back when things had quietened down a bit. Besides, he felt ashamed of his outburst at Wally. Then his stomach began to rumble so he changed his mind and headed for the kitchen. Old Man Rogers, fork in hand, was presiding over a pan of sizzling sausages.

'Hurry up, lad, it's gone nine.' He motioned Larry to a seat with a wave of his fork.

Wally was sitting at the table, his head bowed over his plate as he ate. Larry touched his shoulder. 'Sorry. Wal,' he said, 'I'm a bit mixed up this morning after my fiasco last night.'

His friend raised his head and after a second's hesitation grinned and nodded. 'Don't give it a thought, me old amico. Sit down and grab some bangers, they're great.'

Larry was well into his breakfast before April made her appearance, followed by June who had dark shadows under her eyes. With a kind of resignation he watched the secret glances she exchanged with Wally. Well, that's that, he thought.

76

He turned his gaze to April who winked at him and whispered hoarsely 'Don't worry about Ma, I've got that old bugger's number.' Larry smiled half-heartedly, unable to believe that anyone could ever get the better of that Tyrannosaurus Rex.

The door opened and Ma Rogers came into the kitchen. 'It's half past nine and you're still having breakfast.'

Wally stood up. 'I've finished, Ma,' he said, smiling at her.

'It's not you I'm talking to, Wally,' she said, 'It's these others.'

'Fee, fi, foh, fum,' chanted April, her cigarette jerking up and down in rhythm.

Mrs. Rogers glared malevolently at her, opened her mouth to reply, then abruptly changed her mind and left.

Old Man Rogers looked up from his chair by the fire where he was fondling the cat in his lap. 'Fee, fi, foh, fum?' he queried. 'Funny you should say that. We had the giant from *Jack and the Beanstalk* staying here three years ago. He *was* a big feller.'

'I know,' choked April, starting to cough.

'Yer,' said the old man reflectively. 'Never came down to breakfast. She used to take it up to him. First time she's ever done that.'

April spluttered over her breakfast plate, and seeing Larry's perplexed look, went into a paroxysm of coughing and laughter.

'What was all that about, then?' asked Wally as he and Larry left the room.

'Something to do with Ma Rogers, I think.' Larry was beginning to see what April was laughing about.

'Oh,' said Wally, not really caring, now that he knew they weren't laughing at him. 'Coming to the theatre later to see if there's any mail?'

'I've got a bit of shopping to do first,' said Larry, wanting to be on his own for a while.

'OK, mate, see you there about half twelve.' Wally gave a thumbs-up sign and mounted the stairs to his room.

Larry watched him go, admiring his easy charm and hating him for having slept with June.

He wandered around the city centre, 'shop-window-fuddling' as his mother called it, jingling the small change in his pockets as he walked aimlessly along. He crossed the main road to a tailor's shop and stood drooling before a display of suits and sports jackets and bolts of cloth. He had never had a suit made to measure, and the only clothes he possessed were his chalk-stripe demob suit and raincoat, and a sports jacket he'd bought off the peg in Swansea High Street with some of his army gratuity.

He fancied himself in the dark blue blazer with brass buttons which stood proudly on a stand in the front of the window. It was the sort of jacket he had always associated with officers in mufti, with cream flannels and week-end house parties, braying laughs, and strawberries and cream served outdoors on croquet lawns.

'Anyone for tennis?' Tillson stood at his shoulder, an empty brown paper carrier bag under his arm.

'Oh, hello.' There was no warmth in Larry's greeting, but Tillson seemed not to notice. He sucked his teeth reflectively. 'Fancy that meself,' he said, nodding towards the blazer. 'Still, no use dreaming. Anyway, me animal would soon make a mess of that. He'd claw it off me back, would Simba.'

Larry remembered the somnolent beast he had stroked and wondered why Tillson kept up the pretence that his lion was savage. He merely nodded, still looking at the shop window.

'Seven quid for a blazer. Bloody hell!' said Tillson, suddenly seeing the price tag.

'I wouldn't mind paying that much if I could afford it. It's non-utility, mind.' Larry blurted out his thoughts. 'If you'd spent six years in uniform you'd want to wear something with a bit of style that doesn't rub your neck raw. I got fed up with bloody khaki suits and flannel underwear. I'm due for a bit of the sweet life.'

'You're out of your depth, son.' Tillson's tone was laconic. 'If I was you I'd settle for a fresh battle dress for the next few years and leave this business to them who can do it. You're nothing but a bleeding NAAFI comic, and there's plenty of them about these days.'

'Bollocks!' exclaimed Larry, from the depths of his soul.

'Very clever repartee, that,' the lion man chuckled. 'You'll be topping the bill at the London Palladium soon with that kind of material. Well, better go and get the meat for me act tonight. Want to come for a walk to the slaughter house?' He waited for Larry's reply to this unexpected offer.

'Ah, well, I'm off then.' He sounded genuinely disappointed.

Larry watched the figure in the dirty raincoat as it shambled away down the street. His mind seethed with the clever insults he might have hurled at the retreating Tillson, but they got as far as his throat and choked him.

I'll show the buggers, he thought for the second time that morning, but with an increasing lack of conviction.

There was no mail for Larry at the stage door and his depression was deepened by the fact that the stage door-keeper got his name wrong again.

'Nothing for you, Mr. Power,' said the one-armed custodian, looking in the 'P' slot.

'Gower,' said Larry through gritted teeth.

The door man gave the 'Bs' a cursory glance. 'Nothing for him either.'

From where he stood, Larry could see that neither was there anything in the 'Gs'.

'Well, give me the key to number 12.'

'It's not here, Tillson's got it.'

Larry walked away onto the stage, not really wanting to go to the dressing-room anyway. Time enough to go up there and brood, he thought.

Simba sat in his cage staring into space, his mind on food. His stomach rumbled loudly as Larry walked towards him. The lion focused with difficulty on the approaching figure, reluctant to relinquish his dreams of herds of fresh meat on the hoof. He recognized his new friend and rolled on his back to be tickled.

Larry scratched the sparsely-haired belly, murmuring endearments he had used on the family cat. 'Who's a lovely boy, then?' he crooned, still awed at the fact that he was tickling a real live lion. Simba purred with the imprecision of an engine missing on a couple of cylinders, his front paws hanging limp and his eyes closed in ecstasy.

'Don't suppose you've ever had a lady friend,' said Larry. 'All that lovely wedding tackle going to waste.'

He eyed the lion's sexual equipment and was suddenly reminded of the joke about the old lady in court who shouted to the suspected rapist in the dock 'You ought to be bloody well hung.' 'I am,' was the calm reply.

He snorted with laughter and without thinking gave Simba a playful rub in this most sensitive area. The reaction surprised him. The lion's eyes turned upwards in their sockets and he let out a broken roar of bliss.

Larry backed away from the cage, startled. He hadn't meant to arouse the lion in that way and felt shocked at his own temerity. 'Sorry, boy,' he said. 'Don't get the wrong idea.' Simba's reply was to rotate his hind legs like a cyclist going uphill, his eyes now fixed on Larry with an expression of abiding affection. 'It looks like we're engaged. We'll get married as soon as we can, and live in a Lyons Corner House.'

Larry gave the lion's mane a friendly tug and left. Simba's eyes followed him with their expression undimmed. Love had come into his life at last.

Wally came through the stage door just as Larry was preparing to leave.

'Come on round to The Grapes,' he said excitedly. 'Ted Edwards is in the saloon. I'll introduce you to him—I worked on the bill with him before the war when he was just about to make the big time.'

'Ted Edwards?' Larry was very impressed. He had always been a great fan of the famous comic. All through the war years the radio show built around Ted Edwards had helped listeners to forget their troubles, and he had become a folk hero. His catch-phrases and funny voices were imitated by all the young comedians and there was more than a hint of his style in Wally's act.

When they entered the saloon bar they found Ted Edwards surrounded by a group of people who were laughing loudly. He was of medium height and slim build, although the brown camel-hair coat slung loosely over his shoulders gave them an illusory breadth. In his right hand he held a glass of whisky, from which he took large sips at each pause in his narration.

His face, which Larry remembered from a thousand press photographs and cinema newsreels, was coarser in real life. He felt a sense of disappointment, too, at the sound of the voice which had brought him and his family so much pleasure over the radio.

'Get a couple of drinks for us,' whispered Wally, 'It's no good interrupting him in the middle of a joke—I'll introduce you to him when he's finished.'

Larry ordered two bottles of Guinness and as he paid for them he eyed his change with alarm. He'd soon be broke at this rate. Wally accepted the drink with a quick smile and resumed his attentive listening to the comedian's gags. Larry stood beside him, sipping his Guinness.

'This feller goes into the toilet, y'see, and finds this coloured bloke lying on his side having a slash. "Why're you doing it like that?" he says. "Well," says the Sambo, 'I've got a bad back and the doctor said I wasn't to lift anything heavy".'

Edwards's admirers laughed wildly, and the comic took another swig from his glass, his eyes hooded as he appraised their reaction.

Wally tapped him on the shoulder. 'Hello, Ted—remember me? Wally Winston.' He held out his hand.

Edwards ignored the gesture. 'Oh yes, I remember you. Second spot at the Met., Edgware Road when I was topping the bill there. Nice little act. Always in the wings when I was on. They tell me that you've nicked one of my routines.'

Wally blushed and gave a strangled laugh. 'You know how it is, Ted. Got a bit carried away one night and slipped in one of your gags without thinking. It went so well I kept it in the act.'

'Well take it out again, son.' Edwards's face was red with anger. 'Too many bleeding upstarts in this business. Find your own material.' He turned back to his audience. 'Bloody profession's full of army concert party comics and poufs.'

'That's a nice thing to say, dear.' Jimmy Long had come in unobserved and was leaning languidly against the bar.

Larry, who had been secretly enjoying the scene until the reference to 'army comics', nudged Wally. 'This looks interesting,' he said.

His friend stared venomously at the back of Edwards's neck. 'Big-headed bastard,' he muttered, at the same time making sure that the comic couldn't hear him.

Edwards turned to face Jimmy Long. 'Now there's a lovely sight.' He clapped his hands in mock delight, after carefully handing his whisky to a bystander. 'Jemima is wearing her off-the-shoulder tweed jacket with twin set and pearls.'

Jimmy pirouetted and dropped a curtsey. 'And Edwina is looking lovely in her camel-hair coat with the open-work truss and peep-toe sandals.' He grinned wickedly. 'Show us your war wound, Ted.'

There had been a lot of publicity about Edwards having been injured by a piece of shrapnel while on a visit to France in 1944 for the services. Newspapers had featured pictures of him lying in a hospital bed surrounded by bandaged soldiers and giving the thumbs-up sign. The photographs had gone a long way to increasing the popularity of the 'Ted Edwards Radio Show.'

'Shut your trap, you big queen.' Edwards was really angry now, and the bantering tone was gone from his voice.

The bar went quiet, and Larry was reminded of the usual scene in a Western when hero and baddie face each other for the final showdown, although in this case he wasn't quite sure who was wearing the white hat.

Jimmy took a long drink and set the glass down on the bar. He dabbed his mouth with a white handkerchief, and looked Edwards up and down.

'Healed nicely, hasn't it? Not a mark anywhere. That can be *seen*, that is.'

The other man growled and took a step forward, his fists clenched. 'I'll smash your teeth down your throat.'

'I wouldn't do that if I were you, duckie, or I might tell these friends of yours what really happened to you.'

Edwards's face was livid, but he stood wavering indecisively.

This was the second piece of blackmail Larry had witnessed that morning, and eager to see what his erstwhile idol would do, he pressed forward. Someone jogged his elbow, and his glass of Guinness poured over the front of Edwards's camel-hair coat.

'I'm sorry, Mr. Edwards.' Larry was appalled at what he'd done.

'You great, clumsy git!' Edwards clawed the coat from his shoulders. 'Look what you've done! Cost me a bleeding bomb, this coat did.'

Larry patted the stain ineffectually with his grimy handkerchief. 'Sorry,' he kept repeating.

'Get off!' Edwards shoved him away and Wally took Larry by the elbow. He was shaking with laughter. 'That'll teach the bastard. Come on, let's get something to eat.'

Larry was only too glad to leave. 'I didn't mean to do it, somebody pushed my arm.'

Wally laughed again. 'Of course—*I* did, mate. Wanted to get my own back, didn't I?'

Larry stopped in his tracks. 'You mean you deliberately jogged my elbow so that I'd spill the beer over his coat?'

'That's right, me old 'oppo.'

Larry could hardly believe that Wally was capable of such a thing. He opened his mouth to protest, then, thinking better of it, he shook his head in wonder and started laughing too.

'And I've still not been formally introduced to the great Ted Edwards.'

'You should be glad, dear, he's not your type. Although you certainly made an impression on him.' Jimmy Long had joined them, and together they walked to a café which had been recommended to Wally.

'Where's George?' asked Larry as they sat down at a reasonably clean table.

'Not too well today, so he's having a morning in bed. I'll take him some sandwiches back for his lunch. He's not a big eater, anyway.'

Jimmy sounded like a wife talking about her husband. Larry felt uncomfortable.

'What's all this about Ted Edwards's war wound?' he asked, changing the subject.

'Oh—didn't you know?' Over the egg and chips, Jimmy told them the story. 'We were all together in an ENSA show in France, me and George, Ted Edwards, a couple of girl dancers and Mavis Jenkins, who called herself a soubrette but was forty if she was a day. She'd played a piano accordion in her act for so long we all used to say she'd got pleats in her tits from the pressure.

'Anyway, we were billeted in a little estaminet outside Caen, and Ted, who was always chasing the crumpet, got a bit tight one night in the bar after the show, and had a go at one of the dancing girls. Well, she wasn't having any of his nonsense and her partner—forgotten her name now—*she* wouldn't have anything to do with him either. So there's old Mavis in the corner by the fire knocking back half a pint of cherry brandy and not looking too bad in the half light, and Ted goes over and starts pawing her. Up to this time he hadn't taken any notice of her other than complain that she got more laughs than he did when she did her "Oh Johnny" number at the end of the show and went into the audience to sing it, sitting on the officers' laps. Mind you, I thought it was common, and so did George.

'Still, he fancied anything when he'd had a few, did Ted— nasty customer in drink, he was—and Mavis was only too glad to get some attention. To cut a long story short, they went upstairs to his room and we all nodded knowingly at each other and went on with our drinking. Suddenly, some time later, when we'd forgotten all about it, there was a terrible scream from upstairs—from him, not her.

'George and I were nearest the stairs and we rushed into Ted's room. Well, talk about laugh! There was Mavis in her knickers with her tits round her ankles trying to lift the window off Ted's John Thomas. He'd got no toilet in his room, and never being one to worry about niceties like that, he'd hung his old thing out of the window to take a leak before getting down to more serious matters. He was always boasting about the size of it, and from what I saw that night, he had every reason to.'

Jimmy's eyes misted over reflectively for a moment, then he continued hurriedly. 'As he stood there, letting it all hang out, he stretched his arms in the air and turned his head towards Mavis, who was struggling with her bra by the bed—she told us all this as we tried to help—"Look," he said, "No hands." Well, at that very moment a heavy lorry went past in the street—rattled the window—the sash cord snapped—it was only hanging by a thread anyway—and the bottom half of the window slammed down on his Palethorpe.

'We could hardly get him free for laughing. He was groaning away, and I must say he had plenty to groan about. Eventually we got him on the bed and sent for the M.O. of the nearest unit. He got an ambulance right away and took him to the Army General Hospital.

'Of course, the ENSA people couldn't let the true story out, but as Ted Edwards was news, the correspondents soon found out he was in hospital, so a statement was put out saying he'd been wounded by a bit of shrapnel. We were all sworn to secrecy over it and for poor old Mavis' sake we never let on.

'He was ever so badly bruised, though, and was in dock for a few weeks. Funny thing was, an American General came visiting some G.I.s in the same hospital, handing out Purple Hearts, and nearly gave one to Ted by mistake. The ward sister said "It's not his heart that's purple, General—it's something else." Edwards didn't think it was funny at all.'

Larry and Wally bent double with laughter over the cluttered table, and Jimmy smiled as he stirred his tea. 'That's your great Ted Edwards for you. Still, it was naughty of you to push Larry's elbow, Wally.'

'Didn't think anybody had seen me.' Wally stopped laughing and shrugged his shoulders. 'Serves the bastard right, anyway.

Old Larry didn't mind, did you, mate?' He patted his friend on the shoulder.

'No,' said Larry, wondering if he meant it.

Jimmy watched them carefully as he drank his tea. 'Come on then, lads. You can pay for this magnificent meal, Wally. That'll teach you to take advantage of your friend's good nature. Don't forget George's sandwiches.'

Wally muttered something inaudible and stayed behind to settle up as the other two sauntered out into the grey street.

'He's ambitious, is our Wally,' said Jimmy lightly. 'But then, aren't we all?'

'Yes, I suppose we are,' replied Larry thoughtfully.

Larry went to the theatre early that evening. As he began to walk upstairs to the dressing-room, Lovegrove called to him. He stood at the foot of the stairs, his hands on his hips and his legs wide apart. 'Gower!' he shouted.

'Give the gentleman a cigar, he's got the name right!' Larry was past caring what the manager thought of him. Jimmy had told him on their walk from the café after lunch that if he had not been replaced with another act by Tuesday morning, they would have to let him stay for the week.

'Don't give me any lip.'

'What would you say to a full set of teeth, then?'

Larry started down the stairs towards Lovegrove, his body tense. He was a strong lad, and his years in the army had left him in pretty good shape.

Lovegrove dropped his hands from his hips and assumed a less arrogant stance. He was a physical coward and like all bullies quick to recognize strength and determination in others. It did not mean that he was equally quick to capitulate, only that he would change his tactics and adopt other, more subtle means of getting his own back. At one time he had carried on a vendetta against his wife's only brother—with her he had no chance—and was not averse to writing him poison pen letters. Under the guise of 'a well-wisher' and 'an advocate of fair play' he had

86

accused his brother-in-law, who was an undertaker, of reclaiming the brass handles and other accessories from the coffins of the deceased before they were consigned to the flames of the local crematorium, and of using them over and over again. The letters had succeeded for a time, until one Saturday night in an over-confident mood induced by drink, he had used the theatre notepaper on which to write his accusatory note. His brother-in-law, who had suspected him all along but had temporarily suspended the activities of which he was accused, took the letter along to Lovegrove on the following Monday morning and in front of an approving Mrs. Lovegrove made him eat it, envelope, stamp and all.

He now watched Larry descend the stairs and made a mental note to send him one of his 'you stink' anonymous letters, care of the stage door.

'All right, son,' he said quickly. 'I just wanted to say that I saw your act second house last night. It was a bit better—not much, mind you—so I've decided you can stay.' He kept to himself the fact that Head Office had told him there was no chance of getting a replacement at the amount of money Larry was being paid, and therefore he'd have to put up with his act.

Larry stopped one step above Lovegrove and looked at him uncertainly. He was glad to hear that he now had the chance of finishing the week and would be spared the ignominy of being taken off the bill.

Lovegrove sensed his relief and seized the opportunity to take another dig at the aspiring young comic. 'Mind you, a word from me in the right direction and I can make or break you.'

Lovegrove waddled off quickly before Larry could work out whether this was a threat or a promise. He stood on the stairs for a while, wondering at his own aggression. He usually had no difficulty in controlling his temper but the frustrations of the past few days had sharpened its edge and forced him into actions which were alien to his easy-going nature.

On reflection he realized that though he had spoken sharply to some of his new male acquaintances, he still had a healthy respect for the females. This observation was quickly borne out before he'd reached the next landing. Julie Tempest came out of her dressing-room with a newspaper in her hand. Her face under the white turban was grotesque with half-applied stage make-up. She waved the paper at him. 'Where's Lovegrove?'

Larry backed away. 'Er—I've just seen him by the stage door. I think he's gone to his office.'

Her husband came out of the dressing-room and touched her shoulder tentatively. 'Don't get upset over the notice, love. There's nothing we can do about it.'

Larry looked puzzled. 'What notice?' he asked.

Julie Tempest hurled the paper at him. '*That* bloody notice in there. The write-up of the show. *You'd* better read it, too. He's torn you to pieces.' She threw off her husband's restraining arm and stormed back into her room.

Her husband picked up the paper from the floor near Larry's feet and reassembled it carefully. 'She's mad as hell with the reporter. He's knocked everybody in the show except Wally Winston, and that ain't good for business. It's her they're paying to see and the public take notice of what the critics say these days. Mind you, things didn't go too well for her last night.'

Larry remembered his part in the débâcle and shuddered involuntarily.

'Lovegrove promised us we'd get a good notice. The editor's supposed to be a friend of his. Must have sent the wrong feller along last night to review the show. Probably the war correspondent, to judge from the way he's shot up the acts.'

'What's he said about me, Mr. Tempest?'

'*Mr. Tempest?* Listen, sonny Jim, I'm a performer in my own right.'

Larry had touched Tommy on a raw nerve.

'Just because I'm married to the cow, it doesn't mean that I have to take her name.' In spite of his anger Tommy had dropped his voice and was looking furtively over his shoulder towards the dressing-room. 'Barratt's my name. Tommy Barratt, and don't you forget it.'

'Sorry, Mr. Barratt, it was a slip of the tongue.'

Tommy's face unexpectedly creased in a grin. 'It's all right, son, everybody does it. It's part of the cross I have to bear.'

Larry's eyes were on the newspaper in Barratt's hand. 'What does it say about me?' He felt his mouth go dry.

'Here, read it for yourself. Julie won't want to keep it, anyway.' Tommy handed it over. 'Don't take what he's said too much to heart, lad. It's on the third page under the notice for the Empire.' His voice was kind.

In the solitude of his dressing-room Larry found himself trembling. It took him several minutes to pluck up enough courage to turn to page three and read what was there.

It was headed 'Last Rites at the Royalty Theatre'.

'Those of us unlucky enough to have been at the Royalty Theatre last night should today be wearing black armbands. The reason is simple. We were all present at the death of Variety. The last rites were administered at 6.15 p.m. and continued until 8.30 p.m. There were no flowers, although at one time tomatoes were considered.

'The chief mourners were Miss Julie Tempest, who described herself as "nude but nice". Nude she certainly was, nice she was not. I could have forgiven the acre or so of goose pimples she revealed to us—they were no doubt caused by a zephyr wafting across the stage from the direction of the glue factory. But the presentation of her act was unforgivable and though mistakes were made by the stage staff, Miss Tempest's act was a complete shambles. Let us draw a veil over the details of her performance, wishing only that she had done likewise over her too ample frame.

'The other acts on the bill, with one exception which I shall come to later, were entirely forgettable. April and June—where, one wonders, was May?—opened the bill with a dancing routine which boded ill for the rest of the proceedings. They finished their act with at least sixteen bars to spare, which, under the circumstances, the audience considered a bonus, even if the orchestra could ill afford them. It appeared at some passages in the music that the trumpet player was only using one lip—no doubt saving the other one for tomorrow evening's performances.

'They were followed by a certain gentleman called Barry Flower.'

Larry turned his eyes to heaven, brought them down, and with trepidation read on.

'What he was trying to do escaped me. It was definitely not comedy as far as I could make out, and judging from the audience's bewildered reaction they were equally in the dark. It would have been kinder if Mr. Flower's act had been in the same lightless condition. He is, I'm afraid, without talent and the sooner he takes up some kind of useful trade, the better.'

Larry felt as if he had been hit by a runaway tank. Someone had told him that it didn't matter what they said about you in the Press as long as they got your name right. He was not even allowed that tiny piece of consolation. His first reaction was to flee—to run as far away as possible from this drab theatre, this bitchy back-biting profession and—and what? There was nothing else he could do.

He wallowed in a mire of self-pity, his head buried in his hands, the newspaper spread over the dressing-room table like a potential shroud for his dying hopes.

Joe Armsworth knocked on the door. 'Tillson—are you in there?' He entered the room. 'That animal of yours—' He stopped and looked at Larry's face and then at the newspaper. 'Oh aye—seen bloody notice, 'ave yer? Don't worry, lad, you'll get worse than that before you top the bill at t'Palladium. Remember, there's three hundred million Chinese that don't know nor care what they've said about you, and that applies to the good notices as well as the bad 'uns.'

Larry forced a smile. 'I might do better if I were to play a week at the Peking Empire—the reception couldn't be any worse than the one I've been getting here.'

'Never tha mind, son. They're a tough lot of buggers here, and at least the critic's roasted everybody else on the bill as well as you, except for young Wally.'

'I haven't read that far yet.'

'Well, don't—it might make you jealous. By the way, where's Tillson? His lion's getting restless down on stage. A bloody mongrel got in through the stage door somehow, and he barked so much at Simba that the poor thing's frightened out of its life. He'll need a bit of settling down before the act.'

'I'll have a go at soothing him, Joe. I seem to get on better with him than the audience.' Larry was glad to have an opportunity to take his mind off his misery.

'Come on, then. I'll be calling the half in five minutes.' Armsworth looked at the battered pocket watch he had taken from his bulging waistcoat. 'They should all be in the theatre by the half hour before curtain-up, you know. The artistes, I mean. It's in your contract, is that.'

He led the way down to the stage.

Larry could see that Simba was in a bad way. The lion was padding up and down the cage at a frantic rate, uttering short grunts.

'What's up, old mate?'

At the sound of Larry's voice the animal stopped its pacing and peered uncertainly in his direction. Larry patted its head and crooned to it. Soon the agitated flanks resumed a steadier rhythm and Simba lay down on his back to be tickled.

'Well, I'm buggered,' said Joe Armsworth in admiration. 'If you can get that lot out there to do same for you, you'll be a star in no time.'

'What are you doing with that beast?' Tillson careered across the stage toward them, his arms flailing wildly.

Larry stopped stroking the lion's belly, and stood up.

'It's all right, Tillson. I asked him to settle the poor bastard down. A dog frightened the life out of it,' said Armsworth, interposing his great bulk between the two men.

'I don't like anybody going near him. He could tear your arm off if you're not careful.' Tillson stank of whisky and his face was working furiously. 'Stand back, I say.'

Simba looked up at him resignedly, rolled over, shook his mane and raising one leg, broke wind.

Larry and Armsworth burst into laughter, and Armsworth clapped his hands. 'Well said, Simba.'

As they walked away from the angry Tillson, Joe warned Larry 'Watch him, son. He can be a dangerous customer. Used to be a good circus act at one time, mind you. Worked for Bertram Mills for years until drink and his temper put the skids on him. Very unpredictable, that's his trouble.' He glanced at his watch. 'Arthur, call the half hour,' he shouted.

Larry looked at his own watch. 'It's only twenty to six.'

Joe smiled. 'You can tell you're new to this game. We always call the half thirty-five minutes before curtain up. "Overture and beginners" is called five minutes before the show starts.'

'Thanks for telling me.' Larry was glad that Joe had been the one to impart this new piece of stage lore. God knows he needed to learn everything while he still had the chance. He might be an apprentice brick-layer next week, the way things were going.

They met Wally as he was coming in through the stage door.

'You're cutting it a bit fine, aren't you?' Joe looked up at the clock.

'Plenty of time, Joe.' Wally was full of smiles and bonhomie. Larry noticed the paper under his arm and felt sick again. 'What a rave review, eh? Sorry he had a go at you—still, you'll get over it, Larry. Read what he says about me?'

Before Larry could answer Wally had the paper open and was reading aloud. ' "The one bright star in the Stygian blackness of the sky over the Royalty—" '

'What's Stygian mean?' asked Sammy, the pimply stage-hand, who was standing nearby hoping to see the girls come down for the warm-up before their act. There was always the chance of a glimpse of thigh as they twirled round in practice.

'I don't know—I think it's Greek or something.' Wally was annoyed at the interruption. He read on. ' "Wally Winston, a young comic in the true tradition of the music hall, soon had the audience eating out of his hand. His style is crisp and very funny. A combination of a young Ted Edwards and Max Wall at his best." '

'That's because he's nicked half their material,' said Joe Armsworth dryly.

Wally glanced at him sharply, decided to say nothing and continued. ' "This young artiste restored my faith in the future of comedy. Though he alone could not redeem a disastrous evening's entertainment, his performance bore the hallmark of stardom and we shall be hearing a lot more of this young man." '

Tillson blew a raspberry as Wally finished. 'Big-headed bastard,' he said as he pushed past.

Larry found himself smiling in spite of his misery and for one fleeting moment was in sympathy with Tillson. Then he was prodded in the back with a hard forefinger. 'Keep away from Simba. I'm warning you.'

'Piss off,' retorted Larry.

'You've got a gift for repartee, son, I'll say that for you.'

Tillson went on up the stairs, chuckling to himself. As he turned the corner of the first landing the girls could be heard coming down the steps in their tap-shoes. There was a little scream, a slap and April and June came into view. April was rubbing her bottom.

'If it's not Lovegrove it's that dirty old man. My arse will be black and blue before the week's out.' She flashed a quick smile at Larry. 'Hello, sunshine,' she said. 'I see Wally's been reading his notice to you. Did he read you ours?'

June went past without a word and threw her arms around Wally. 'Who's going to be a big star, then?'

He gave her a quick peck on the cheek and held her off. 'Watch the make-up on the suit, love.'

June pouted. Wally whispered something in her ear and she smiled slowly. 'That would be nice.'

Joe Armsworth broke up the gathering. 'Come on, let's get this shambles of a show on. We must give our new star a chance to shine again tonight.' He gave a mock bow to Wally who returned it with a smile, but his eyes were like steel.

'Roll on the Palladium,' he said.

Larry gave his first performance of the evening to a restless, sodden house. It was raining heavily and the brave souls who had made it to the theatre were beginning to regret it, especially those with free seats. People with complimentary tickets were notoriously harder to please than those who had paid.

He was prepared for indifference by this time, and taking Jimmy's advice, he slowed down his delivery. This resulted in a few more laughs than he had yet managed to glean and when he finished his act, the applause at least covered his exit from the stage. From the orchestra pit Dan gave a little encouraging nod as Larry took his call at the side of the stage, even though the clapping had ceased by the time he had straightened up.

April was waiting for him as he came off. She gave him a squeeze and said 'That's a bit better, lovey.'

He squeezed her in return and was unexpectedly roused by her answering thrust against his body.

'Hey—get out of my bloody corner if you're going to do that sort of thing.' Joe pushed them good humouredly to one side as he gave the lighting cues for the next act.

Larry felt good for the first time since the week had started. I'll show them, he thought yet again. In the darkness backstage he seized April roughly and pressed his lips to her eager ones. His hands sought the soft flesh of her breasts with a sudden urgent need. But then he became aware of a snuffling sound from nearby. He stopped his fumbling and looked over April's shoulder, in time to see Sammy beating a hasty retreat. His ardour suddenly cooled.

'What's up, love?' April sounded disappointed.

'Sammy was watching us.' Larry felt unaccountably ashamed of himself.

'Don't worry about him.' She snuggled up to him again.

'Well, we can't do anything here, anyway.'

'Ooh! What do you want to do then, naughty boy?'

Larry was in control of himself now. The throbbing in his loins ebbed away in direct proportion to the increasing archness of his companion.

'I've just remembered, I promised to see how George Short is—Jimmy said he wasn't feeling too well today.'

94

'Not turning queer on us are you, duckie?' April demanded sharply.

'Good God, no,' said Larry in real alarm, and to emphasize the point took her left nipple between his fingers and applied gentle pressure.

'That's all right, then.' April was somewhat mollified. 'Play your cards right in the digs tonight, honey, and you may win the jackpot,' she said in a Mae West voice and swinging her hips. 'I do fancy you, though,' she added quickly, kissing her reluctant lover on the cheek.

He laughed, genuinely touched by her affection, and patting her bottom lightly, he went off to look for Jimmy Long.

His and George's dressing-room was the brightest place in the whole theatre, and it give Larry a feeling of real pleasure to enter it. Both men were already made up. George was sitting in front of the mirror, smoking his pipe as he adjusted his false eyelashes, and Jimmy was wriggling into his gown.

'Give us a hand here with this zip, Larry dear. That's it. Now those hooks and eyes at the top. Thanks. How was the act tonight?'

'I think it went better. Not a sensation by any means, but at least I felt I was getting somewhere. I took your advice about slowing down my patter, and I'm pretty sure that that's part of my trouble—speaking too quickly, I mean.'

'You'll be all right, son.' George's deep voice once again came as a surprise.

'Thanks. By the way, how are you feeling now? That's what I really came to ask.'

'He's not right, poor love.' Jimmy answered for his friend. 'It's his stomach, you know—where the shrapnel got him. Hardly touched those sandwiches at lunch-time.'

'I'm fine, don't fuss me.' George stood up and reached for a sequined dress, wincing as he did so. Around his middle he wore a surgical corset, Larry noticed. The dizzy feeling of unreality which had hovered round him so often these past three days descended once more. Alice in Wonderland, that's me, he thought. Here I am, helping a man into an evening gown and accepting the fact without blinking. And over there is a bloke in a wig and false eyelashes, smoking a pipe.

'If we had a couple of flamingoes we could play a spot of croquet,' he said brightly.

George caught the allusion and laughed. 'Alice in Wonderland, eh? I suppose that's how you feel, watching us strange creatures get dressed. Got a bit of a dream-like quality about it, I've no doubt.'

George had begun to struggle painfully into his dress.

'That pipe can't be doing your stomach any good. Give it to me.' Jimmy took it from George's mouth and tapped the tobacco out into an ashtray.

'Women are all alike, aren't they, son?' remarked George, with a chuckle.

Larry nodded assent. 'Some more so than others,' he said without thinking.

George and Jimmy looked at each other and back to Larry. 'Yes, I suppose you're right, dear,' they said together in their camper voices and laughed.

'By the by.' Jimmy spoke before Larry could retrieve his last remark. 'Don't worry about the write-up tonight. The critic didn't even mention us—that's sometimes worse than being panned.'

'And three hundred million Chinese neither know nor care that I died a death last night.'

'Who told you that?' asked George.

'Joe Armsworth, the home-spun philosopher,' Larry grinned. 'I'm getting the right slant on things. Hey—get it? Chinese—slant? I say, I say.'

'The boy's working well tonight. There'll be no holding him soon. Come on, George, it's "magic" time.' Jimmy pushed Larry out of the door. 'Poor old George really is rough tonight. I'll have to watch him carefully,' he said in a low voice.

Larry nodded in sympathy, putting his arm affectionately around Jimmy's shoulders. Almost immediately he jerked his hand away. 'Sorry,' he said hastily.

'It's all right dear, you don't have to feel ashamed of yourself for consoling an old queen. We're not lepers, you know.'

Jimmy spoke lightly, but his voice was full of hurt. He turned away and called to George. 'Henri Lamarr must be about to drop his last club. We'll be off.'

With a hurried apology, Larry took the opportunity to disappear from the scene, angry with himself for having put his arm round Jimmy's shoulder, angrier still for snatching it away so quickly. He had devalued a genuine gesture of friendliness by his reflex action. Where ought one to draw the line in normal relationships with queers? He was confused by the whole situation. A lion was casting sheep's eyes at him because he had inadvertently squeezed the animal's nuts, April was panting after him, tongue hanging out, and now Jimmy Long seemed to be taking a fancy to him. While the people whose affection Larry craved—the audience and June—could not be more indifferent.

Wally was in the dressing-room when Larry returned. He looked up.

'What a notice, eh?'

The paper was spread out before him and he had obviously been reading his part of the review again. Savouring every bloody word, thought Larry.

He forced a smile. 'There'll be no stopping you now, Wal.'

'No sir. I rang Lou Hyman and he's tickled to death with everything—especially now that they've changed the running order, too.'

'What do you mean?'

'It's all right—it doesn't affect you. Armsworth told me this morning that as I went so well and they're a bit short for time, I'm closing the first half. Long and Short are doing another spot after Henri Lamarr, and I've been given an extra five minutes. There's the new running order—on the mirror.'

He brushed his hair with his silver brush, checked his make-up in the mirror and grinned at Larry. 'Move over Max Miller. Watch out Tommy Trinder. The lad's on his way!'

Larry looked at his watch, his smile wearing a little thin. 'You'd better get down there—Jimmy and George are already on.'

'Getting matey with those two, aren't you?' Wally put one hand on his hip and waved a limp-wristed salute with the other. 'See you later, dear. Got to meet my public.' He minced out of the door, almost colliding with Tillson.

'Watch the suit with that bloody meat.' Wally's voice changed abruptly as he inspected the front of his jacket for stains. 'Scruffy sod!' he shouted as he left.

Tillson grunted indifferently, slapping a large, smelly chunk of horse meat in the sink and turning on the tap.

Larry said nothing, not wishing to start any more arguments. He forced himself to ignore the pungent combination of odours from Tillson and the meat, and looked at the new running order.

OVERTURE	2 mins.
APRIL & JUNE	3 mins.
GOWER	8 mins.
HENRI LAMARR	10 mins.
LONG & SHORT	10 mins.
W. WINSTON	15 mins.
Interval—15 mins.	
GIRLS	5 mins.
TILLSON	12 mins.
LONG & SHORT	15 mins.
MISS TEMPEST	25 mins.

Artistes are requested to keep to these times.

Signed: *J. Armsworth*,

Stage Manager

No wonder Wally was so happy. He had virtually been elevated to second billing with this new position. Even Larry knew the significance of this place at the end of the first half of the programme. It also meant that Jimmy and George had lost some prestige by dropping their place in the order. However, at least they had another spot to compensate. Nobody had bothered to tell Larry—obviously he was not affected by the change—and the fact emphasized his lowly position in the hierarchy of his chosen profession.

The smell in the room became stronger as Tillson moved around, muttering to himself. He took the meat from the sink, weighed it in his hand, and putting his head back, placed it over his face. Larry looked at him in amazement.

'Does it fit?' Tillson's voice came through muffled. 'It's got to fit all over, otherwise Simba might take a chunk out of me face.'

'Just a minute,' said Larry. 'Put your head back a bit further and I'll have a look.' He tip-toed out of the room.

Tillson remained in position waiting for Larry's verdict, until it dawned on him that he had gone. 'Bleeding ponce,' he growled as he removed the meat from his face.

An unfamiliar figure was watching him with interest. 'Hello, old chap. I'm the Church of England chaplain. That must be a nasty black eye you've got there.'

Tillson's reply was unprintable.

'Oh, I say,' said the chaplain blushing furiously. 'You must be a Roman Catholic.'

Larry spent the time before his second performance in wandering about outside the theatre, trying to get away from his thoughts and the smell of Tillson.

By the time he came back, the room was full of cigar smoke. Wally sat in his chair, puffing away at a large Corona. 'Trying to get rid of Tillson's pong,' he said, coughing. 'It's disgraceful that I—er, we—should have to put up with him. Why can't Joe Armsworth put him in with Henri Lamarr? They're two of a kind.'

Larry, who had only exchanged a couple of words with the juggler, sympathized with Wally's anxiety to get Tillson out of their room, but privately doubted that anyone could be as bad as the lion tamer.

'Old "Droppo" 's French, y'see,' said Wally by way of explanation. 'Eats lots of garlic and all that pongy stuff. They say he was in the Resistance during the war—he should be able to handle Tillson all right. Don't see why he should have a dressing-room all to himself. He's only got his clubs to look after. I'll have a word with Armsworth to shift things around.'

But Armsworth was quite adamant when Wally approached him. Larry stood uncertainly behind his friend.

'He stays where he is, sonny.'

'But there's three of us in that room, and Lamarr's on his own. Come on, Joe, after all, now I've got the second star spot I'm entitled to a better dressing-room.'

'Listen, Tommy bloody Trinder, I made out that dressing-room list on Monday, and that's how it's going to be until Saturday. Just because you're doing well this week you're not going to take over the sodding theatre. Now bugger off.' Joe's voice was without venom but there was enough finality in it to make Wally stop arguing and turn away. 'I'll let you have some carbolic for the room from the cleaners—that might keep old Tillson's perfume under control.'

'I suppose Joe has a good reason for not letting Tillson share with Lamarr.' Wally was less belligerent now and a little chastened by the stage manager's remarks.

Observing him as they stood together side stage, watching the preparations for the second performance, Larry was intrigued by his friend's changes of mood. It seemed that to survive in show business, you had to fight for everything you wanted, and if you did not get it you didn't sulk—you simply rationalized the situation and pretended to have gained a kind of victory. Resilience, that was the quality necessary for survival. He wondered whether he would ever acquire it, remembering how swiftly and utterly his confidence and resolution had been shattered when he'd read his first notice a couple of hours earlier.

As if reading his friend's mind, Wally said 'If you don't speak up when you want something in this game, mate, nobody'll do it for you.' He laughed. 'They'll not tread all over me if I can help it. The Lord helps them that help themselves.' He grabbed June round the waist as she and April came up. 'See what I mean?' he said, pulling her towards him.

100

'Yes, mate,' replied Larry, doing the same to April, wishing it was June, but forcing himself to rationalize the situation.

'You're getting the right idea, me old china.'

'Hello chaps!' The chaplain approached the cuddling foursome.

'If you can't marry us, Vicar, how about saying a few words over us for the week-end?' April gave him a saucy wink.

The clergyman laughed good-naturedly. 'I'm supposed to look after your spiritual and moral welfare when you're on tour, but I don't think any of you are in any danger at the moment.'

'Ah, but you ought to hear about *his* reputation.' Wally pointed at Larry. 'No woman is safe with him, padre.'

'Ooh!' said April, giving a mock shiver. 'Lovely!'

Larry blushed. 'Don't you believe them, sir.'

'Sir, eh? You must be an ex-serviceman. So am I. Ex-chaplain to His Majesty's Forces. Perhaps we can have a chat one night this week—might even recruit you into the Actors' Church Union.'

Wally threw up a salute. 'I'm already a member, sir.' He still kept one arm round June.

'So am I,' said April.

'I know that, I have your names from Head Office, that's why I'm here to see you. Well, I won't bother you now, you're obviously very busy. See you later on in the week—unless you want to see me before. I don't listen to confessions or any of that sort of thing—might embarrass me.' He winked. 'I can offer you a nice cup of tea, though, and the wife makes fairly reasonable Welsh cakes. So perhaps we can entice you along, Mr. Flower?'

'Gower,' said Larry resignedly.

'That's funny, that's where my wife comes from. Probably have a lot in common, you two.' He turned to go. 'By the way, that fellow in the lion act wasn't in the services, was he?'

'Wouldn't take him. The lion had flat feet.' Wally was losing interest in the proceedings.

'I say, that's clever. Wish I'd said that.' The padre gave a cheery wave and left them.

'Was he being sarcastic?' Wally looked peeved.

'Can't tell with vicars,' said Larry. 'By the way, Wal, why did you join the Actors' Church Union?'

'Because of the digs. They have a list of digs which they publish and you can guarantee that they're all OK.' Wally was enthusiastic.

'Anyway, I like to know that somebody's watching over me,' said April, looking up at Larry.

'Yes, I suppose it is a comfort.' Larry disengaged himself hurriedly, uncertain whether or not that 'somebody' began with a capital 'S', and looked at his watch. 'Hey! They'll be calling the "Overture" soon. It's nearly five minutes to curtain-up.' In his own ears he sounded like a character in a Hollywood movie, but the others reacted normally to his words.

'Come on, June,' said April. 'Let's practice that bit at the beginning of "The Toy Drum Major". Leave her alone for a minute, Wally, we've got work to do.'

June gave Wally a lingering kiss. Larry watched them jealously and then felt ashamed of himself.

'Lovely girl, June,' he said, as she walked lazily away.

'She'll do for this week, anyway,' replied Wally carelessly, donning his 'man of the world' air as he left Larry.

Larry was shocked at his friend's attitude but secretly pleased that at some other time, at some other theatre, when Wally was not on the bill, perhaps. . . .

Joe Armsworth interrupted his reverie. 'Seem to have lost some of yer nerves then, old son. You're looking more relaxed.'

Larry tensed up again as he came back to reality. Seeking to change the subject he asked Joe why he had turned down Wally's request to have Tillson moved to Henri Lamarr's dressing-room. 'Not that *I'm* worried, mind you,' he added.

Joe looked at his old pocket watch and gave Arthur the signal to call the 'Overture' before replying. 'It's a long story. I might tell you tomorrow if you're a good lad.'

He would say nothing more, and Larry soon forgot his curiosity as he steeled himself for the second performance.

The girls' act was greeted with an untoward burst of applause and shouts from a small section of the not very full house.

With a sinking heart Larry recognized, even from the wings, the Welsh accents in the audience, and remembered that this was the night his schoolmaster acquaintance had arranged to come with some friends.

'Noisy lot of buggers in the circle,' panted April as she came off.

Larry had no time to reply before he found himself stumbling on stage with leaden feet to the accompaniment of cheers and cries of 'Cymru am Byth'.

Far from being strengthened by the presence of his fellow countrymen, whom he knew were only trying to help, his confidence was weakened. His timing, which had slowly been improving after Jimmy Long's advice, was blurred by the sudden resurrection of his own Welsh accent. He found himself talking like a machine gun and at one time looked down to see Dan frantically trying to slow him with his baton.

Apart from the noisy encouragement from the circle, the rest of the audience was angrily silent, resentful of this partisanship and unable to understand a word that Larry was saying.

When he got to the duet with himself, his supporters, hearing music, cried 'Sospan Fach' and 'Sing us a Welsh song, Larry boy.' They joined in his chorus and when others did not, became aggressive. At the end of his act there were more cheers and applause than Larry had ever received but the enthusiasm was confined to about twenty seats in the circle. He was forced to take a second curtain—something he had never done before —because of the insistent clapping of frenzied Welsh palms, a Cardiff Arms Park reception in miniature.

When he had retired finally to the side of the stage, Joe Armsworth gave the cue for the music and lights for Henri Lamarr. 'Got a few friends in tonight, then?' Joe grinned at Larry as he stood breathing heavily in the corner.

'With friends like that, who needs enemies?' Larry was angry and pleased at the same time. He was annoyed that his act had been thrown out of gear by his Welsh supporters and yet warmed by the knowledge that wherever he went the fact that he was Welsh would attract some of his fellow countrymen to the theatre. To belong to a minority ethnic group might be good for his career. Harry Lauder had been a very successful professional Scotsman; there were plenty of Jewish comedians; Irish tenors were always in demand, and Paul Robeson wasn't doing too badly. So far, though, Welsh comedians were few and far between, he thought. Perhaps he would be the one to make it.

His thoughts were cut short by the sound of squeaking shoes which stopped abruptly in front of him as he was about to mount the steps to his room. Lovegrove stood before him.

'You brought those bloody hooligans in tonight, didn't you?'

'I knew some people were coming to see me, but I didn't know that they were going to behave like that.' Larry was on the defensive immediately, reluctant to push his luck too far by antagonizing the manager again, and feeling guilty about his undeserved reception.

'Just count yourself lucky you're not slung off the bill, lad—there's still time. After that notice you got tonight and that rowdyism you caused just now, I might be forced to change my mind.'

Larry bowed his head to hide the anger in his eyes. Lovegrove, mistaking his action for one of submission, could not resist a final, wounding shot.

'Never did meet a Welshman who was any bloody good.'

Having delivered this last salvo, Lovegrove squeaked away, little realizing how close he'd come to strangulation as Larry gripped both hands around the iron stair rail to prevent himself from doing the same thing to the manager's throat.

'That'll teach him to give me lip,' crowed Lovegrove to himself, resolving to write Larry's poison pen letter before he left for home.

Larry dressed hurriedly, grateful that there was no one in the room to whom he would have to talk. He checked the money he had left and decided he'd go to the pub near the theatre for a drink before going back and facing Ma Rogers. Picking up a stick of grease-paint he wrote a message on the mirror for Wally. 'See you back at the digs. Larry.'

He knew he had made a mistake as soon as he entered the public house.

'Here he is, boys,' a voice shouted, and before he could say a word he was being pummelled by hard, welcoming Welsh fists.

The schoolteacher he had met on Monday came to his assistance. He was merry but not drunk. 'Sorry we made a mess of your turn, Larry bach,' he said, genuinely apologetic, 'but the boys got a bit out of hand. It's seldom we get a chance to cheer on one of our own, d'you see?'

'It's all right, mun,' Larry stammered in reply, still bruised by his welcome, and lapsing immediately into a broader Welsh accent than he was accustomed to using. 'Why aren't you in the theatre for the rest of the show, then?'

'We got thrown out, boy.' A large, broken-nosed face thrust itself into his.

'No we didn't, Idris,' said Elwyn Thomas, 'I don't think anybody would try to do that.'

Larry, looking round at the company, was not surprised. A few of them were short men with heavy shoulders—the rest were six footers of enormous proportions.

'We left quietly and of our own volition.' The speaker, a curly-haired giant, waved the back of a theatre seat in the air.

'Ianto Price, used to play rugby for Swansea before he came up here to sell insurance. Doing very well, too—nobody would dare not to buy a policy from him.' The schoolteacher was at Larry's side again. He handed a large glass of whisky to Larry. 'Drink up, boy bach. You must need that after your performance.'

Larry took a hearty swig, at the same time not quite sure how to take the last remark.

'You ought to concentrate a bit more on your singing. Mind you, I appreciate what you're trying to do—break away from the tradition of the stand-up comedian, isn't it?'

Before Larry could reply an argument started at the bar and Thomas left him to act as referee in the dispute. 'Like school kids they are, this lot. No harm in them, but they can be a bit boisterous at times.'

The broken-nosed man he had met a moment ago handed him a pint of beer. 'Put that whisky in here, Barry. Best thing in the world for the voice.' Broken-nose took his whisky from him and poured it into the pint of beer. 'We always get together on a Tuesday night. It's a sort of Cymrodorion Society, although it's not official—just a bunch of poor home-sick Welsh lads getting together for a bit of "hiraeth". Most of the boys play rugby on Saturdays and it takes until Tuesday for us to feel well enough to meet each other again.'

'Come on, drink up.' Elwyn Thomas was back with another whisky for Larry. 'That's from Llewellyn Probert over by there.' A man whose shoulders measured fully three feet lifted his glass in salute from across the bar. 'Solicitor, he is. Doing well for himself, but he tends to fret when he's away from Wales for too long. His father was the finest tenor this side of Carmarthen—and there's *nothing* this side of Carmarthen.' He laughed uproariously at his own joke. 'Now there's one to use in your turn, eh? Nothing this side of Carmarthen. Duw, Duw. Have to do better than that. No! No! Llewellyn, put the man down! Stop showing off.'

The wide solicitor was lifting a terrified man horizontally in the air to rhythmic shouts from his companions. 'One, two, three, four.' At the count of four he heaved his victim, who appeared to pass out with fright, across the bar to Ianto Price who caught him neatly and lowered him gently on to the counter. 'That was a forward pass,' shouted someone. 'Scrum!'

Larry found himself in the middle of the mêlée as the Welsh contingent, who by now had the saloon to themselves, pushed and shoved for possession of a non-existent rugby ball. Before the game could get too rough the schoolteacher took a whistle from his waistcoat pocket and blew it hard. The combatants sorted themselves out quickly and stood, panting, against the bar. 'It's getting a bit too rough, lads. Now let's get some fresh air and try somewhere else later on.'

Cries of 'Let's go to the Dragon' greeted this exhortation and the bunch of laughing, shouting men, carrying Larry along with them, headed out of the door and up the street, much to the relief of the publican. The two police constables for whom he'd sent, who had prudently stayed out of sight until the mob had gone, then marched bravely into the saloon bar, asked where the trouble was, took down particulars, and retired with helmets under their arms to a back room where they commiserated with the landlord over a couple of foaming free pints.

Meanwhile, the Welsh invaders continued on their way to the Dragon. It was kept by a fellow countryman, Ivor Williams, who, upon hearing their noisy approach, cleared his saloon of customers. They were only too ready to leave. 'I'm getting to hate Tuesdays,' he said to Gwyneth, his wife.

'Oh, I don't know. We always have a good old sing-song at the end of the night.' She patted her hair and smoothed her skirt. 'Wonder if Ianto Price is coming tonight?'

Her husband gave her a strange look.

Larry was carried away by the tide of Welshness, feeling no pain now that he had had a few drinks. He found himself pushed up against the bar and was about to order for everybody when he remembered his dwindling resources, and instead started to sing a chorus of 'David of the White Rock'. His companions joined in with gusto, automatically dividing up the song into part harmony, making the glasses on the shelves ring in sympathy and Gwyneth turn to jelly.

'There's lovely,' she cried, tears rolling down her face. 'The drinks are on the house for that. Ianto Price, what are you having?'

'You, if there's any bloody chance.'

There were roars of laughter at Ianto's reply, and a tight-lipped Ivor Williams started handing out drinks. 'Tuesdays,' he muttered to himself, 'I hate bloody Tuesdays.'

Larry accepted another Scotch which, added to those drinks he had already consumed, rid him of the last of his inhibitions. From then on he was the leader of the pack. He invented a game which involved leaping from table top to table top on one leg, an idea dredged up by drink from his experience on an army assault course; and he did an extremely funny impromptu routine with a couple of Scotch eggs and a sausage from the bar counter. He was the hit of the evening—of the year—for his new-found friends.

'You're good enough to be on the stage,' said Gwyneth.

'I am on the bloody stage.'

'There you are, I told you, Ianto.'

'I know, mun, I saw him tonight. But he's a damned sight funnier here that he was at the Royalty.'

Larry was too far gone to be annoyed. 'You haven't seen anything yet, folks,' he shouted and did an impression of a nervous surgeon doing his first operation, using the food on the bar counter as his props.

'Bloody Tuesdays,' wailed Ivor Williams as he watched Larry pretend to remove a salami sausage from the stomach of his imaginary patient, sniff it, and throw it over his shoulder. Ianto Price caught it and made an unmistakable gesture to Gwyneth.

'That's enough of that.' All five feet three of Williams quivered with outrage.

'Oh, go on Ivor, he's only playing.' Gwyneth was enjoying herself.

'Well, it's not nice is it?' Ivor's tone was more conciliatory as the towering Ianto handed him back the sausage with a bow and a click of the heels.

Larry, sensing he was losing his audience, struck up one of the bawdier rugby songs. The response was immediate and one song led to another and one drink led to another and all was noise and whirling lights as Larry gradually slipped under the table. The last words he heard were those of Ivor Williams.

'Hey, Ianto Price is having his way with my Gwyneth on the stairs.'

And with the charitable hope that they were carpeted and not linoleum-covered, Larry passed out.

'Come on, bring it up, you'll feel better for it,' said the same voices that previously that evening had enjoined him to 'Get it down you, it'll do you the world of good.'

108

He heaved again and felt his stomach contract as it rid itself of another quart of unwanted liquid. The shudder that passed through him shook him from head to foot.

'My glasses, anybody seen my glasses?' Larry was panic-stricken. Without his spectacles the world was a blur—comforting when he wanted to escape from it, but frightening when he sought to rejoin it.

'Here you are, boyo.' The schoolteacher reached into a pocket and taking out the glasses, placed them uncertainly on Larry's nose. The greasy lenses revealed to him a back street in which various figures lay scattered like the aftermath of a battle. He staggered to his feet with the assistance of Elwyn Thomas, the School.

'What happened?' he enquired with a throat aching from an overdose of singing and retching.

'Ivor called the police, the bugger. Good job they were a couple of Welsh lads. Could have been nasty if somebody hadn't started singing "Hên Wlad fy Nhadau" half way through the scrap. Nice baritones, those two coppers. Naturally, after the Anthem we couldn't start fighting again—wouldn't have been patriotic somehow. So we all left peacefully. Mind you, there's one or two the worse for wear, as you can see.' Elwyn indicated the groaning figures around him. 'Still, it was a bloody marvellous Tuesday—best we've ever had, thanks to you, Harry.'

'Larry.'

'That's right. We brought you out between us, Ianto and I. You were dead to the world, boy bach.'

'You mean Ianto wasn't arrested?'

'What for—having it off with Gwyneth on the stairs? Never.'

Ianto emerged from the gloom and came to stand under the lamp post to which the other two were clinging for support. 'Thanks for making it possible for me to achieve my lifetime's ambition. If it hadn't been for your singing she'd never have let me.' Ianto wrung Larry's hand, making him wince with pain.

Larry remembered his last thought before passing out. 'Were they carpeted or did they have lin—lin—' It was no good. 'Oil cloth,' he said. 'Was there oil cloth on the stairs?'

'Thick pile carpet, mun.' Ianto was indignant. 'Wouldn't have been fair to the girl otherwise. Cold on the bum, oil cloth.' He, too, deliberately avoided the word 'linoleum'.

'Linoleum,' corrected Elwyn Thomas, enunciating carefully.

'I wish I'd said that,' Larry murmured.

'Ask him to say "oil cloth",' said Ianto.

'Bollocks,' replied the schoolteacher with dignity, and the three of them clutched each other, helpless with laughter.

'One for the road,' said Ianto, pulling a flat half bottle of whisky from his back pocket. Larry forced himself to take a drink, hoping it might settle his stomach, and all around them the prone and semi-prone came to life. Ianto went from one to another administering sips from the bottle like Sir Philip Sidney on the battlefield. Gradually they all got to their feet and dispersed in little groups.

'Got to be up early in the morning.' Elwyn looked at his watch. 'Half past twelve . . .'

'Good God!' Larry was aghast, remembering that he had no key and that Ma Rogers bolted and barred the door.

'Well, all the best, Larry,' said Elwyn, getting his name right at last. 'I'll drop in on you at the theatre in the week.'

'Come alone, please.' Larry was anxious not to repeat the night's experience, exhilarating as it had been.

'Of course. We won't dare get together at the Dragon for a week or two until Ivor calms down again. Find your way home all right?'

Without waiting for a reply, Ianto and Elwyn left Larry standing under the lamp post, vomit-stained and confused as to his whereabouts. Fortunately there was still enough alcohol in his veins to prevent his feeling depressed about the situation. He set off in search of the digs, doing the Cockcroft walk and singing little snatches of 'Men of Harlech'.

When Larry finally arrived at the digs at half past one, there was no sign of life. The window of his own room, which faced on to the street, was firmly locked and looked as though it had not been opened for years.

He stood back and surveyed the front of the house, swaying slightly. The long walk had caused the alcoholic fumes to rise anew in his brain and he found it difficult to think. From where he stood he could see that the window of the room above his was slightly open. Who sleeps in there? he wondered, trying to remember the lay-out of the house. It was an even chance that it was the girls. A drainpipe led down past the window from the roof.

Should I ring the bell and risk the twin savagery of Mrs. Rogers and her Alsatian, or should I climb the drainpipe and risk breaking my neck? he pondered.

The answer was obvious.

He started his perilous journey with a head that spun and legs that seemed made of rubber. He had just clawed his way past the top of his own window when a head suddenly appeared at the window above.

The shock made him lose his grip and he fell backwards into the privet hedge in the sparse garden below. The bushes broke his fall and as he lay supine, he heard April's voice calling anxiously 'Are you all right, love?'

He waved his fingers at her to show that he was alive, but was unable to speak, the wind having been driven from his body.

April opened the door carefully and led him into the passage, motioning him to be silent. In spite of his condition, Larry had enough sense not to arouse the snarling guardian of the kitchen.

He lay on the bed in his room as April clucked over him. She began to undress him, and after a few half-hearted attempts to stop her, Larry submitted. She was about to remove his underpants when Larry giggled. He looked down at himself.

'Ooh!' said April in wonderment, 'I didn't know there was a Welsh Eiffel Tower.'

She took off her dressing-gown. 'Seems a pity to waste it,' she said.

Wednesday

L arry was awakened by a knock on the door. He tried to say 'Come in,' but he could only manage a croak. His head felt terrible and he was unable to raise it from the pillow.

The door opened and April entered, carrying a cup of tea. 'How do you feel this morning, darling?' She sat down on the bed, and, leaning over, gave Larry a hearty kiss. 'Tea's up.'

The taste of tobacco on her lips made his stomach heave again. With difficulty he restrained himself from being sick.

'What about last night then, you cheeky devil.' April slapped him playfully across the chest and he *was* sick.

She held his head as he poured the remainder of his night's excesses onto the floor beside the bed.

'That's right, love, let it all come up.'

He tried to comply with all his heart and soul, and fell back exhausted on the pillow.

'I'll clean it up, ducks. I've told Ma Rogers you've got a touch of gastric 'flu so she'll expect a bit of mess.'

She left the room and came back a few minutes later with a mop and bucket. 'You were a naughty boy last night, weren't you?' She winked at him conspiratorially as she worked. 'I don't mean all this lot, either. Ooh, you were fierce.'

He smiled wanly, not quite understanding what she meant.

April finished her job of mopping up his mess by sprinkling disinfectant around the room. 'If Ma Rogers suspects it's drink and not 'flu that's keeping you in bed, she might turn nasty.' She stopped and looked down admiringly at him for a moment before leaving the room. ' "All through the night" was never one of my favourite songs, but after last night it's the top of my hit parade.' She blew him a kiss and shut the door gently behind her.

Larry was too exhausted to work out what all these exaggerated endearments meant and fell asleep again.

The next time he awoke, Wally was standing over him. 'Feel all right now, lad?' He sniffed the air suspiciously but said nothing about the lingering odour of stale whisky. 'We missed you last night at supper. Old Man Rogers made a casserole for us. Tasty, too—plenty of nice gravy and meat and a suet pudding with jam for duff afterwards.'

Larry retched weakly. Wally jumped back from the bed. 'Watch the suit, mate.'

His concern was unnecessary because there was nothing left for Larry to bring up.

'Take it easy, me old amico.' Wally waved a salute. 'Got to go and ring Lou Hyman. Things are moving pretty fast for me this week.' He sniffed the air again. 'Not starting to use perfume, are you? April said you had gastric 'flu when we were at breakfast. Wonder how she knew about it?' He gave Larry an approving nod and slyly tapped the side of his nose. 'You're certainly learning a lot this week—are you giving lessons in exchange?' He laughed good-naturedly and went out.

Larry lay there wondering weakly what his friend was getting at. Then he sat bolt upright as the memory of the previous night's activities came flooding back to him. 'Good God—no!' he groaned, holding his head in his hands. There was much he could not bring into focus, but quite enough was returning painfully to his consciousness.

He remembered some of the endearments he had murmured in the night and tried unsuccessfully to turn aside the memory of the acrobatics he had engaged in. 'Engaged!' Was he? Had he? The thought that he might have plighted his troth in his cups was too appalling to contemplate. 'Oh Mam, Mam, what have I done?' He turned his face into the pillow and wept tears of self-pity.

His watch read two o'clock the next time he came to and he forced himself to get up and dress. The task was almost too much for him, and as he was resting, preparing for the assault on his shoe laces, April came in. She was dressed in her best and her eyes shone with new-found happiness. 'I'll tie those for you, sweetheart.' She knelt at his feet and fixed his laces, now and then glancing up at him with adoration.

He avoided looking into her eyes by closing his own and pretending he was worse than he was. Actually, he was gaining strength by the minute, and the urge to get away and work this thing out by himself was overcoming his nausea.

'Shall we go walkies, then?' said April solicitously as she sat by him on the bed.

'If you don't mind, I'd rather be on my own for a while.'

April pouted, an expression which ill-fitted her normally cheerful countenance. 'After last night I thought you wanted to be with me for ever and always.'

Larry keeled over on his side, just saving himself from complete collapse by hanging on to the bed rail. He sought desperately for an excuse. 'I have to see the padre—the chaplain you know. I've got to see him this afternoon.'

'So soon!' April clapped her hands.

'No! No!' Larry started to say. He was interrupted by Mrs. Rogers, who came in unannounced.

'Ha!' she cried, pointing at the two of them sitting quite innocently on the bed. 'I thought so. Gastric 'flu, is it? Sex, that's what it is.' She sniffed the air like a war-horse scenting battle. 'Whisky and sex.'

'Shut up! We're engaged. Larry's actually going off to see the vicar this afternoon.' April held on to his arm in triumph as they stood before the landlady.

Even Ma Rogers was taken by surprise. 'Oh. That's a bit sudden, isn't it?' Her voice was comparatively mild.

Larry could only nod dumbly, overwhelmed by the turn of events and unable to think. He patted April's hand abstractedly and, pointing towards his neck as if to indicate a clerical collar, stumbled from the room and out of the house.

The situation was definitely out of hand, he decided, as he

sat shivering on a bench in the little recreation ground where he had met Elwyn Thomas. As the wind blew cold around his ankles, resurrecting grimy leaves in brief melancholy dances, he considered what had happened to him.

He had slept with April last night and she now considered that they were engaged. By saying that he was going to see the vicar he had compounded the misunderstanding. But surely, he thought, she must have been to bed with a bloke before. After all, she seemed pretty experienced. It must have been something he'd said to her, some words in the heat of the moment she'd been longing for someone to say. For the life of him he could not remember what they were, although he had a vague idea of what he had done.

He was not a natural philanderer; indeed, there was a strong streak of Welsh puritanism running through him. How he wished he could be more like Wally. 'Love 'em and leave 'em' was Wally's dictum. Instead, Larry's instinct after such an episode was to wear the hair shirt of guilt and beat his breast like those characters in the Bible.

Thinking of the Bible brought him back to the vicar. Perhaps, after all, he should go and see him, talk to him man to man and get some advice. He had been a choirboy for years until his voice broke and he was given the job of pumping the organ. That's what got me into this mess, he thought ruefully.

He rubbed his chin thoughtfully. The bristles reminded him that he had not shaved. Going back to the digs was not an attractive proposition. Still, if he was going along to see the vicar he'd better look a bit decent. His suit was surprisingly clean, he found. April had obviously sponged it for him last night—no, there had been no time for that, he recalled with a stab of guilt, it must have been this morning.

A shave in a barber's shop would be the answer. Another expense he could ill afford. He took out his post office bank book from his inside pocket and considered the balance. Twenty-three pounds and fifteen shillings was all that was left of his army gratuity—with married life staring him in the face. He shuddered and got to his feet.

There was a small post office-cum-sweet shop in the main street behind the recreation ground, and there he drew out three pounds, the limit he could get on demand. As he came out of the shop he saw a barber's pole about a hundred yards down the street. He headed towards it.

The hot towels and administrations of the barber rekindled the spark of life in him and he began to feel hungry. The vicar had said something about his wife making nice Welsh cakes. His stomach rumbled with anticipation as he enquired from the barber the whereabouts of the Church of St. Bartholomew.

He found it easily enough. It was a pleasant, though grimy, church built in mid-Victorian times to assuage the conscience of a city businessman who had made a fortune out of the Crimean War. The vicarage, a large house with a little garden in front, was next door.

Larry hesitated before pushing the bell button. What am I going to tell him? Perhaps I'll just say that I would like to join the Actors' Church Union—and then ask his advice about April. But how can I talk to an unknown vicar about having carnal relations with a woman? There was a lot to be said for the Catholic confessional box.

The door opened as he was about to turn away. 'Saw you coming through the gate. Come in, come in. This *is* an unexpected pleasure, I must say.' The Reverend Philpotts was casually dressed, and without his clerical collar.

Larry felt a little better. It would be easier to talk about his shortcomings to a clergyman out of uniform, so to speak.

The vicar propelled him along a wide passageway towards a door at the far end. The gloom of the house was relieved by the pictures on the walls and the bright red runner on the floor.

'You're lucky today. My wife has some of her Welsh friends in for tea. You'll be most welcome, I must say.' He opened the door and swept Larry inside. The room was gay, with a chintz-covered settee and matching armchairs. Four ladies, one of whom was Gwyneth Williams from the Dragon, were seated at a table weighed down with plates of cakes and sandwiches.

A plump, jolly woman with dark hair and eyes detached

116

herself from the group at the table and came towards him.

'This is—now let me get it right this time—' The vicar thought for a moment.

'Larry Gower from the Royalty Theatre,' said Gwyneth from the table. 'I had the pleasure of meeting him last night.'

The plump lady shook his nerveless hand. 'Well, well. Delighted to meet you. I'm Betty Philpotts, and these are some other people from our part of the country. Gwyneth, of course, you've met.' Gwyneth smiled sweetly at Larry who stared blankly back.

'And this is Muriel Evans, our local Probation Officer'—a matron with close-cropped grey hair nodded firmly—'and last, but not least, Myfanwy Price, our organist.'

A tiny lady with rimless glasses bobbed up and down in her chair in greeting.

'That's Ianto's sister. You met him last night, remember?' Gwyneth's voice held no trace of warning, and Larry, in secret wonderment, bowed politely to each of them.

'Get another chair, Nicholas, and make some room at the table for Mr. Gower.'

'Larry,' said Larry.

'That's right. Don't stand on ceremony. We once named a cat Ceremony just so we could say that when anybody stepped on it. But it was too difficult to get your tongue round when we had to call him, so we had to change his name to Llewellyn.' Betty Philpotts chuckled happily. All the time she was talking she busied herself setting a place at the table for Larry to join them.

'There now,' she said. 'We're all settled. Say grace, Nicholas. This young boy looks as if he's starving.'

Larry, who was about to sink his teeth into a Welsh cake, hurriedly put it down and bent his head as the vicar blessed their food. As his head came up again he caught Gwyneth looking at him. She gave him a big wink and smiled. Larry, beginning to loosen up and accept the situation, smiled back. Let him who is without sin cast the first stone, he thought, reaching for another Welsh cake, secure in the knowledge that at least there would be no boulders from Gwyneth's direction.

'Do you sing?' enquired Myfanwy Price, in a bird-like tone which matched her darting movements as she spread jam on a piece of bread.

Larry, who was stuffing a slice of home-made cake into his mouth, nodded an affirmative.

'Tenor or baritone?' Muriel Evans was in the latter category, her voice as low as a man's.

'He's a lovely tenor, Muriel. Ivor and I had the pleasure of listening to him sing last night. Made me cry, he did, with his "David of the White Rock".'

'You must come and sing for us tomorrow afternoon. We're having a little social for the old folks of the parish, and we'd be thrilled if you could do a little turn for us.' Betty was carried away with enthusiasm. 'Perhaps some of the others from the theatre would come along, too.'

'Steady on, dear.' The vicar, who had taken no part in the conversation except to smile and nod, raised his jammy knife in protest. 'We'll have to get permission from the theatre people first and this young lad doesn't even belong to the Actors' Church Union yet.'

'That's really what I came to see you about,' said Larry, growing cold with the memory of his true reason for coming to the vicarage. He resolved to leave his man-to-man talk to some time later in the week.

'Are you Church of England? If so, there's no problem at all.'

'I was a choirboy for years,' said Larry proudly. 'From the time I was seven until my voice broke, taking a stained glass window with it.' He laughed at his own joke. The Probation Officer permitted herself a slight smile.

'Ooh! That's funny.' Myfanwy Price bobbed up and down on her chair with glee.

'That's nothing,' said Gwyneth. 'You should see what he can do with a couple of Scotch eggs.'

Larry choked.

'You must do that for us at the social. I'll make some specially for you. There's clever you must be. I've always liked juggling.'

The vicar's wife turned to her husband. 'You must ask Mr. Lovegrove to let them all come to entertain us.'

'All right, dear, if Larry's agreeable I'm sure some of the performers will be delighted to do something.'

Larry was by no means so sure but he committed his own services to the social.

'Who is the principal artiste?' asked Muriel Evans. 'Someone we all know?'

'Julie Tempest, the strip-tease artiste,' said the vicar. 'A little past it now, but still a fine figure of a woman.'

'Disgusting, that's what it is,' the Probation Officer rumbled her disapproval.

'Oh, I don't know.' Betty was more disposed to be generous. 'Last time I saw her perform during the war at the Swansea Empire she didn't show much more than you could see on Caswell Bay sands any August Bank Holiday.'

'There's too much of that sort of thing pervading our society today. Heaven knows I see enough of it in my job. Girls getting themselves into trouble, then having to leave home. They drift into crime before they know where they are.'

'Wish I had the nerve to do it.' This came from Miss Price, who giggled as she fluttered over the crumbs on her plate.

'What, get yourself into trouble?' Muriel Evans was incredulous.

'No, love, do a strip-tease she means.' Gwyneth stood up and stretched herself. 'Wouldn't mind having a go myself.' She posed provocatively.

'Ooh!' said Myfanwy in admiration.

'Ach-y-fi!' boomed Muriel.

'This isn't like a vicarage tea party at all,' laughed the vicar. 'Must be your influence, Larry, bringing the aura of show business into our drab lives.'

Larry smiled weakly, thinking of how he had contributed to a young girl's delinquency, or at least encouraged her in the nature of her ways. His fellow sinner, Gwyneth, seemed unperturbed by what had happened to her the previous evening. Perhaps the sort of resilience needed to survive in the variety theatre was also a requisite of a publican's wife. He'd have to think about it.

Betty began to clear away the tea things and Larry looked at his watch. It was five fifteen and time to be making tracks for the theatre. The vicar promised to bring the Actors' Church Union form to the theatre for him to sign.

'I haven't any here at present, but I can soon get one.'

Betty handed Larry a carrier bag. 'Here's some cakes and sandwiches to take back with you. Don't forget the social tomorrow. I know it's short notice, but if you can get some of your colleagues along we'd be tickled pink. Myfanwy will play for you, just tell her what you want to sing. She'll fix the keys with you tomorrow if you come a bit early. And I'll make some Scotch eggs for you to juggle with.'

'I shouldn't bother about the eggs,' said Larry, blushing. 'I need plenty of room for that act.'

Betty looked disappointed.

'Perhaps I could teach it to Ianto. He can do wonders in a small space they tell me.' Larry looked at Gwyneth as he spoke.

'Yes, if there was an opening, Ianto would be through it in a flash. Finest wing three-quarter Swansea ever had.' Myfanwy was full of sisterly pride.

'Yes, that's right,' said Gwyneth. She kept a straight face but her eyes were twinkling naughtily.

Larry thanked Betty for the tea and shook hands all round, noting painfully that Muriel Evans had the grip of a man. 'I might give a solo tomorrow,' she said.

' "Asleep in the Deep", perhaps?' Larry couldn't help himself.

'Ha, ha.' The vicar's arm was round Larry's shoulders and with a frown from Muriel and a wink from Gwyneth he was out in the hallway.

'I say, that was rather funny.' Philpotts allowed himself a hearty laugh. 'She is rather mannish, isn't she? Betty was thinking of buying her a shaving brush for Christmas as a joke, but I persuaded her not to. Welsh humour is sometimes a little cruel, don't you think? By the way, you and Gwyneth seemed to be sharing some little secret between you. Won't ask you what it is, but I believe you all had a good old time at the Dragon last night. My church warden is a regular there—he told me about the fun you all had.' He shook hands with Larry and patted him on the shoulder. ' "Have a good time while you can" is hardly in tune with Christian dogma, but I think there's no harm in enjoying yourself.' He laughed and shook a finger at the young comedian. 'As long as no one gets hurt in the process, mind you.'

He closed the door, and Larry was left to do some soul-searching as he walked to the Royalty, clutching his bag of cakes like a small boy returning from a Whitsun Treat with his free orange and apple and a sticky bun.

Joe Armsworth found Larry feeding bits of Betty Philpotts's cake to the lion.

'Give us a bit of that cake, son. Too good to waste on bloody lions is that, from the look of it.' He took a slice of jam tart from the carrier bag on the ground beside the cage. 'By God, that's bloody tasty.' He smacked his lips and eyed the silent Larry thoughtfully. 'You're a bit quiet for a lad that's just got himself engaged.'

Larry's head whipped round. 'Is that what she's told you?' His heart sank. He had hoped that somehow he might persuade April to say nothing until he had time to sort things out, but then he remembered that Mrs. Rogers was a party to the knowledge.

'Trying to stop a woman telling everybody she's going to be married is like trying to tell that lion to take his head out of that carrier bag.'

Larry looked behind him. Simba had taken advantage of their inattention to finish off the rest of Betty Philpotts's home-baking. He looked up at Larry, crumbs stuck in the hairs around his muzzle. If anything, the love-light in his eyes was even stronger than before.

'Have you told Simba you've been unfaithful to 'im? He's going to take it hard, y'know.'

Larry could summon only a faint grin. 'It's all happened a bit fast, Joe.' He hesitated, not wanting to confide too much in anyone and at the same time needing advice desperately. 'I was late getting back to the digs last night and . . .' He got no further.

'Larry darling!' April rushed across the stage to him. 'I've been looking everywhere for you. What did the vicar say?'

Joe looked at Larry in surprise. 'You're not calling the banns already? "Larry Gower, spinster of this parish" and all that nonsense?'

'Well, not really.' Larry shifted his feet uncomfortably. 'Can't do that. We're not members of this parish.'

April grabbed his arm. 'I know that, love, but there's ways of doings things if you know how.' She looked into Larry's face with such earnestness that he had no ready reply.

Even though he had been a member of the Church of England all his life, his knowledge of the laws concerning marriage and the run-up to it was pretty sketchy. As for April, Larry's mentioning that he was off to see the chaplain that afternoon was enough to seal her conviction that their marriage was imminent. She was a simple girl in spite of her experience in the theatre, only too ready to believe anything that would take her nearer to the altar, and Larry had been the first man to show her any genuine affection, or even to simulate it in love-making. It blinded her to the reality of the situation.

And so, faced with a seemingly insurmountable problem Larry took the easiest way out. He smiled gamely and gave April a peck on the cheek. 'That's right,' he said ambiguously.

Joe Armsworth, a married man with three grown-up children, shook his head slowly at him over April's shoulder. Larry raised his eyebrows helplessly and allowed April to lead him away. Simba's gaze followed them mournfully.

Larry accepted the congratulations of the stage staff as April paraded him around. He felt he was living in a nightmare and at the first opportunity disengaged himself and sought the sanctuary of his dressing-room.

Wally was the first to greet him. 'Congratulations, me old mate! Why didn't you tell me? Engaged already and only three days in the business!'

'Stop it, Wally, it's a bloody mess.' Larry felt terrible as he sat down heavily on the chair in front of the mirror.

'Come on then, let's have it, son.'

Larry haltingly described the events of the previous night, leaving out certain details but preserving the essence of his experience. 'And now she thinks we're engaged,' he concluded almost tearfully.

Wally, who had heard him through without interrupting, whistled loudly. 'If I carried on like you every time I had a bit of the other, I'd be the most married man in the business.'

'It's all right for you—but what do I do now?'

'You say Ma Rogers was there when you talked about going to see the vicar?'

'Yes, but I didn't mean it like that. I was just looking for an excuse to get out of the room.'

'You might just as well have signed the marriage licence there and then, chum. She's got a witness.'

'That's right, laddie,' said Tillson, swaying through the door, bearing his night's supply of meat for his act. 'You're a dead duck. She's probably doing you a favour. Leave the business and open a dancing school. "Happy Feet—I've got those happy feet".' Tillson shuffled round the floor in a dreadful parody of a tap dance.

'Pissed again, then?' asked Wally.

'Pissed and bloody happy with it.' Tillson took Wally's silver hairbrush and tossed it in the air, missing it by a foot as it fell to the ground.

'You've got a nerve! That's silver, that is.'

'I'm so sorry, my lord.' Tillson bent and picked the brush from the floor, nearly falling over as he did so. He handed it back to Wally who was quivering with fury.

'Don't push me too far,' rasped Wally, threatening Tillson from a safe distance.

'I could push you through that bloody wall, son, old as I am.

123

I've held off a jealous lioness with one hand. Look at that.' Tillson rolled up his sleeve, revealing a livid scar which Larry had already wondered about. 'There was a time when I had twelve lions in the act, all of 'em bloody savage—not like that poor bugger down there. I know I'm a sodding joke to you bastards, but I've been up on top of the bill in my day and don't you forget it. I'm on the way out now, but at least I've been somewhere.' Tillson had assumed a kind of dignity during this outburst which Larry grudgingly admired.

Wally looked deflated. 'Well, just watch it, then,' he said lamely, replacing his brush on his part of the dressing-room table.

Larry had nothing to say and turning his back on the other two began to prepare for the first performance.

He called in on Jimmy and George on his way down to the stage.

'Congratulations, dear boy,' said Jimmy with a trace of disbelief. 'I thought you were saving yourself for me. Frankly I'm surprised. You hardly know the girl.'

'Leave the boy alone, Jimmy. "When love comes along, time stands still".' George stood up with difficulty and shook Larry's hand.

'What do you mean "When love comes along, time stands still"?' asked Jimmy sharply.

'You remember. That's a line from *Cinderella* when Buttons is alone with Cinders before she goes to the ball.'

'No it isn't. "Time has no meaning" is what he says.' Jimmy seemed to be getting annoyed.

'Thanks, anyway.' Larry left them arguing. The news of his surprise engagement was having a strange effect on the company, he thought. It had indirectly started two arguments within five minutes.

He timed his arrival in Joe's corner to coincide with the

beginning of the girls' act. The last thing he wanted to do was to see too much of April until he had decided on a plan of action.

Sammy, the pimply stage hand, edged up to him. 'Hey, I saw you in the wings last night, kissing and cuddling.' He nudged Larry with his elbow. 'What's it like? Y'know.' He winked hugely.

'Wonderful. Too beautiful to describe,' said Larry. 'Don't ask me, though—ask Miss Tempest. She's the one who can help you. You know the projector she uses in her act?' Sammy nodded, his eyes bright with expectancy. 'Well—next time she comes on stage, go up to her and say "Can I be the one to see that nobody touches it for you?" She'll understand what you mean. Get me?' He left Sammy working it out.

The girls were just going into 'Colonel Bogey', and as he watched April's sturdy legs flying in a vain attempt to keep up with the relentless stick of the conductor, he could understand why she was so anxious to trap him in the net of matrimony. There was no hope for her in the business; her dancing was not good enough to keep her in work for long. Even Larry's inexpert eye could see the difference between her laboured efforts and the easy, lazy grace with which June performed their indifferent routine. He was sorry for her, but more sorry for himself.

The girls panted into the wings. April, unable to speak and wheezing painfully, gave him a big sloppy kiss as the orchestra struck up his opening music. He went on stage vigorously rubbing her lipstick from his face, as though by removing the stain he would get rid of her, too. He faced the audience which crouched out there in the dark, waiting to devour him.

'Well, hello there!' he said brightly, a David face to face with Goliath, hoping he hadn't left his sling-shot in the dressing-room.

His desperate personal situation, coupled with the success he had achieved with his Welsh audience in the Dragon the previous night, had somehow purged him of his on-stage fear. He worked more easily, and found that the audience was responding with awakened interest instead of the sullen silence he was now beginning to accept. There were no great bursts of laughter, but enough steady chuckles and occasional isolated guffaws to give him confidence in his future.

'That's a bloody sight better, my lad,' said Armsworth. 'If that's what love does for yer, you ought to get engaged once a week.'

April claimed him at once. 'I watched you all the way through again,' she said proudly. 'I understood nearly everything you said tonight.'

'That's nice.' Larry tried to sound enthusiastic.

'Oh, you're sweating, love. You mustn't catch cold.' She clucked and fussed over him all the way back upstairs. He managed to persuade her to let him go to his own room to change, promising to see her afterwards.

Wally was examing the back of his silver hairbrush for dents in its surface. Tillson was not in evidence, although his aroma pervaded the room.

'He's got to go, that Tillson. I can't see why Lamarr should have a room all to himself while we're stuck with *him*.'

Larry began to take off his stage suit. 'Well, you know what Joe Armsworth said.'

'He's not the final authority on dressing-rooms.' Wally looked knowingly at Larry. 'I'll get Lou Hyman to sort things out.'

'Anything you say.' Larry was getting a little fed up with Wally's 'big-time' attitude. 'What am I going to do about April?' he said, getting on to his own problem.

'You've already done it, mate.' Wally chuckled. 'I don't know what you did or said on Tuesday night, but according to what April told June, you're Errol Flynn and Charles Boyer all rolled into one.' He regarded his friend with new interest. 'I had no idea that you were so good at it.'

'Oh, stop it! Tell me what I can do to get myself out of this bloody shambles.'

'Best thing to do is play along with her until the end of the week and then—"Goodbye darling, sorry it didn't work out".'

126

'But the poor girl really believes I'm going to marry her, Wally. She might do something desperate if I let her down like that.'

'Come off it, mate. Don't be so bloody simple.' Wally was scornful.

'She's got a witness, too—Mrs. Rogers. You said that yourself. Can she get me for breach of promise or something? Honest to God, Wal, I'm at my wit's end.'

Wally began putting on his make-up, turning away from Larry to the mirror. 'I'm afraid it's your problem, my son. I can only tell you what I'd do in the circumstances.'

'That's a lot of good, that is.' Larry knew he would have to go elsewhere for advice. The vicar would be the one, he thought. I'll try again to talk to him. He suddenly remembered the church social. 'By the way, do you fancy doing a charity show for the vicar at the church social tomorrow afternoon? I said I'd ask some of the acts to go along. The vicar said he'd get permission from old Lovegrove for us to appear.'

'A church social?' Wally was indignant. 'Not on your nelly, boy. Never do anything for nothing if you can help it. Not offering any money in "readies" are they? 'Course they're not.'

Larry left the room, not trusting himself to speak. April met him in the corridor. 'I was on my way to see you, Larry.' She hugged him close and momentarily removing her cigarette from her mouth, kissed him passionately. 'I can hardly believe it's happening to me,' she murmured.

'Neither can I,' said Larry with a fervour which she misunderstood.

'There's so much to talk about, and there'll be a ring to buy, won't there? "Diamonds are a girl's best friend" they say, don't they?'

Diamonds, thought Larry, bloody diamonds! He changed the subject rapidly. 'I promised the vicar that I'd go and entertain at his church social tomorrow. Would you and June care to come along?'

'Anything for you, dear, and we'd better keep in with the vicar too, hadn't we?' She squeezed his arm. 'I don't know about June, but I can do a solo spot if you like. I've been rehearsing my own act for some time. June doesn't seem to care too much about our act these days. Between you and me, I'd be better off without her.'

Larry remembered watching April's efforts first house and groaned inwardly. 'If you'll excuse me, I'll go and ask some of the others if they'd like to do something.'

'You're not leaving me again, are you?' April was plaintive.

'Must keep in with the vicar, like you said.' Larry kissed her quickly, feeling like Judas.

'Off you go, then.' She hugged him again. 'I can't wait to be Mrs. Bower.'

'Gower,' said Larry sharply.

'That's right,' she agreed.

Larry sat with Joe Armsworth in his cosy little den under the stage. They were drinking beer from a barrel which Joe kept in a corner. 'Can't stand bottled beer,' he said. 'I always keep a small keg of Tetleys in my room. Come down and have a pint— Arthur can take the corner for a while. He knows the show now.

'I don't know how to advise you, old lad. Women are funny bloody creatures. Need handling carefully. I should know, I've been married for nigh on twenty-seven years, and I still don't know anything about 'em.'

Larry sat back in his chair and puffed out his cheeks in an expression of defeat. 'There's no way out as far as I can see, and it gets worse every minute. She's already talking about a bloody diamond engagement ring, and she can't even get my name right.'

Joe laughed at Larry's expression of comic dismay.

'What about this social tomorrow, then? I'll come and give a hand if you like. They'll probably need a bit of help with the tabs and lighting. I know that Church Hall, it's not too bad for sound, but they're a bit short on backstage equipment. I'll have a word with Philpotts meself.' He shifted his bulk in the comfortable-looking leather armchair. 'Who've you asked to perform?'

'Wally's not interested, April's coming, not sure about June—and there's myself. There's no point in asking Tillson, he'd frighten the life out of them and I couldn't ask Jimmy and George somehow. Their act and Julie Tempest's are hardly the right sort for a church social.'

'What about old Henri Lamarr?'

'I've hardly spoken two words to him since I've been in the theatre.'

'I'll ask him if you like. He's not a bad bloke when you get to know him.'

'You were going to tell me about him, incidentally. I still can't understand why he has to have a room all to himself. Wally's talking of ringing his agent about it.'

'He's getting too big for his boots, that lad.' Joe was unperturbed. 'He can ring who he bloody well likes. It's in Henri Lamarr's contract that he has to have a dressing-room of his own.'

'But why?'

'It's very simple, sonny Jim. Because Julie Tempest has to have somewhere to have it off with him, that's why.'

'She's married, though,' Larry protested, 'and Tommy's with her. Hasn't he got any pride?'

'He's had to learn to swallow it over the years. I don't suppose he's been able to satisfy her for a long time, and Julie eats men like him before breakfast. So, Henri Lamarr worked on the bill with them one week a couple of years ago, did her a favour between shows one night, and he's been a regular fixture on her tours ever since. Of course, Tommy knows.'

'But why doesn't Lamarr just live in the same digs as them?'

'She always stays in hotels and she likes to pretend to the public that she leads an exemplary life. "The stripper who's a lady underneath" she calls herself. Then when she wants "servicing" she nips along to his dressing-room and Bob's your uncle. From what I can gather she's a tigress with her fellers. She needs a big strong bloke like old Henri to keep her happy. No wonder he keeps dropping the clubs. It's a miracle that he can get the buggers up in the air.' Joe chuckled into his beer. 'So now you know their little secret—keep it to yourself, mind. I'd better get back upstairs and see what kind of a balls-up Arthur is making of the show.'

Larry lurked in the shadows like a criminal, hoping to make it through the stage door undetected and find a pub for a quiet drink.

'Boo!' April jumped out at him from behind a fold of curtain. She was wearing her Indian costume with the feather for the second half's opening. 'Me wantum see white man's totem pole.'

'Now, April,' said Larry. 'That's not nice.'

'I'm sorry, pet, I didn't mean to be vulgar.' April was contrite. 'But when I think about last night I go all shivery. Don't you?'

'Yes, I do.' There was conviction in Larry's voice. 'Have you asked June about the social tomorrow?'

'Yes, and she said she'd rather not come because Wally's promised to take her to the pictures. So I'll do my solo. It'll be good practice for when I branch out on my own.' April was struck by a sudden thought. 'Maybe we could form a double act. I could be your stooge and we could do a sort of Nat Mills and Bobby.'

Larry was shocked at the suggestion that he should share the stage with anyone. Having to make headway on his own was trouble enough; to be saddled with a partner would be like wearing a millstone round his neck.

April saw his look of outrage and put her head on his chest. 'I know how you feel, darling, you want to be the breadwinner of the family. That's OK by me. I'll stay at home and have your supper ready for you when you get back from the theatre at night.'

Larry gave a loud roar. The feather had got up his nose as she unfolded the picture of their happy wedded bliss, producing a combination of sneeze and groan of despair.

'Bless you.' April took a hanky from her bra and handed it to him.

'Thanks. I think it's a bit stuffy in here. Better get a bit of fresh air. Won't be long.'

April watched him go with a faint dawning of suspicion in her mind. She dismissed it quickly and, hugging herself, hummed a few bars of 'The Wedding March'.

Larry picked a pub a couple of streets away. He sat in a dark corner where he hoped his make-up, which he had forgotten to remove, would be unnoticed.

A little man in a cloth cap came in and sat near him. He nodded at Larry, took a swallow of beer and peered closely at him. 'Hey! Aren't you the feller from the Royalty?'

Larry nodded.

'By gum, tha' nearly had me laughin' when you were on. Took me all me time to keep a straight face. What's your name again?'

'Flower,' said Larry. 'Barry Flower.'

'Ah, that's reet. Should have done a bit of juggling, though. They like juggling 'ere.'

'So I've been told,' said Larry, drinking up.

The first person to greet him as he came into the theatre was Sammy. He was holding his hand over his eye.

'I said what you told me to say to Miss Tempest and she thumped me. Look.' He took his hand away to reveal a nasty swelling. He grinned. 'I'm not mad at you though. As she swung her fist her dressing-gown fell open. By gum, she's well built, is that one.'

'Sorry, Sammy,' said Larry. 'It was only meant as a joke.'

'Never mind. It was worth it.' Sammy walked away, bearing his swollen eye like an honourable wound won in battle.

April trapped Larry at the foot of the stairs. She sniffed his breath. 'That's not fresh air you've been out for, it's Tetley's best bitter. You naughty boy!'

Larry was amazed at the way April had been transformed overnight from a happy-go-lucky girl with a bawdy sense of humour to the simpering love-struck ninny he now saw before him. He could hardly believe that he alone was responsible for this change in her and yet he knew he was. 'Aladdin and his Magic Lump' they ought to call me, he thought in self-contempt.

'I've ordered some of that wine you like so that we can have a little celebration back at the digs tonight. Mrs. Rogers was quite nice about it, too. "All the world loves a lover" they say, don't they?' She took his arm and began to lead him off.

'Baa-aa,' he said.

'What, love?'

'I was doing an impression of a sheep.'

'Oh, you are clever, Larry.'

Between shows Joe told him that Henri Lamarr had agreed to perform for the vicar's social.

'That's a surprise,' said April, who now followed Larry everywhere and was determined not to let him out of her sight except when he went to his room, where Tillson's smell drove him out again.

'He's quite an obliging bloke when you get to know him.' Joe Armsworth looked at Larry for confirmation.

'So I've heard.'

'Lovegrove told me that the vicar has asked for permission and he's got no objection—though I bet he tried bloody hard to think of one. I'll get over to the Hall in the morning and set things up. Dan said he wouldn't mind playing for the acts.'

'I promised to rehearse some Welsh songs with the organist.' You know, fix keys and that.'

'I hope you're going to do "All Through the Night". I love that song. Perhaps we can go over it together tonight in the digs?' April looked meaningly at Larry.

'There's no piano there.'

'Who needs a piano for a song like that?' April's eyes were shining.

Larry found the second house audience even better than the

first, probably because he was eager to face them and forget his worries.

April was ready for him with a towel when he came off. He accepted it and the kiss that accompanied it with resignation—it would have been churlish to refuse either under the circumstances. But he realized once again that he would have to do something pretty soon to straighten out this mess.

When they all set off for the digs that night, Larry and April walked briskly ahead of Wally and June. He told April he liked walking fast, it was a legacy from his army days, he said. Actually, he didn't fancy being forced into some dark corner on the way home for a bout of necking. The night presented a big problem. April no doubt expected the treatment as before, and he didn't feel capable of it, physically or mentally.

Ma Rogers greeted them herself at the door to the kitchen. She arranged her features in a welcoming smile which looked ghastly in its unfamiliar surroundings. 'Has he bought the ring yet?' The piercing glance she shot at April's left hand ricochetted into Larry's eyes.

'It's a sort of an unofficial engagement really, isn't it, April?' Larry smiled awkwardly.

April wasn't so sure, but decided not to argue about it for the moment.

Wally and June came in.

'You two are next for Cupid's bow and arrow.' Mrs. Rogers was horribly arch.

'Ha, yes,' said Wally nervously. 'You never know your luck, do you? He caught you with it, didn't he?'

June said nothing, watching him carefully.

'That wasn't Cupid's bow and arrow, mate,' said Mr. Rogers behind his wife's elbow. 'That was me flaming hatchet in Bradford.'

'You vulgar swine!' Mrs. Rogers lost her brief good humour. 'All right, I'll have one quick drink with you and then I'm going to bed.'

They took their places at the table which Mr. Rogers had set out with the best china and cutlery. Two bottles of wine stood among the sauce bottles and the shining salt and pepper pots.

Wally poured out the wine and lifted his glass. 'A toast to the happy couple. May they live as long as they want, and want to as long as they live.'

'Hear, hear,' said Ma Rogers, raising her glass delicately and putting it down empty.

'Cheers,' said June, lazily.

'Speech,' said Mr. Rogers. 'Let's have a few words from Larry.'

'Oh no!' Larry was panic-stricken. He stared along the line of faces. Wally was smiling at his discomfiture; June looked uninterested; Ma Rogers was furtively drinking another glass of wine; her husband stood with an expectant, toothless grin, and April— As he looked at her his heart turned over. In her upturned face there was hope, love and desperation, making her look almost beautiful. A single tear started a slow journey over her flushed cheek.

He gulped his wine quickly and refilled his glass. 'Here's to us, then,' he said and sat down. April took his hand and squeezed it.

'That's the sort of speech I like. Now for the grub. I had to sell my soul to the butcher for a bit of stewing beef.' Mr. Rogers placed the meal before them with the air of a man who had produced a miracle.

Mrs. Rogers poured another glass of wine and excused herself, reminding them all tipsily that engagement or not, there was to be no hanky panky that night.

April chattered happily throughout supper, unaware of Larry's comparative silence. Wally egged her on to talk about her trousseau and her bottom drawer. June said very little, occasionally snatching a contemplative look at Larry as if seeing him in a new way.

Mr. Rogers told lurid stories about married life in the theatre as he sat near the fire feeding his cat with scraps of meat left over from the meal.

Larry wondered what his parents would think of it all. Their life together had been one of harmony and peace, a million miles removed from the alliances he had come across this week —Julie Tempest's ménage-à-trois, Mr. and Mrs. Rogers, and the relationship between Jimmy and George, to say nothing of Gwyneth and Ivor Williams.

He knew that his mother would take April to her bosom, dyed hair, heavy make-up and all, and he could imagine his father giving her a big welcoming hug. But he couldn't see April fitting into his scheme of things. Apart from the fact that he felt no love for the girl, he was at the beginning of his career and there was no room for a partner. Besides, it would be a pretty stiff price to pay for one night of pleasure and he was determined that it would stay at one night, in spite of what April's hands were doing to him under the table.

The others were not long excusing themselves for bed, Jack Rogers being the last to go. 'I usually let that bloody Alsatian of hers come in here of a night-time to guard the place, but I won't bother tonight.' He winked and left them.

As soon as Rogers had closed the door April was in Larry's lap, nuzzling him. 'I thought they'd never go.'

Larry stroked her hair absently. He was searching for an excuse not to go to bed with her. She wriggled on him lasciviously and, despite his good intentions, he stirred.

'If all Welshmen are built like you, it's no wonder they're keeping a welcome in the hillsides.' April's eyes were closed.

Larry stood up abruptly, almost throwing her to the floor. He helped her to her feet.

'That's it,' he said, a sudden idea coming to him.

'That's what?' April was upset and puzzled.

'In the part of Wales where I come from it is the custom for engaged couples to keep themselves pure until their wedding night.'

'You mean that we can't sleep together tonight?' April's voice went up an octave.

'We can kiss and cuddle, but that's all. Then, when we do get married it will be that much better for waiting.' Larry was improvising madly.

135

'I've never heard of that before.' April's voice was suspicious.

'It's like a knight in the old days pledging to honour the woman he loved by swearing to abstain from the sins of the flesh until they were able to wed. The practice isn't widespread in Wales, but it's very strong where I was brought up.'

'You mean, like Sir Lancelot and Guinevere and all that lot?' The idea didn't appeal to April very much, but she was prepared to go along with it. At least he was proving that he didn't want her for her body alone. Pity though.

'King Arthur was Welsh, you see, and I suppose that's why the tradition started.' He took her hand and kissed it gallantly, then, taking her arm, led her gently from the room.

He stopped outside his bedroom and pressed a chaste kiss on her forehead. 'Good night, my dear. Sleep well.'

April grabbed his face and planted her lips on his. She released him just before he was about to swoon from lack of oxygen. 'Good night, Lancelot. I'm sorry you've put your lance away for the time being, but I love you all the more for respecting me.'

April turned away from him and went upstairs to bed feeling nun-like. Larry watched her go, glad that his hastily contrived excuse for celibacy had worked for the time being, yet ashamed of his own duplicity.

Thursday

L arry lay in bed watching April press his trousers. She had come in early with a cup of tea, her hair neatly brushed and her face already made up.

'Good morning, Sir Lancelot,' she'd chirped, planting a wet kiss on his lips. 'I'd better iron your suit for this afternoon's social. It looked a bit crumpled last night.'

Despite his protestations she had borrowed Mrs. Rogers's iron and board and was now busy creasing his trousers. 'I used to do this for me Dad when he was alive.'

Larry was secretly relieved. At least he'd have no angry father to contend with. He settled himself more comfortably on the pillow. 'Dead then, your Dad, is he?'

'Yes, died when I was fourteen.' April stopped ironing and looked vacantly into space. 'He was lovely to us kids, though him and Mother didn't get along too well together. They were always arguing.' April resumed her task.

'Where's your mother now?'

'She's dead too, killed in an air raid on Liverpool. I'd already left home by then.'

'What happened to your brothers and sisters, then?' Larry asked, almost gaily. No would-be mother-in-law either, he thought.

'There were only two of us. Me and my brother Bill, William McDonald. There's Scottish blood in the family somewhere along the line.' She looked at him with a tender smile. 'And soon there'll be Welsh blood.'

Larry grinned back mirthlessly. 'What's Bill doing now?'

'He's a policeman. Big, strong lad. Takes after my father's side of the family. He was a commando in the war. Worships his little sister he does.' She laughed. 'He never liked me going on the stage. Said it was a wicked profession.'

'Ha, ha!' Larry's laughter was unnaturally loud. The bed had gone suddenly hard.

Wally was finishing his breakfast by the time Larry and April arrived for theirs. June had just begun.

Wally was more subdued than usual. He felt that he had pushed his old friend perhaps a little too far along the road to matrimony—and also rather guilty about refusing to help with the social that afternoon. Noticing Larry's coolness towards him he declined a second cup of coffee from Mr. Rogers and beat a hasty retreat.

April chattered on to June like a magpie, unaware of the uneasy relationship that had developed between the two comedians. Nothing escaped Mr. Rogers though, and he remarked on it to Larry as he cleared away the plates.

'Had a bit of a barney, you two lads?'

'Not really.' Larry did not want to discuss the matter.

'I've known young Wally since he first came here with Jack Graham's Little Sailor Boys before the war. He was only thirteen then, and a right little bugger. Dead keen to get on, but there's no real harm in him. There's bound to be a bit of needle between comics—always was and always will be. You're young and inexperienced and he's got a few years of audiences behind him. From what I saw of you on Monday, though, you've got what it takes. It's raw, mind yer, but it's there.'

'What are you two talking about?' April interrupted her description of the wedding gown she was going to have—'all white and mediaeval like the dresses Lady Guinevere wore'—if she could get enough clothing coupons.

'Nothing,' said Larry, getting up from the table and looking at his watch. 'Think I'll get along to the theatre and see if there's any mail.'

'Hang on.' April was up, brushing crumbs from her skirt. 'I'll come with you, love. See you later, June. Thanks for

138

breakfast, Mr. Rogers.' She kissed the old man, who rolled his eyes.

'If Larry changes his mind, I'll have yer,' he cackled as the door closed behind them.

'She might be back on the market sooner than you think,' drawled June, taking a packet of cigarettes from her dressing-gown pocket.

Rogers was all agog, but before he could ask her what she meant the Alsatian crept in and started eating the scraps he had put down for the cat. By the time he'd chased it out with an oath and a badly-aimed slipper, June had gone.

'Bugger it,' he said, annoyed at missing a bit of gossip.

The one-armed stage door-keeper held up a letter for Larry. 'You're lucky this morning.' He handed one to April. 'One for you, too, Miss McDonald.'

'It's from Bill,' squealed April. 'Just wait until I tell him about me being engaged.'

Larry shivered at the thought. He examined his own letter. The envelope was addressed to him in ill-written capitals and the postmark was a local one. Inside was a piece of lined paper from a cheap exercise book.

'I SEEN YOURE ACT LAST NIGHT AND WHAT A LOT OF COBLERS IT WAS. I THINK YOU STINK AND SO DID EVERYBODY ELSE. GO BACK TO WALES WERE YOU BELONG AND LEAVE THE BISNESS TO THEM WHO CAN DO IT. SINCERELY WELL WISHER.'

'Bloody hell!' exploded Larry in sudden fury.

'It's one of those poison pen letters, is it?' asked Lovegrove, who had been hanging about near the stage door in order to watch Larry's reaction. He exulted inwardly as he saw Larry's face. That'll teach the little bastard, he thought, his piggy eyes bright with malevolent glee.

'We've had a few of them over the past few months,' remarked the door-keeper. 'It's about time somebody did something about it.'

'Give it to me,' said Lovegrove, holding out his hand. 'I've got all the others in my office, and one of these days we'll have an investigation.'

Larry put the note in his pocket. 'It's not worth making a fuss about,' he shrugged.

'Yes, well, perhaps you're right,' said Lovegrove. 'It's all part of the game and after all, you're not exactly Vic Oliver, are you?' Seeing Larry's grim expression he decided he could afford to be a bit magnanimous. 'I've managed to get permission from Head Office for you to do that social this afternoon. Took a bit of persuasion on my part, but they finally agreed.'

As a matter of fact Fred Brotherton had merely grunted 'Please your bloody self' when he had made his enquiry, adding 'Got any tips for the two-thirty at York? I lost a packet at Doncaster last week.' Lovegrove was able to pass on a reasonably priced winner to the theatre owner and felt subsequently more secure in his job.

'Don't be late for first house, mind,' he admonished, waddling away.

April, who had been absorbed in her brother's letter, oblivious to what had passed, looked up at Larry's face. 'Had some bad news from home, pet?'

'Nothing too serious,' he said, dismissing the subject. 'Let's go and find Joe and see what's happening.'

Joe was in his room under the stage, making a list of things he needed for the afternoon.

'Hello, you two. Dan's in the band-room, April. He'd like a word with you about what you want him to play for your act. I've heard that piano they've got at the hall and it's bloody murder, by the way.'

'I'm trying out some new routines today,' said April proudly. 'For when I do my solo act. That is, if I ever need to now that I'm going to be married.'

'For God's sake don't try anything clever. Dan's not a bad pianist but don't give him too much to think about.'

'Don't worry, I've got my music. He won't have to bloody well busk it,' retorted April with a touch of her old spirit. 'Sorry,

Larry. I didn't mean to be awkward.' She was all sweetness and light again.

'What have you done to that girl?' Joe Armsworth asked Larry in wonder after she'd gone.

'It's frightening the life out of me, whatever it is, and it's getting more complicated every minute. Diamond engagement rings and wedding gowns—and I've just found out she's got a big brother in the police force.'

Joe tried not to laugh. He was getting to like the young lad very much and didn't want to hurt his feelings, but the situation was a bit comical.

Larry took the letter he'd received from his pocket and showed it to Joe. 'And on top of it all, I've just had this.'

Armsworth read it carefully. 'D'you mind if I hang on to it, son?'

Larry had no objection.

'There's been a few of these lately from what I've heard, but this is the first one I've been able to have a good look at. Leave the note with me—I've got a vague idea I might be able to trace the author.'

He refused to elaborate and, hitching his trousers up over his huge belly, reminded Larry that it was time he was off to the Church Hall.

The sound of clubs thudding on the floor mingled with French oaths came from the stage as they went upstairs. 'Old Henri must have been at it again yesterday,' Joe observed. 'Anyway, he was good enough to volunteer for this afternoon. You'd better thank him.'

Larry approached the squat, sweating juggler as he was stooping to pick up another fallen club. 'Bonjour,' he said, risking his school French.

'Ah, shwmai,' replied Lamarr, unexpectedly.

'Good God!' exclaimed Larry. 'You're not from Wales, are you?'

'No, boy, I am from Brittany, but before the war I used to sell onions in your country. I was what you call a "shoni onion" boy. They are very similar, your language and Breton.' He shook Larry's hand firmly, giving him a blast of garlic at the same time. Wally was right, thought Larry uncharitably, he and Tillson would go well together.

He remembered the short, bereted figures of the 'shoni onion' boys pedalling up and down the hills of his home town, their handle-bars festooned with strings of onions. They had been very popular in Wales before the war.

'I learn to juggle from a circus man when we are together in the Maquis—the Resistance. Always I am keen to be in show business. Look at this.' He put his hands on his head and moved his huge biceps up and down in rhythm as he whistled the 'Marseillaise'. 'I move also other muscles to the music—watch.' The Frenchman removed his sweaty T-shirt, revealing a massive hairy chest and stomach. Larry watched, fascinated, as Lamarr expanded and contracted his muscles in time to his whistling.

When Henri had finished he clapped in genuine admiration. 'You ought to do that in your act,' he said enthusiastically.

'Miss Tempest would never allow it. I must only juggle with these bloody clubs. Is in the contract.' Lamarr put his shirt on and picked up his clubs. 'She is my manager, you understand.' He avoided Larry's eyes.

'Why not have a go at your muscle routine this afternoon? She won't be there. Give the old dears a treat.'

Lamarr's face brightened. 'That is an idea. I will ask the conductor if he will play the music for me as I perform. Yes, I will do that.' He nodded vigorously. 'But first I must practise again with these clubs. Last night I drop four of them. The lights are too strong in my eyes, I think.'

Larry left to look for Dan and April, the thud of falling clubs loud in his ears.

'Who's playing for you this afternoon, Larry?' Dan enquired as the three of them sat over a plate of spam sandwiches and three halves of bitter, for which Larry had paid.

'The organist at the church, Miss Myfanwy Price. She knows a lot of Welsh songs and it's just a question of fixing keys. No

142

offence meant, Dan—I don't have any piano copies, you see.'

'No, no, lad. I'm not very good at busking. Tell you what I've noticed lately in your act—' He paused to take a fresh sandwich from the plate. It was a race between him and April as to who would finish them first, Larry noticed with dismay. They seemed to be inhaling the sandwiches rather than eating them. He hoped he wouldn't have to order more—the three pounds he had drawn from the post office on Wednesday was nearly gone.

'I've noticed,' continued Dan, flicking a crumb from the end of his large nose, 'that your act's improved a bit since Monday. You seem to be taking more time over your delivery for one thing.'

'I've noticed that, too,' said April, delicately feeding another sandwich into her face. Larry had already observed that she ate heartily at the digs, but as he wasn't paying for it he had not been concerned at her intake. However, her appetite had now become something to worry about—it might seriously affect his pocket.

Dan swept the last large triangle of bread and spam from the plate, looking in faint surprise at the willow pattern revealed beneath it.

'Oh, they've all gone, Larry.' April, with a lump of sandwich wedged in her cheek, regarded the empty plate with evident disappointment.

'One o'clock—it's time we were gone, too.' Larry indicated his watch. 'We're supposed to start at half past two and I haven't been over the songs with Miss Price yet.'

'Sit down, lad,' said Dan expansively. 'These things never start on time. Get some more of those sandwiches and three more halves. We'll work better on a full stomach.' He made no attempt to put his hand in his pocket.

April gave Larry a pleading look. 'Dan and I have worked ever so hard this morning.'

Larry gave in and ordered a fresh round of food and drinks. He sat down sullenly and watched his two companions start round two of their contest. The fact that April won added to his resolve to be rid of her at the first opportunity—big brother or not.

The Church Hall was gradually filling up by the time they arrived.

'Thank heavens you're here,' said Betty Philpotts as she bustled about. 'Mr. Armsworth and Mr. Lamarr have arrived and Myfanwy is anxious to go over your songs, Larry. Come along, dear, we've got a little room put aside for you to dress in.' She whisked April away, introducing herself as she did so.

Myfanwy Price was bobbing up and down with excitement on the piano stool.

'I think we'll try "David of the White Rock" first,' said Larry nervously.

'Off you go then and I'll follow you. What key?'

'I've no idea.'

'Try C, that's pretty reasonable.' Myfanwy played a bright introduction and nodded at him to start.

He sang one verse, trying to keep his voice down. The frail curtain that Joe Armsworth had fixed up was blowing in the draught from the open door of the Hall's front entrance, and Larry could see the cloth-capped and floral-hatted audience looking curiously at him between gusts.

'I only know one verse,' he said as Myfanwy played on.

'Welsh or English?' she asked, her head on one side, looking for all the world like an inquisitive sparrow.

'Well, I know the same verse in both languages.'

'That's it, then. Sing the Welsh verse first and then sing it in English.'

With that settled they fixed the key for 'Gwyneth Gwyn' which Larry had never sung except with a choir. He was aware of slight discrepancies in his version, but the bird-like accompanist assured him she would go along with whatever he did.

'That'll have to do now, Larry,' Joe Armsworth said. 'Henri's getting cold feet about doing his muscle-twitching act, whatever the hell that is. He hasn't had a run-through with Dan yet.'

Henri spoke to them from the side of the little stage. 'I think perhaps I 'ad better do my usual act.' He was bare to the waist, his huge muscles quivering under the massive growth of hair. Larry wasn't sure whether he was practising or just nervous.

Dan stood next to him. 'He's got nothing to worry about,' he said calmly to Joe. 'I know the "Marseillaise" backwards, so he doesn't have to rehearse it with me. All I have to do is follow his muscles. What key are your biceps in?' He laughed heartily. The lunchtime beers and the large whisky he'd persuaded a reluctant Larry to buy him before leaving the pub were having a marked effect.

'All right. Then I will finish with the lighted clubs.'

'That'll be awkward,' said Armsworth. 'You need a black-out for that. I'll just have to throw the main switch, that's all.'

'Ooh, I say, aren't you lovely and hairy!' Gwyneth Williams from the Dragon felt Henri's arm and feigned a shiver. 'I wouldn't like to meet you on a dark night. Oh, I don't know, though.' She giggled as Henri stared at her. 'Hello, Larry. I've come along to give a hand. Anything I can do for you?'

'No thanks,' said Larry, grinning. 'They've got stone stairs in this place.'

'Naughty!' Gwyneth giggled again.

Henri's puzzled stare suddenly gave way to an expression of delighted recognition. 'Mais—how is it possible—little Gwyneth Jones from Bishopston!' he cried, crushing her to his hairy chest.

Gwyneth was momentarily lost from view in his embrace. When she came into sight again she was flushed with delight. 'Duw, Duw—Henri the "shoni onion" man!' she shrieked. 'Every Spring, regular. Once every five weeks when Mam was out.' She threw herself into his arms again.

'Excuse me, chaps, but I'm afraid we'll have to start the proceedings in a few minutes.' The vicar clapped his hands. 'Gwyneth, put that gentleman down.'

'He's an old friend of the family, Vicar. He used to call at our house before the war, selling onions.' Gwyneth's eyes were shining as she patted her hair back into place.

'That is right. She lived on the common. The most beautiful bungalow you ever see, eh, cariad?'

Larry lifted his eyebrows. 'No stairs, then?'

'Dad built a cellar for the coal,' said Gwyneth.

'The black bottom, the black bottom,' sang Larry.

'Really, we must get cracking,' the vicar insisted patiently. 'Mr. Armsworth has given me the running order. April goes first with her little dance, then Miss Muriel Evans will render her solo, Larry will do his turn, and we'll finish with Mr. Lamarr's juggling act—if we can get him away from Gwyneth. Ha, ha.'

The audience was becoming restless as the stage was cleared and Dan took his place at the piano. He flexed his fingers, cracking his knuckles like pistol shots. 'I'll do a little overture to get the show off to a good start,' he told Mr. Philpotts.

The vicar agreed with alacrity. 'Fine, fine. But first let me introduce you to the audience.' He gave a cue to Joe and the curtains jerked away.

'About time,' grumbled one old dear in front. 'Hurry up and get on with it. We want our tea.'

'Yes indeed, don't we all?' The vicar was jaunty but firm. 'First we are going to have some entertainment from our friends at the Royalty Theatre, who have so kindly agreed to come along free of charge this afternoon.'

There were groans from some of the audience. The only reason they came to these monthly social gatherings was because they could be sure of a good blow-out on the sandwiches and cakes provided by the vicar's wife and her friends. They looked longingly over their shoulders towards the back of the Hall where the tea was laid out ready on trestle tables.

'And off we go with an overture by the Musical Director of the Royalty Orchestra—Mr. Dan—er—'

Dan ignored the meagre applause and bent over the piano. He had decided to play Gershwin's 'Rhapsody in Blue', and as he began the first notes the old upright piano became a concert grand behind which sat the whole of the London Symphony Orchestra. This kind of fantasy had originally been a means of escape from the plethora of wrong notes produced by his orchestra; it was now an ingrained part of his everyday life. His ear heard only what he desired it to hear; he would surely

146

otherwise have been driven insane by the indifferent musician-ship of his players. His fingers flew over the cracked yellow keys, only occasionally making contact, while he hummed aloud the orchestral accompaniment which rang in his head. The effect was bizarre.

The vicar turned anxiously to Joe. 'Do you think he's all right?'

'Don't worry sir, he's enjoying himself.'

The audience undoubtedly was not. Impatient cries of 'Get him off' arose from cracked old windpipes. There was no sign of Dan giving in—he was not even aware of the hostility. In his mind the brass accompaniment was over-reaching itself and he took one hand off the piano with which to make a 'shushing' gesture.

The vicar took this as his cue to announce April. 'Miss April McDonald,' he proclaimed loudly, pointing into the wings.

Unfortunately Dan had *not* finished. He was merely sitting with his hands at his sides, his eyes closed in concentration, waiting for the London Symphony Orchestra to reach the part where he came in again.

Wearing a fixed stage smile, April tapped her way on from the wings to music which bore no resemblance to that which she had rehearsed with Dan. She tried to improvise to Gershwin but had difficulty in getting her feet to follow the staccato bursts from the piano. In desperation she started doing cart-wheels round the stage, which brought some enthusiastic rounds of applause from the male members of the audience for whom a well-filled pair of knickers was a rare sight.

The clapping coincided with the end of Dan's solo. He stood up, bowed and departed the stage, leaving April high and dry. She did a quick leap in the air and finished with the splits.

'Great presence of mind,' said the vicar to Larry, who had been watching the whole scene open-mouthed. Not having seen April rehearse with Dan that morning, he wasn't sure what the act was all about, but he was left in no doubt that something was wrong as April came off sobbing and threw herself into his arms.

'He ruined it, *ruined* it! He never even played the right music, the mad sod. He's buggered up me speciality. And I so wanted to do well for your sake.'

Larry patted her half-heartedly on the back. 'There, there,' he murmured.

Gwyneth came up. 'Never mind, love. I thought you were great, especially when you did the splits at the end.'

'That's another thing,' said April tearfully, 'I didn't mean to do that but I had to finish on something, and that stage is full of splinters.'

'Come with me to the Ladies. I've got a pair of tweezers in my handbag.' The two girls disappeared through a door at the side of the stage.

Myfanwy Price replaced the disgraced Dan at the piano and Mr. Philpotts introduced Muriel Evans, who appeared in a man's top hat and tail suit with a silver-knobbed cane under her arm.

'I'm Burlington Bertie, I rise at ten thirty,' she sang as she strode up and down.

'Who's the feller?' asked Joe, who had missed the introduction to the act.

'It's not a bloke, it's the probation officer, Miss Evans.' Larry was quite impressed.

'She's pretty good, y'know—for an amateur,' Joe conceded grudgingly. 'The audience have woken up anyway—listen to 'em.' The sound of singing came to them from out front, as the old folk joined in choruses they had sung in their youth.

'Oh I do like to be beside the seaside,' sang the vicar happily. 'I say, she really knows her stuff, old Muriel. Hardly think she could do this kind of thing, eh Larry? I believe she used to perform at prison concerts when she was down South, before she landed the job up here—Betty says she was a pro for a short while but her parents made her give it up. Well, she's about finished, chaps. You're next, Larry. Good luck.'

Larry took off his spectacles and put them in his pocket. He was introduced as an up-and-coming young comedian just out of the forces. 'Out of the frying pan and into the foyer,' laughed the vicar, and without waiting for the audience to react, went on 'And here he is—Larry—er—LARRY!' he cried, raising his voice at the end of his announcement.

Myfanwy Price went straight into 'David of the White Rock'.

'Not yet,' hissed Larry out of the corner of his mouth as he passed her. The sparrow stopped playing abruptly and cheeped in embarrassment.

'Good afternoon, folks! Sorry I'm late—I've been to a Scottish wedding. You could tell it was Scottish, the confetti was on elastic.'

'You're keeping us from our tea, young man,' muttered a slavering old lady loudly.

Larry, who had decided to tell a few jokes rather than attempt his stage act, quickly abandoned the idea and announced 'David of the White Rock'.

Myfanwy Price's accompaniment was excellent and Larry found himself singing better than he thought possible. Joe Armsworth turned to the vicar. 'It's more singing he ought to be doing in his act. The public don't seem to understand his comedy, although I must say some of it appeals to me.'

'I think he's a nice young chap,' said Philpotts. 'I only hope he's not too sensitive for your profession.'

'Well, if he wants to get on as a comic he'll have to lose some of that. You can't burst into tears every time you get a bad reception. It's all right for you, vicar—you don't have to rely on applause at the end of your sermon.'

'It might be better if we did. We could do with a bit more enthusiasm in church. Might help the collections along, too. By the way, is that one-armed stage door-keeper of yours C. of E.?'

'I've no idea, sir. Why do you ask?'

'Thought he might make a good church warden. He'd be very useful for handing round the collection plate, eh?' Philpotts nudged Armsworth and winked. Joe looked at him blankly. 'Only one hand, you see,' the vicar began to explain. 'Wouldn't be able to take anything off the plate. Ha, ha. Just a joke.'

'Oh yes, I see.' Joe's face remained unsmiling.

'Good heavens, Larry's about to finish.' Philpotts rushed

forward on to the stage, applauding Larry's last note of 'Gwyneth Gwyn'.

Joe grinned at his back. That'll teach him to tell jokes to me, he thought.

Larry came off feeling very pleased with the way things had gone. The accompaniment had been perfect and had brought out the best in his voice. He wondered whether he should put a straight song in his act instead of just finishing on the duet with himself.

'Where's Dan?' Joe was looking around anxiously.

Henri filled the wings with his powerful frame, and with the smell of garlic and nervous perspiration. 'I do not go on without music. There must be music for my muscles and my clubs.'

The vicar had already announced Henri, and was looking off-stage enquiringly. His aged flock were beginning to get to their feet and he feared a stampede on the food-laden tables.

Dan was nowhere to be found. Myfanwy Price came to the rescue, twittering with excitement at the expanse of Henri's bare torso. Lamarr handed her the music for his clubs routine and asked her if she knew the 'Marseillaise'. She nodded brightly and fluttered back to the piano.

The sound of her playing halted the senior citizens in their tracks long enough to give the helpers time to get them back to their seats. The appearance on stage of Henri in all his bare-chested glory brought whistles from wrinkled lips and as he went into his muscle act there were 'oohs' and 'aaahs' which brought a sigh of relief from the vicar. 'I think he can hold them until Betty's had time to boil the water for the tea,' he remarked to Gwyneth who had just returned from the Ladies with April. They stood on the opposite side of the stage from Joe and Larry.

'Henri could always make my water boil just by looking at him,' said Gwyneth in an aside to April. 'He used to sell us onions, you know.' She explained to April how they had met.

'What part of Wales are you from, then?' April seemed to be meeting more Welsh people in a week than she had in five years.

'The same part of the world as Larry. Just outside Swansea,' said Gwyneth, her eyes on Henri's stomach which was flapping in and out against his backbone.

'Quaint customs they have there, don't they? They tell me that after they're engaged the men and women down there keep themselves pure until the wedding night. Must take a lot of self-control.' April eyed Gwyneth expectantly.

Gwyneth tore her gaze from Henri, who was now flicking his Adam's apple in time with Myfanwy's pianistic variations on the 'Marseillaise'.

'Who told you that?' Gwyneth was almost indignant.

'Larry did. We're engaged you see, unofficially.'

'He's having you on, girl. I suppose some couples like to keep themselves in suspended animation, but I wouldn't say it was a custom, indeed. I'm certain my Ivor never heard of it, I'm glad to say.' She giggled and returned her gaze to Henri's antics.

'I see.' April's mouth closed in a thin white line and she asked no more questions.

In the opposite corner Joe was getting ready for Lamarr's grand finale. It was what he normally finished with, but Joe was not sure whether it would be very successful in the Hall. Henri required lots of room in case of error and that was one thing they were short of this afternoon. In a complete stage black-out, Henri was about to juggle with three lighted clubs. It was not exactly a sensation in the theatre, but at least it allowed him to end his performance with a fair amount of applause.

He came to Joe's side of the stage for his clubs. Larry handed them to him. 'Your muscle bit went very well,' he said admiringly.

'I am very content, boy bach.' Henri was beaming with success. 'Now I astonish them with my clubs.' He had shown Larry how to screw in the bulbs at the head of each club and they now shone brightly in the gloom of the tiny wings.

Joe Armsworth said 'Here goes,' and pulled the main switch as Henri walked on juggling. The lights went off everywhere, including the one on Myfanwy's piano. She stopped playing and screamed. No one had prepared her for a black-out and memories of the Blitz were still fresh in her mind. Perhaps it was the Russians this time. Had she not had her back to Henri, she would have seen his lighted clubs. As it was she flew off her chair and ran straight into him. It was unfortunate that all three clubs were in the air at the same time. They rained down on Henri's head.

Pandemonium was just beginning to break out amongst the old folk in the body of the Hall when Joe finally got the lights back on. The shouting stopped and everyone looked towards the stage where a strange tableau was revealed.

'By gum, that's more like it,' drooled one old man in a raincoat.

Henri Lamarr lay prostrate on the stage straddled by Gwyneth, her skirt up over her thighs as she bent over him, her lips glued to his.

'Good Lord above, what's going on?' Mr. Philpotts was shaken enough to invoke Head Office.

'I'm giving him artificial respiration, vicar. He's unconscious and that's what they taught us to do in the Red Cross.' She resumed her task of resuscitation.

'Oh,' said the vicar uncertainly, and ordered Joe to draw the curtains.

Larry knelt at the juggler's side. 'I thought you only did that to people who're supposed to have drowned,' he said to Gwyneth. 'As far as I can see he's just had a bump on the head.'

Henri's left eye opened and winked at him.

'It seems to be working, anyway,' said Larry.

Betty Philpotts had a tea-table ready for the performers and fussed over Henri, who had a sizeable lump on his head.

'Don't worry too much about him,' her husband observed dryly. 'He's had expert attention.'

Myfanwy was very apologetic about having precipitated the panic but soon cheered up and was chirping with pleasure at the compliments on her piano playing from Larry.

'It was delightful to hear you singing so nicely,' she returned.

Muriel Evans received her due share of praise from Joe Armsworth. 'I really thought you was a feller when you started,' he said.

The probation officer winced slightly, but acknowledged the intended compliment with a nod of her cropped head.

'By the way, what happened to Dan? Where did he disappear to?' Larry looked at April as he asked the question.

'I'm sure I don't know,' she replied, without pausing in the transfer from plate to lips of a slice of cake, poised for demolition. Her experience had certainly not affected her appetite, thought Larry, but her manner was surprisingly subdued. When he came to think of it, those were the first words they had exchanged since she had come off the stage in tears. He wondered vaguely what was the matter.

'I expect old Dan felt a bit ashamed of making such a mess of April's act and went home. He'd had a few anyway— perhaps he wanted to sleep it off before the first show.' Joe pulled out his pocket watch. 'Come on, we've got to get our own show on the road, as the Yanks say. Out in the street might be a better place for it, according to our local press.'

Mr. Philpotts and his wife thanked them all profusely and the vicar once again promised to drop in with the Actors' Church Union form for Larry to sign.

Henri gave his word that he would visit Gwyneth at the Dragon and gave her a rib-cracking squeeze before he left.

'I've always liked my men big and strong,' said Gwyneth breathlessly to Betty.

'But your Ivor is quite small.'

'Or small with a forgiving nature,' added Gwyneth wickedly.

Larry stayed behind for a word with the vicar. As the others went off to collect their coats and props he took him to one side. 'Would you mind if I came and had a word with you?' He felt awkward.

'About what? In some kind of trouble are you?' Philpotts showed concern.

'No. Well—yes, in a way.'

'The sooner you come the better, then. How about between your shows tonight? I've got a confirmation class at six thirty in the Vicarage, but from seven o'clock onwards I shall be free.'

'I'll do that, thanks.' Larry shook the vicar's hand and joined the others who were waiting for him at the door of the Hall.

'April's gone on ahead,' said Joe. 'She wants to get her leg make-up on.'

Larry was glad to be free of her suffocating company for a while and enjoyed the stroll back to the theatre with the two men.

'You did well with that singing of yours. Why don't you put a proper song in your act? Then, if your comedy doesn't go too well, you can always be sure of some claps at the end. Like old Henri here with his lighted clubs.' Joe turned to Henri. 'That was a bloody good finale you put on this afternoon. I think I did you a good turn throwing that master switch. Met that piece before, then, have yer?'

Lamarr rubbed his head and smiled. 'Oh, yes, mun. I certainly 'ave. She was a very loving girl when she was sixteen and I used to visit her with my onions.'

Joe laughed. 'That's a new name for them.'

Julie Tempest was waiting for them when they got through the stage door. Tommy stood behind her.

'Where have you been, then?' Her eyes were blazing as she confronted Henri. 'You're under bloody contract to *me*.' She struck her ample bosom with a beringed hand. 'What do you mean by pissing off and doing charity shows without my permission?'

Henri lowered his great head and made no reply.

'You can blame me, Miss Tempest.' Joe Armsworth leaned against the wall of the passage and picked his teeth with a matchstick as he spoke. 'It was for the vicar and it's usually up to the artiste himself whether he wants to do it or not, provided the theatre manager has no objection.'

154

'He's right, love,' ventured Tommy timidly from the vicinity of her left elbow.

'Not in this case, he's not.' She pointed a shaking finger at Lamarr. 'I own that bastard's contract. He can't make a move without my say so.'

The juggler looked up slowly. 'Some day I will kill you.' He spoke quietly.

Julie Tempest went white, turned on her high heels and strode off, her leopard-skin coat flying out behind her. Tommy stayed just long enough to raise his hands in a conciliatory gesture, then hurried after her.

'I mean it, Joe.' It looked as if Julie Tempest's demise was imminent as Lamarr clenched and unclenched his powerful, hairy fists.

Larry cleared his throat nervously. 'Well, better go and get the glad rags on.'

Joe's watch came out. 'Half an hour, please,' he called up the stairs.

'How did it go this afternoon?' Wally was eager to be friendly again. 'Sorry I didn't come with you, but it's one of the things I'm funny about—doing charity shows.'

'That's OK, mate.' Larry smiled at him. 'It was a bit of a lark, anyway. Dan was a bit strange, though. Have you seen him?'

'Yes, met him as I came in. He was apologizing to Joe for something—he seemed all right to me.'

Larry told Wally what had happened. His friend chuckled. 'See what I mean? Do something for nothing and you come a cropper.'

'April did, right on her behind. It must have hurt her, because she was very quiet after it happened. Hardly spoke two words.'

'Does she still think she's your fiancée?' It was the first time anyone had spoken the word in connection with April and it had an air of grim finality about it. Larry felt nervous again.

'I've arranged to talk to the vicar between shows to see if he can give me any advice.'

'Good luck then, old son.' Wally's interest in the subject waned. 'By the way, I've had a bit of good news today. Lou Hyman is coming up tomorrow with one of the big West End producers—Morrie Green. It seems that a few people from the agency business have been in this week and they've all been raving about my act. There's talk of a big new revue opening in the West End and they're looking for somebody new as second comic. If it comes off it'll be my big chance.' He rubbed his hands together with excitement.

Larry tried to look suitably impressed, but his new-found envy of his friend's success made it difficult. 'Good for you, Wal,' he said, none too heartily.

But Wally was too wrapped up in his own thoughts to notice Larry's lack of enthusiasm. He hummed to himself as he brushed his hair in the mirror, examining his face for spots at the same time.

Tillson made his usual entrance with the lion's meat wrapped in newspaper. He dumped it in the basin with a grunt. 'Horse meat's getting more bloody expensive every day. It's this bleeding Labour Government that's doing it—Attlee and his crowd. Ration books, clothing coupons—anybody'd think we *lost* the war not won it.' He took off his coat and slung it on a hook. 'It's your fault they're in—the Socialists. You buggers from the services voted for 'em. Old Churchill wasn't good enough for you after he'd finished off Hitler.'

'We wanted a change, mate. Churchill did a good job in the war—fine! But now it's all over we need fresh ideas. We want people in Parliament who are young and think the same way we do—want the same things we want. I spent nearly six years being told what to do, now I'd like to give a few orders myself.' Larry found himself voicing thoughts he had never before expressed.

'Hallo, hallo!' Wally was amused at Larry's outburst.

'And I feel the same way about the theatre and comedy, too. Far too many people in the business have had it all their own

156

way for too long. Give *us* blokes a chance. We've got *new* ideas for comedy, some of us.' He looked at Wally. 'I don't think just standing there telling a string of gags is the only way to be a comic. There's a lot of so-called "NAAFI comics" coming out of the services at the moment, and we're all new to the profession, but that doesn't mean that we've got to conform to a bloody formula. And the audience will be younger, too—they'll want something a bit fresher. I'm not exactly slaying 'em this week, but at least I'm trying to give them something different.' Larry was shaking as he finished. 'Sorry, Wally, I wasn't getting at you when I talked about gag routines.'

Wally raised an eyebrow. 'Let's face it, me old amico, you wouldn't be here this week if I hadn't fixed it with Lou Hyman.' He turned away to the mirror.

'Ungrateful git,' Tillson snorted, taking a gulp from a hip flask. 'Communists, that's what you are. Your mate here gives you a chance and you tear into him.' He offered Wally his flask. It was declined with a shudder. Tillson shrugged and put it away.

Wally turned back to Larry. 'Look, china, you've got to give the audience what they want. That's what I'm doing this week —that's why I'm tearing the balls off 'em. The answer is out there. People don't like too much change, they like the same old stuff. Listen to radio and what do you hear? Catch-phrases every week. "After you, Claude"; "Can I do you now, sir?" and all those ITMA sayings. The resident comics on Variety Bandbox—Reg Dixon, Frankie Howerd, Derek Roy—they all have some catch-phrase that the public knows 'em by because they plug them week after week.'

'Giving the public something to recognize you by is OK—that's what it's all about. But what I mean is, there's only *one* Max Miller, there's only *one* Tommy Trinder—they're the originals. I want to be the first Larry Gower, not a carbon copy of somebody else.'

'You'll be the one and only Larry Gower, son, that's for bloody sure,' sniggered Tillson, dumping himself on the broken chair. 'From what I've seen of your act the business couldn't stand another one like it—Christ!' The chair collapsed under him and he fell over backwards, his partly-removed trousers waving in the air. The hip flask flew from his pocket and was caught by his outstretched hand in an almost impossible save. 'How's that?' he cried in triumph and farted noisily where he lay.

When Larry came back into the wings after his act he was relieved to find that April was not waiting for him. 'I'm going to the vicarage between shows, Joe. The vicar said he'd have a chat with me. Is that all right?'

'It's OK with me, old lad, but don't be late for second house.' Joe gave the first lighting cue for Henri Lamarr's turn.

Larry lingered a little. 'What did Dan say about this afternoon?'

'The poor old feller was very upset. He got so wrapped up in his overture that he was in a trance when he finished. He walked through a door at the side of the stage and when he came to he found himself on a bus going to Huddersfield. And to make matters worse,' confided Joe, 'he was conducting it.'

'Pull the other leg, it's got bells on,' Larry said.

'You ask him, then,' Joe grinned. 'Old Dan's OK—just had a couple too many, that's all. It's this feller I'm worried about.' He nodded towards a grim-faced Henri who was flinging his clubs about with a controlled fury. 'He hasn't dropped any yet, and that's a bad sign. It means he's mad. I hope we won't see any bloody fireworks tonight. If Madam pushes him too far he might do something a bit drastic.'

'Come into the study,' said Philpotts when Larry arrived at the vicarage.

When they were seated he poured Larry and himself a glass of sherry and sat back in his leather chair. 'Now then, Larry. What's this trouble you're in? It's not Gwyneth Williams, is it?'

Larry nearly choked on his sherry.

'Thank heavens for that, then,' said the vicar, breathing a

sigh of relief. 'She has been a bit of a trial since she came to the Parish. A heart of gold, but a little wayward.'

'No, it's not her, it's April—you know, the dancer in the show.'

'You mean the one who had some difficulty with the pianist? What came over him, by the way? Someone told me that they saw him on the Huddersfield bus this afternoon. He must have had an urgent appointment elsewhere. Now, tell me what's worrying you.'

Larry spilled out his story, sparing none of the details, glad of the opportunity to get it off his chest. When he had finished Philpotts drummed his fingers on the arms of his chair for a while and then poured them both another glass of sherry.

'So the poor girl quite naturally considers herself engaged to you, and has a witness in the form of Mrs. Rogers, your landlady. Well, I don't think we have to worry about a breach of promise action, but let's examine the facts. Now then, she seems quite a simple girl and without guile, but my knowledge of her is confined to what I have seen of her over the past day or two— hardly enough to assess her character. One thing is reasonably certain—no girl wants to be married to a man who doesn't love her, however much she may love him. But you took advantage of her sexually and in your half-drunken state you must have told her things which led her to suppose you were in love with her.'

Larry nodded miserably.

'Cheer up, old man. They can't hang you for what you've done,' said the vicar with a smile.

'They can in the Middle East,' Larry remembered.

'Really? I thought they just chopped off a hand or something. Never mind, let's continue our summing up. You then made matters worse by leading her to suppose that you were coming to see me about an impending marriage. This you did in front of a material witness.'

'A very substantial one.'

'It was decent of you to pretend that some ancient Welsh custom prevented you from going to bed with her the following night. Nice touch, that.' Philpotts chuckled for a moment. 'So far in your relationship you have not told her that you have no love for her and have no intention of marrying her—which is the true state of affairs. Right?'

'Correct,' said Larry.

'Then you must do so.' Philpotts slapped his hands on the arms of the chair for emphasis. 'There is no other way out. Any other solution would be a cowardly one. Tell her as gently as you can that it was all a misunderstanding and that you are deeply sorry for what you have done. She will undoubtedly be upset for a while, but it is better that you tell her now before it becomes too late. Throw yourself on her mercy.'

'What about her brother Bill? He's a policeman in Manchester.'

'That, I'm afraid, is one of the penalties of indiscretion. Anyway, I doubt that she's had the opportunity to write to him yet. It's only Thursday today.' Philpotts radiated reassurance.

Larry stood up and shook his hand warmly. 'Thanks for the advice, sir. I'll act on it tonight. It'll be hard, I suppose, but I'll do it.'

The vicar led him out of the front door and on the way back to his study bumped into his wife.

'Poor boy,' she said, shaking her head sadly.

'You weren't listening at the door again? Shame on you, Betty. That's not playing the game.'

'Oh, go on, Nicholas. I feel sorry for the boy.'

'You should be feeling sympathy for the girl, surely?'

'I do, of course, but I'm more sorry for Larry. April phoned her brother from here this afternoon to tell him about her engagement. He's coming along to see her at the theatre on Saturday after playing Rugby League for Hunslet.'

'Oh dear me,' said the vicar, pouring himself another sherry. 'Poor boy, indeed.'

As Larry walked back to the theatre he mused on the lot of some of the married men he had met that week. There was old

Jack Rogers living in a divided house, imprisoned in his bright kitchen like a fly in amber; Ivor Williams, who wore the horns of cuckoldry like a small, neutered stag; and Tommy, who was perhaps the most pitiful of all, permanently humiliated by his domineering wife and forced to run after her like a lap-dog. What an advertisement for marriage! Another thought struck him—*all three husbands were shorter than their wives*. Perhaps stature had something to do with it. His own parents, now—his father was definitely taller than his mother and they were happy enough together. He tried to remember how tall April was. Her Indian feather had tickled his nose when he had kissed her, so she must be shorter than he was. Unless— Ah! She was *deliberately crouching and bending her knees* when they were together to give the impression of being shorter—then, when they were walking down the aisle after the wedding ceremony, she would suddenly rise to her full height and look down on him triumphantly. 'Got you,' she'd cry, and he'd finish up locked in a kitchen with a cat for company, forced to stand aside and watch an endless procession of lovers stream up the stairs to her bedroom.

There seemed to be only one solution for a happy marriage, as far as a man was concerned. *Marry a shorter partner*. Or, alternatively, wear secret lifts in your shoes, like the Hollywood film stars.

His thoughts had slowed the pace of his walking and it was not until he caught sight of a clock over a men's-wear shop that he realized he was late. He had ten minutes in which to get to the theatre and change. Fear pumped adrenalin into his calves and he arrived breathless at the theatre with five minutes to spare. As he tore up the stairs Joe Armsworth's angry words followed him. 'You're bloody late, son.'

'Cutting it a bit fine, aren't you?' Wally sounded smug as he watched, without offering to assist, Larry's frantic change.

'That's the first thing a pro has to learn. There's no excuse for being late. When that blind goes up you just have to be there. We're not doing army concert parties any more, this is for real.'

'Oh, belt up,' panted Larry as he struggled into his trousers.

161

'Don't bloody preach to me. I'm sick and tired of having sermons about show business crammed down my throat.'

'You're nearly on!' Joe's voice came urgently from the stair-well.

'Your flies are undone,' said Tillson, who had viewed the proceedings with a sozzled leer from his position near the sink.

Larry looked down. They *were* open. He began buttoning them as he left the room.

'Leave 'em open,' suggested Tillson. 'You might get your best laugh this week.'

'Balls!' yelled Larry in frustration.

'Did you hear that shaft of wit?' Tillson asked Wally. 'I tell you, that boy's got a wealth of material up his sleeve.'

Joe was furious with Larry. 'When I say get back in time for second house, I want you bloody well back here by the time I call the half.'

'I know—"there's no excuse for being late".' Larry sounded flippant without really meaning to be.

'That's right. Just remember it, then at least you'll have learned something this week.' Armsworth emphasized the word 'something', his voice tight with anger.

April and June clattered into the prompt corner from the stage and Larry, sick at heart, went on and gave his worst performance of the week.

He was confused by what had happened to him, and it showed. Mistiming bits of business with which he had begun to have some success as the week progressed, and even making a mess of the duet, he stumbled his way through his act. The audience sensed his nervousness and fidgeted uncomfortably throughout his performance. They were glad to see him go.

Joe, who was now feeling sorry for him, gave him a friendly pat on the arm as he came off. 'All right, old son, just write that one off to experience.'

Larry, close to tears, nodded and made for the comforting darkness at the back of the stage.

162

April joined him. He instinctively made to reach for her, needing the comfort of a woman's arms, then, remembering, dropped his arms to his side. Strangely enough, she made no move towards him. Instead, she waited with folded arms until he had composed himself.

'I was speaking to Gwyneth this afternoon—told me she used to live in your part of the world.' Her voice was unnaturally high.

Larry knew what was coming and was somehow glad. 'And she told you that there's no such thing as a tradition of keeping yourself pure until your wedding night. I'm afraid that she's right.'

'Why did you lie to me, then? After you'd had your pleasure you went off me, didn't you? You take advantage of a girl and then cast her aside like a—a—'

'Worn-out glove?' offered Larry.

April hit him hard across the face.

'There's no need to be bloody funny about it. It's no laughing matter. You tell me you love me one minute—we're unofficially engaged and you're off to see the vicar. Then the next night you tell me a fairy story so you won't have to go to bed with me.' Her face crumpled and she began to sob quietly.

Larry stood helplessly by.

'I'm sorry. Really I am. It's all a big misunderstanding. I don't know how it all got out of hand like this.' He put his arms around her, but she stiffened within them until her sobbing began to die down, and then she shrugged him away.

The music of Henri Lamarr's act came to them muffled by the curtains. Larry's eyes were more accustomed to the darkness now and he could see April's tears falling to the floor with almost the same frequency as the juggler's clubs. At least he's not mad this house, Larry thought distractedly.

'And I've told everybody we're engaged, too. I'll be the laughing stock of the business. What will Mrs. Rogers say?' She wailed quietly. 'What will our Bill say?'

The hair on the back of Larry's neck suddenly rose. 'You've told him, then? He knows, does he?'

She nodded. 'He's coming to the theatre on Saturday night. He says he wants to see my fiancé for himself.'

'But can't you tell him it's all off now?'

'Yes, and when I do he'll be here to give you a damned good hiding.' April whirled away from him in a fresh burst of tears and rushed off.

Larry was stunned and bewildered. He had not imagined it happening like this. He had meant to take April aside after supper and tell her gently that it was all wrong, that he was not good enough for her. In his mind he had seen himself stemming her flood of tears with a gentle kiss and consoling her that 'in spite of what had happened he would never forget her, never, ever'. Instead of which he had had his face slapped hard, and looked like getting a further beating at the hands of her big brother.

A furtive movement behind the curtain caught his eye. He pulled it aside. Sammy stood, clutching himself.

'You'll go blind if you keep that up,' reproved Larry.

'Not likely,' Sammy giggled slyly, 'I can see well even in the dark.'

Jimmy stopped Larry on the stairs. 'I don't know what you've done to that April, but she's crying buckets.'

Larry had stayed down in the stage area and in his misery had sat talking to Simba about his troubles. The lion had purred and rumbled with pleasure and Larry was comforted by the knowledge that at least he had one friend he could talk to. He had waited until Wally had begun his act before going back to the dressing-room.

'If I were you, ducky, I'd get off to your digs and lock yourself in until morning. You've had quite a day, I believe.' Jimmy's eyes were kind as they saw the young man's anguish. 'You know, you'd be far better off if you joined our gang,' he said, twitching his hips to make Larry smile. 'Don't worry—I'm not recruiting new members this week. Anyway, it's not much fun being a queer these days—should have been born an ancient Greek, I suppose. I'd have looked lovely in one of those togas.'

'How's George?' asked Larry politely.

'I think he's worse than he lets on.' Jimmy's voice grew sombre. 'When we came off just now it was all he could do to climb these steps. I'm very worried about him.'

Larry looked suitably solemn. 'Hope he's better tomorrow. Well—better get off, like you say. "Hell hath no fury" and all that. Still, I really am sorry she's upset. Everything's gone wrong somehow this week.'

He bounded up the remaining stairs to the dressing-room, which was mercifully empty, and changed back into his street clothes.

'Didn't expect you so soon.' Jack Rogers was sitting by the fire reading a newspaper with the cat on his lap. He got up slowly and put the cat on the floor, its tail waving furiously in disapproval. 'Where's April? Not had a lovers' tiff, have yer?'

'Something of the sort,' said Larry. And as Rogers poured him a cup of tea, which he said was all he wanted, he told the old man what had happened.

Rogers sucked his gums and tut-tutted. 'Pity, that. She's a nice young kid, is April. Always good for a laugh and got a right healthy appetite, too. I like to see that in a woman.'

Larry remembered how she had gone for the sandwiches at the pub and the way she had tucked into the food at the social— in spite of the fact, he suddenly realized, that she must by then have known about his duplicity. He began to feel a little better. At least he'd save a few bob on lunches the rest of the week.

'Before I forget,' said Rogers. 'Could you let me have thirty-five bob for the wine you had on Wednesday night? I got it on tick at the off-licence, like April asked me to. I promised to pay him in the morning.'

Larry forked out the money sullenly, then, hearing footsteps outside, hastily said 'Goodnight' and hurried into his bedroom. He would never have believed that the seedy room could look welcoming, but that night, as he heard April sniff her way past his door accompanied by variations on the 'Never mind, love' theme from Wally and June, it was a sanctuary—a refuge from the outside world.

Friday

He was awake early. Reaching automatically for his spectacles, he looked at his watch. Six thirty. He decided to be up and away from the house before anyone was about. The thought of April's tear-stained, accusing face confronting him over the breakfast table was more than he could stomach. The business of washing and shaving would have to be done later—any movement on the stairs might bring Mrs. Rogers out from her lair. No doubt April would have told her the news, and the sooner he made himself scarce the better. Women stick together on these occasions, he reminded himself.

He opened his door quietly and crept into the passage. The front door presented him with noisy problems and as he drew the last bolt he had the feeling that someone was watching him. He turned round and beheld the awesome figure of Ma Rogers in her dressing-gown, standing like Brunhilda at the top of the stairs.

'Monster!' she hissed. 'You swine! What have you done to that girl?'

'The same thing the giant did to you—fee, fi, foh, fum!' Larry gave her a two-fingered salute and shot out of the door like a bullet. He wondered whether he would ever dare to go back.

The morning was bleak and he shivered as the cold wind struck his face. It was dark and the street lights were still on. In the distance a factory hooter mournfully called the faithful to work. He made up his mind and strode resolutely along the main street towards the railway station where he knew he could at least get a cup of tea,

The darkness gradually lifted as he walked and he looked in despair at his surroundings. During his two years in Italy he had revelled in the bright shop signs, the brilliant colours of the awnings and shutters, the gaiety of a people who had fought a war, been defeated, and without pausing for breath had joined the winning side. Here in this town he felt he was among the losers. The faces of the people who passed him on their way to work, head-scarved, muffled against the wind, were pale and tired. There was a lack of friendliness about at this hour of the day and he was glad to reach the bustle of the railway station.

He paid for a cup of strong tea and a cheese roll which put up a tough battle against his snapping teeth, and in defeat made its presence felt down every inch of his gullet. The station buffet was sprinkled with army uniforms, some of them displaying the same divisional sign as he had worn up until a few months ago. For a while he envied the easy camaraderie of the soldiers as they smoked their NAAFI-issue cigarettes and swapped tall stories about Nobby Clark at the Sangro and old Chalky White on leave in Rome. Nostalgia for his army days began to overwhelm him.

Then a sergeant wearing a red armband with the initials 'RTO' came in. He bawled the soldiers out on to the platform, bullying and chivvying as they grabbed for kit bags and webbing equipment. Larry allowed himself his first smile of the day as he realized his freedom. Good luck, lads, wherever you're going. I'm glad I'm not going with you.

He bought another cup of tea and relaxed with a newspaper which someone had left on the seat beside him. 'Bread ration may be cut' screamed a headline. That'll please April, he thought. 'Less bacon and home meat' proclaimed another. 'Beer supplies to be halved'—now *that* really *is* bad news.

Larry put the paper aside and glanced at the station clock. Eight thirty already. He wondered how breakfast was going at Ma Rogers's. There'd be plenty to gossip about and his name would be mud, he had no doubt. Sod 'em all, he thought. I'll bet the old cow daren't tell anybody what I said to her about the giant, anyway. That was one secret he shared with April.

There was still the whole day to while away and he decided that he would have a wash and brush-up in the Gents and then a nice leisurely saunter to the barber's for a shave.

It was not exactly the best day for sitting in the recreation ground, but after he had had his shave there seemed nothing else to do until opening time. The weak winter sun was out and he sat on a bench out of the wind and raised his face to catch the sun's meagre rays. A black and white mongrel sniffed at the contents of a wire litter basket and, not liking what it found, raised its leg and peed against it.

Larry put his hand out to pat the dog as it passed. It jumped back a pace, snarled and ran off the way it had come, barking over its shoulder. He put his hand back in his pocket. It's funny that I can have a lion eating out of my hand and yet I can't ever get a dog to like me. I'm a 'cat man' like Jack Rogers, he thought. Larry Gower, the King of the Cats, tamer of forest-bred lions, dozed off.

A whistle blown hard at a distance of three feet blasted him awake. Elwyn Thomas stood before him, grinning. 'You're up and about early, bach. I thought actors stayed in bed until two o'clock in the afternoon after a hard night with the landlady's daughter. Perhaps you haven't been to bed yet. Sidling home through the recreation ground after a night of debauchery at the vicarage, is it?'

Larry laughed and moved over to make room for the school-teacher to sit down. 'Just out for a little walk.'

Elwyn shouted to his class of boys to carry on practising scrummaging and sat beside him. 'Have you got over Tuesday night yet? Duw, that was a night, mun—best Tuesday we've ever had. Told you that though, didn't I?' He leant his head back against the seat and sighed happily. 'To be perfectly frank with you, I didn't think you were all that good on the stage. Mind you,' he held up his hand to still Larry's faint protests. 'Mind you,' he repeated, 'we didn't give you much chance that night. It must have been a bit difficult with the boys shouting all the time.'

'It certainly was.' Larry was indignant.

'But when we went to the Dragon and you started messing about with the eggs and things—all that impromptu stuff was great, boyo. Great! And your voice, too. That's a gift that you're not using to its full advantage. Tell you what, I'll write out some piano copies—in your key, of course—of some of the Welsh songs we sang that night. It's a hobby of mine, music—I've got a couple of ideas for you I'll put down, too. Gwyneth told me you did very well at the Church Hall on Thursday with your singing. There's a girl for you, Gwyneth.' The schoolmaster rattled on, hardly stopping to take a breath. 'She's a good old sport—ask Ianto Price. Had her on the stairs, as you know. Never been that lucky myself. Good job Ivor turns a blind eye to her carryings on. Fair play, they say she only does it for Welshmen.'

'I know one Frenchman she's done it for,' interrupted Larry mysteriously.

'A *Frenchman* with Gwyneth?' Elwyn was shocked. 'He must be a Rugby player then. Either that or a top tenor.' He looked beseechingly at Larry.

'He's a juggler who can move his muscles to music.'

'Ah—I knew there had to be something special about him to get Gwyneth's knickers off.'

He looked over at his class, who had taken his order to practise scrummaging only too literally and were milling around in the mud. 'Cockcroft!' he shouted. A familiar figure struggled free of the thrashing arms and legs and loped towards them.

Elwyn stood up and dangled the whistle on its string before the schoolboy's mesmerized ·gaze—a hypnotist working on a willing subject. 'Now then, Cockcroft, bach. If I give you this whistle will you promise to blow it every thirty seconds, regular?'

'Yes, yes,' murmured the mud-stained lad ecstatically.

'I thought you would. Well, don't. I want you to take charge of the class and when it gets to twelve o'clock by the church clock over there—that's when the big hand and the little hand are together on the twelve, remember?—blow the whistle and take the class back to school. Right?'

The boy nodded, without taking his eyes off the whistle. Elwyn gave it to him. Cockcroft hung it round his neck and stood for a moment looking down at it. Then he turned and started back to his fighting school-mates, the unconscious comedy of his half-walk, half-run sending Larry into mild hysterics. When he got back to the jostling scrum, the boy hit out wildly at the others, pointing at the whistle and then back at the schoolmaster.

'Cockcroft's in charge.' Elwyn's voice carried across the recreation ground like a sergeant major's. The fighting subsided immediately at the sound of his command and Cockcroft began to take over.

They watched his antics for a while until Elwyn, looking at the church clock, reminded Larry that the Dragon was open. They left the park, imitating the Cockcroft walk side by side. By the time they reached the main road they were exhausted.

'It's good for the bugger to have a bit of authority, mind,' puffed Elwyn. 'You have to delegate responsibility now and again.'

'That's one thing I can't do,' panted Larry, holding on to a bus stop sign until he got his breath back. 'I can't send anybody else on stage to do my act for me. "No play, no pay" is the term used, I believe.'

'That's true, I suppose, but think of the money you can earn when you *do* play. Some of you buggers get hundreds of pounds a week. Diawch diawl, any silly so and so who can stand on his head, play a mouth organ and juggle a few clubs at the same time can make a fortune.'

'Could *you* do it?'

'I'm going to start practising right now. Mind out.' Elwyn carefully stood on his head against the bus stop sign.

'Let's see how long you can hold that position,' said Larry.

'You're on, boyo.' The schoolmaster was already going red in the face.

A bus drew up alongside them. 'What's up with him, then?' asked the conductor.

'It's all right, he's waiting for a bus to Australia.'

'He'll want a 47 then,' said the conductor, ringing the bell. 'Change at Halifax.'

The Dragon was fairly empty when they finally arrived. They went into the saloon bar and greeted Ivor, who was putting fresh sandwiches under glass covers.

'Oh, hello, boys.' There was a welcome in his smile—as if Tuesday had never been. 'Gwyneth will be down in a minute. What are you two drinking?'

'Two halves of bitter and one for yourself.' Larry felt generous.

'Never touch it during the day-time, thank you.' Ivor put two foaming bitters before them on the counter.

'Are you sure?' enquired Larry, relieved.

'Certain,' said Ivor as Larry produced his last crumpled pound note. 'Never touch beer before six o'clock. I'll have a large Scotch instead.' He swept Larry's oncer into the till and slapped the change down with a swift, continuous movement, which would have done justice to a Mississippi river-boat gambler.

'Cheers!' Elwyn waited till Ivor had poured himself a whisky and raised his glass to Larry.

'Cheers,' said Larry faintly, pocketing his change.

'Cheers.' Ivor took a tiny sip from his glass and put it under the counter. 'I'll have the rest later.'

'Good morning, Elwyn. 'Morning, Larry.' Gwyneth was among them in a cloud of eau-de-cologne, eyes dancing. She lifted the flap of the bar counter and kissed them both heartily. 'Who's in the chair, then?'

'Larry.' Ivor had already whipped a glass under an inverted bottle of gin and was opening a bottle of tonic with his other hand.

'Thank you, love,' said Gwyneth.

'Cheers,' replied Larry, swallowing hard as he saw his silver disappear into Ivor's till.

'Bonjour mes amis, and bore da!' Henri Lamarr's muscular frame blocked the doorway to the saloon.

'Where's the Gents?' asked Larry quickly.

Larry loitered in the lav until sufficient time had elapsed for someone else to have bought Henri's drink. He touched the post office savings book in his inside pocket and decided to draw out another three pounds. It was an expensive game, show business, he reflected glumly for the umpteenth time that week.

To his relief, when he returned to the saloon Henri had been introduced and was buying a round of drinks.

'A large Scotch, please,' said Larry, when asked what he wanted. Ivor handed him a glass of whisky from under the counter. It looked suspiciously like the one Larry had just bought for the landlord, but he decided to say nothing. He knew when he was up against an expert.

'Is this the bloke you were talking about?' Elwyn spoke out of the side of his mouth.

'See for yourself.' Larry nodded towards Gwyneth who was prattling away happily to Henri, feeling his biceps and looking flirtatiously up into his eyes. Ivor, who was serving a newly-arrived customer, had his back to them.

'Aye. I see what you mean. Big bugger, isn't he? That's Gwyneth's type, all right.'

'Doesn't Ivor *really* mind, then, what Gwyneth does?' Larry was anxious to know.

'Oh, I suppose he does deep down, but he's learned to live with it. He makes a fuss now and again when it gets a bit blatant—like with Ianto on Tuesday—but they're very fond of each other. Look at him, now, who else would have that in bed with her? I don't think he's any good in that department, either. He's a hot water bottle to her, boy, a bloody human hot water bottle.' The schoolmaster's voice rose slightly at the end of his sentence.

'Who's talking about hot water bottles, then?' Gwyneth was with them again, holding Henri's hand.

'I was telling Larry that he should buy himself one when he's travelling around, sleeping in damp beds,' Elwyn said smoothly.

'They can be less trouble than other ways of keeping warm, can't they, Larry?' Gwyneth winked at him and smiled. 'Must be cold sleeping in shining armour, too. Have to keep your lance nice and warm, don't you, love?'

'What was all that about?' Elwyn was puzzled.

'Just a little joke between us.' Larry felt a light sweat start from his forehead.

'Never you mind, cariad. Your secret's safe with Aunty Gwyneth. Now, come on, it's my round. Drink up, and Ivor, let's have some sandwiches for the lads. This big boy here wants plenty of feeding.'

Henri laughed proudly and flexed his large biceps.

Here we go again, thought Ivor, as a familiar spasm gripped his stomach. It's not the adultery I mind so much, but she gets so bloody generous. He handed plates and condiments across the bar. 'Go easy with the mustard,' he grumbled. 'It's in short supply.'

Larry felt sleepy after his session at the Dragon and, when Elwyn said he had to leave for school, took the opportunity of going with him. Henri stayed behind, performing feats of strength to the delight of the customers who now filled the bar. At least this one is good for custom, thought Ivor, as he bustled between till and counter.

There was no point in Larry's going to the theatre yet, and the digs were out of bounds for the time being. His first job was to draw some more money from the post office.

A cinema attracted his attention after he had undertaken that heart-squeezing operation. Wally had told him that if he said that he was performing at the theatre, he could get in free in the afternoons.

He approached the whey-faced woman behind the glass of the ticket booth. 'I'm from the Royalty,' he announced.

'Oh yes? Where's your card?'

'What card?' Wally had not mentioned any card—typical.

The woman sighed heavily. 'You have to show your card to prove that you're in the profession and then you can get a ticket.'

'How about a quick song and dance, then? That'll prove I'm on the stage.' Larry broke into a little tap dance and started singing.

'That'll be enough of that, young man. Either you buy a ticket or I'll call the manager.' The ticket seller was outraged.

'I give in.' Larry put his hands up in surrender. 'One one and ninepenny please.'

She took his money and he watched the blue ticket curl from the machine in front of her. She tore it off and gave it to him. 'Through the door and on the right.'

'You're very kind,' said Larry. He blew her a kiss and did the Cockcroft walk as he left the foyer.

The tatty commissionaire wheezed up to the ticket booth. 'What's the matter with yon feller, Edith?'

'I think he's bloody barmy. Says he's from the Royalty, but he'd got no card to prove it,' she sniffed. 'Tried to show me he could sing and dance.'

'Like a bit of juggling, meself,' said the commissionaire, scratching his backside through his threadbare uniform.

Larry slept fitfully through a routine Western, woke up for an ice cream at the interval and snored solidly through the first part of an old Cagney movie. A woman behind, who had just come in, smote him sharply on the head with her umbrella to wake him. He was glad she had done so, even though it hurt, because he enjoyed seeing the way Cagney dominated every scene—especially the last, where Cagney took about five minutes to die under a hail of slugs. Good strong stuff, he thought contentedly as he left the cinema. It was now five thirty and he headed for the theatre at a smart pace. He did not want to upset Joe again.

The stage door-keeper handed him a letter as he came in. It was similar to the other he had received, to judge from the writing on the envelope.

'YOU WAS WORST SECOND HOUSE LAST NITE. I THINK YOU SHOLD BE PISED ON FROM A GRATE

HITE. GO BACK WERE YOU CAME FROM. DIS-
GUSTED.'

The handwriting was the same as before. Larry read it
angrily and was about to tear it to shreds when Lovegrove came
into view. His moment of revenge over, he wanted to get the
letter back. The less evidence, the better. He didn't want to be
seen picking up the pieces off the floor for a start, and besides
it gave him a thrill to browse over his collection of nasty notes,
secure in his anonymity. Though not a criminal act, he would
hate Fred Brotherton to find out what he was doing. It would
cost him his job.

'Another of those letters, eh?' He clucked in sympathy.
'Let me have it and I'll see it gets into the right hands. It's time
they had an inquiry about these letters, as I said before.'

Something in Lovegrove's manner struck Larry as odd. On
both the occasions he had received these letters Lovegrove had
been lurking near the stage door, as if he were waiting for him.

Larry put the letter in his pocket. 'No thanks,' he said.
'I'll keep it as a souvenir.'

Lovegrove could not press him further without arousing
suspicion. He grunted to himself and squeaked away, a tiny
alarm bell ringing in his head.

Frowning, Larry watched him go, then took the letter along
to Joe Armsworth who looked at it carefully and put it away
in a drawer.

'Funny thing,' said Larry slowly. 'Each time I've had one,
old Lovegrove's been there when I'm reading it. Yet I rarely
see the old bastard at other times.'

'I'm working on something, Larry old buddy, that may bust
this case wide open.' Joe spoke in a bad imitation of an
American detective.

'You dirty rat,' said Larry in his best Cagney, and they both
laughed.

'Leave it with me. I think I'll have it all sorted out by
tomorrow.' Joe's battered old watch came out. 'Time to call the
bloody half. We live by the clock in this business—as I hope
you've found out this week. What did the vicar say, by the way?

Did you get things sorted out with April?' He ushered Larry from the room.

'It's all over, thank God,' said Larry as Joe shut his door behind them. 'Mind you, I don't think I'm very popular.'

He was not, as he found out when he mounted the stairs to his dressing-room. April passed him on her way down. She had not yet made up and her face looked puffy with newly-shed tears. Larry felt a twinge of conscience and stopped to say how terribly sorry he was, but before he could open his mouth April fired the first salvo.

'I've phoned my brother and he's mad at you.' There was a ferocity in her voice that Larry had never suspected she was capable of. 'He's coming on Saturday, any road—so you'd better watch out, you bloody Casanova.' She flung the words at Larry like a handful of gravel and swept past him, twitching her dressing-gown aside as she did so, as if to touch him would mean contamination.

He pondered once more on the metamorphosis this once jolly, good-natured girl had undergone, first into cloyingly affectionate spaniel and now into vengeful virago. What would be her final role tomorrow? The triumphant harridan, shrieking with malignant glee as her big brother battered him into bleeding insensibility? His scalp prickled at the thought.

Wally was already in the dressing-room. He was fussing around, picking up odd items of Larry's and Tillson's clothing and putting them in some semblance of order. His own clothes hung immaculately on hangers and a fresh make-up towel covered his place at the mirror, which Wally had obviously cleaned as well as he could. The silver hairbrush gleamed in its place of honour and the whole room looked tidier than Larry had seen it all week.

'Hang your coat up properly, mate—don't sling it on my trunk.'

'Sorry, mate.' Larry retrieved his coat from where he had automatically flung it and did as he was asked. 'What's all this in aid of? Having a barrack-room inspection, are we?'

Wally flicked the duster he had borrowed from Ma Rogers

round the room once more and looked at his handiwork with a dissatisfied expression before answering.

'Lou Hyman, my agent—and yours too, for this week at any rate—is bringing Morrie Green here tonight, remember? Can't have the place looking like a bleeding pigsty.' He made a tiny adjustment to his make-up towel and stood back, looking at it.

'Suppose not,' said Larry, starting to take off his street clothes.

'Be careful where you put your things, Larry.' Wally was more nervous and strung-up than his friend had ever seen him. 'This is my big chance—I've *got* to make an impression on Morrie Green. After all, he's very influential in the business. He's producing this new show in the West End but he also does a lot of work in the variety theatres—pantomimes and touring revues for the Number Ones. He's big stuff, is Morrie Green.'

'What are Number Ones?' asked Larry, so impressed by Wally's description of the producer that he took extra care to hang his street clothes tidily before getting into his stage suit.

'Moss Empires and Stoll Theatres, son. They're the Number One theatres. Fifty-two weeks a year of solid work if you get in there. Finsbury Park Empire—that's next to the Palladium for prestige—Golders Green Hippodrome, Chiswick Empire, Wood Green Empire, Shepherd's Bush Empire—that's in London alone. Then there's all their provincial theatres—Manchester Hippodrome, Liverpool Empire, Leeds, Birmingham, Bristol, Cardiff, Swansea, Glasgow—you can play all over the country once you've been approved.' Wally was getting excited at the thought.

'What number theatre is this then?'

'The Royalty? About number six, I should reckon.' Wally was disdainful. 'The good number twos are well worth playing.' He returned to his theme. 'Take the Syndicate Halls in London. Chelsea Palace, The Metropolitan, Edgware Road—that's a smashing shop window for any act, that is—and the Palaces at Walthamstow and East Ham. Brixton Empress, that's another one of theirs. A lot of the big names play those dates. Mind, it

177

don't always mean that if you top a number two bill you can top a number one. You might have to share top billing with somebody else or take second place.'

The recital of all these theatres, the Palaces and Empires, made Larry's head spin. They seemed like misty spires on some unattainable horizon. He felt that his chance of ever working in them was extremely remote, and if he met April's brother on Saturday he might be unable to work for a while anywhere.

'How did things go at the digs last night? I went to bed early —thought it was the best thing to do under the circumstances.' Larry eyed Wally in the mirror.

'Real bloody melodrama, it was.' There was considerable malice in Wally's chuckle. 'Even Ma Rogers was on her side. April was very cut up about it—no kidding. Why didn't you just let things go on until the end of the week and then break it off by post? I would have.'

'That's the cowardly way out,' said Larry self-righteously, privately wishing he'd followed Wally's advice.

'Anyway, it's done now.' Wally was more concerned with the present. 'Look, when they come in—Lou and Morrie Green —do me a favour and scarper, will you? So we can talk business. I think they'll be up between shows. Lou's bringing him to the second house because first house Friday's never any bloody good.'

Wally was right, thought Larry as he battled his way through his act. He was more in command and worked well enough to purge himself of the shame of the previous evening's performance, but he was glad that the moguls from London were not in front to witness the paucity of his final applause.

'They're clapping with one hand tonight,' remarked Joe. 'It'll be much better second house—it's pay-day and the audience should be a bit more cheerful.'

'I hope so. Wally's got his agent and a big producer up from London to see him.' Larry tried to sound pleased for his friend.

'Aye, I've heard. Good luck to the lad, though if he lands a job tonight he'll be bloody insufferable tomorrow.' The stage manager scratched his belly and yawned. 'I've seen 'em come and I've seen 'em go and there's very few that don't lose their heads on the way up. We get a lot of has-beens topping the bill here—like that old cow this week—and they can be a pain in the arse. Nothing's ever right for 'em—the lighting's wrong or the band's too loud or somebody's talking in the wings. Anything to escape the hard bloody fact that they're on the way out. Then you get those who're not quite there yet—perhaps headlining for the first time. They're all anxious to please, ask nicely if they want you to make a change in their lighting or alter their act round. Good tip on a Saturday night. "Thanks, Joe. You've been a great help." A year or two later they become big radio stars and you start reading about them walking out of shows, throwing tantrums and being bloody awkward all round. They stay up there for a while, but they get found out and then I get the buggers back 'ere again. And the lights are all wrong and the sodding band's too loud and somebody's talking in the wings—just like we are. Go on—eff off, the sermon's over.'

'You filthy, scruffy bloody Herbert.' Wally was shouting red-faced at a drunken Tillson. 'Look what the drunken bastard's done,' he screeched at Larry in high-pitched indignation. 'He's dropped his bloody lion's meat on the dressing-table and made a mess of everything.'

Tillson looked drunker than Larry had ever seen him. As he watched, the man took a bottle of whisky from his side pocket and putting it to his lips, drank noisily. He belched, put the bottle back in his pocket and wiped his mouth with the back of his hand.

'We're very house-proud tonight aren't we, darling?' His speech was extremely slurred.

'I've got some important people coming in tonight and I want the place looking reasonably decent, that's all.' Wally grabbed the meat and threw it at Tillson, who caught it deftly in spite of his apparent incapability.

'See that? Who said I'm a drunken bastard? Catch!' he

shouted and threw the chunk of dripping red meat at Larry, who managed to get only one hand to it thus deflecting it straight onto the front of Wally's stage suit which hung on the wall behind him. The soggy horseflesh then fell to the floor, where Wally's newly-shined shoes received it with a wet thud.

Wally was speechless. He stood frozen in horror at the sight of the blood dripping slowly from the lapels of his suit. Tillson took advantage of his shock, retrieved the meat, and brushing it with his sleeve began to leave the room. He turned at the door and shook his head reprovingly at Larry.

'Butter-fingers,' he said.

Larry knew what the incident meant to Wally and tried to think of something to say. 'Ah well, that's show business,' he ventured.

Wally came to life with a fury that startled his friend. 'Show business! What the hell do *you* know about bloody show business?'

'Sorry! Sorry!' Larry lifted his arms to ward off Wally, who was almost in tears with rage and about to take a wild swing at him. 'I'm just a NAAFI comic who knows nothing except the fact that you can get blood-stains off a suit with salt and water.'

'How do you know?' There was a glimmer of hope in Wally's eyes.

'It's an old Welsh remedy. My father used to get nose bleeds sometimes and that's how my mother always cleaned his suit. Sometimes she'd put a key down his neck to stop the bleeding.'

'I'm not bleeding, you berk!' Wally was getting angry again. 'It's blood from the horse meat on my suit.'

'You're right. And it's too late to put a key down the horse's neck. Let's take the suit along to the girls.' Larry stopped. 'On second thoughts, we'd better take it down to Jimmy and George.'

'I can't. They're on stage and I'm on next.' Wally was frantic. 'It's on the trousers as well. Look at those marks.'

'You'll have to wear my suit, that's all,' offered Larry. 'The sleeves may be a bit short on you and the trousers will be big round the waist, but you've got no option, old son.'

He changed quickly and handed over the suit. He watched

Wally's expression of utter disbelief as he put it on and surveyed himself in the mirror.

'It looks bloody terrible,' he groaned. 'The trousers feel all damp round the knees as well.'

'I was sweating a bit out there. Sorry about that but I didn't know I was going to have to hire 'em out when I came off.' Larry felt unaccountably elated.

Wally put his Borsalino trilby on and decided the effect was ludicrous with Larry's suit. He hung it up again. 'Thanks, anyway. Do me a favour and try to get the jacket and trousers cleaned for second house.' Wally took another look at himself in the mirror. 'Christ almighty! I look like a bloody circus clown in this.'

'It's fine from the back,' said Larry behind him. 'Try working in three-quarter profile.'

'Very funny,' snarled Wally as he left.

'One other thing,' called Larry brightly from the door. 'Watch the make-up on the suit.'

Larry leaned against the door and allowed himself a bout of quiet laughter. The sight of the usually dapper Wally crawling miserably down the stairs to face his public in an ill-fitting suit had brought tears to his eyes. He put his street clothes back on.

Still chuckling he picked up Wally's suit and waited outside Jimmy's and George's room until they came up from their act. When they appeared, Jimmy was helping his partner to walk. George seemed in great pain and was holding his side. Larry gave him a hand into the room.

'I don't know how we got through it tonight,' Jimmy panted, easing George into a chair. 'I thought he was going to pass out on me at one stage.' He took off his wig and put it on a wig block, looking anxiously over his shoulder at George, who lay back in his chair, his eyes closed.

'We'll have to get a doctor for him,' said Larry.

George stirred and opened his eyes. 'I'll be all right if you don't fuss me.' His voice was still deep and strong. 'Give me a drop of brandy, Jimmy.' He removed his own wig and handed it to Larry who stood holding it, feeling rather foolish.

Jimmy poured a brandy for George and took the wig from

Larry. 'Thanks, dear. Like a brandy? Might as well all have one now I've got the bottle open.' He set out two more glasses.

'Good health,' said Larry, raising his drink in George's direction.

'Thanks. I think I'll be OK now. The pain's easing off. It's something I've learned to live with, anyway.'

'I still think we should get a doctor for you.' Jimmy hovered over George, looking anxiously into his face.

'Now please stop your damned fussing and let me conquer this my own way.' He patted Jimmy's hand tenderly.

Larry cleared his throat. 'I was going to ask you to clean this suit of Wally's, he's got blood on it, but I shan't bother you with it. You've got enough trouble.'

Jimmy took the suit from him. 'It'll give me something to do, dear.' He examined the stains. 'How did this happen, then? It's in a shocking state.'

Larry told him what had happened.

'That Tillson's a bad lot,' said George, who seemed to have recovered a little. 'Always on the bottle. It's a wonder how the poor lion puts up with him.'

'Perhaps he'll try to get his own back one night. "Simba's Revenge" by Claude Balls.' Jimmy was his sprightly self again now that George was looking better.

'My mother always used cold water and salt to get blood-stains off my father's suit,' said Larry.

'Come from a fighting family, eh?'

'That's right,' laughed Larry, uneasily. He felt it would be almost sacrilegious to discuss his parents with these two.

'Leave the suit with us then. I'll try your mother's remedy on it. Anyway, he'll be lucky to have it by the second house.'

Larry did his best to rub out the blood-stains on the dressing-table and had the place looking fairly tidy again by the time Wally came up from the stage.

He was in a bad temper and complained bitterly as he undressed.

'Cramped my style, not having my own gear on. I couldn't wear the Borsalino with this lot and I forgot how much business there was with it. I felt a proper twat. Ruined my timing—everything went for a Burton. Half my act relies on looking smart.' He held up Larry's trousers. 'How can anybody look smart in these bleeding things?'

'I try,' said Larry with dignity, taking the trousers from him and hanging them up with the jacket.

'If you feel smart, you work well. If I hadn't come to the theatre in a pullover tonight I could have worn my ordinary suit. At least it fits me and it looks good.'

'You might have to go back to the digs and fetch it, then. Jimmy Long says he'll try and clean the blood off your suit for second house, but he can't guarantee it.'

Wally swore and dressed quickly. 'I might just make it,' he said, grabbing for the door-knob.

The door opened on him and a cloud of cigar smoke entered, followed by a small fat man.

'What are you trying to do to me, Wally?' The newcomer waved his cigar in the air and stamped his foot down hard on the floor.

'Lou!' exclaimed Wally in dismay. 'I didn't think you were coming until second house. Don't tell me Morrie Green was out there.'

'We came up on an early train. It was his idea—he wanted to see you working with a normal Friday first house audience to see how you could handle a bad house.' Hyman spat a piece of cigar tobacco from his mouth before continuing. 'Where did you get that suit? Terrible. Terrible.' He shook his head so fiercely that his jowls took several seconds to settle again. 'What have I always told you? Always look smart.' He emphasized the words with his cigar. '*Al-ways look smart.*' Ash cascaded down his fawn Crombie overcoat and he halted his lecture to brush it off with a well-manicured hand.

Wally stood before him like a recalcitrant private before his C.O., arms behind his back. Larry stood near the sink and watched the scene with interest.

Hyman smoothed his thinning hair and started again. 'You came out on stage looking like a bloody yokel. Morrie was not impressed at all. Not at all. I'd given you the big build up all the way up in the train. Lovely performer, I said. Dresses well. Always looks smart. Then you come out looking like *that*.' Hyman stamped his foot again for emphasis. He patted his chest. 'I mustn't get upset. The doctor says I've got to take it easy. It's my heart,' he said, addressing Larry for the first time.

Larry nodded in mute sympathy.

'Who's this? Introduce me.' Hyman waved a hand towards Larry.

'Larry Gower,' he introduced himself. 'You've already met my suit.'

'Oh yers, yers. The army boy. Missed you first house. We only arrived in time to see young Wally here.'

'Can you get Morrie to stay for second house?' Wally pleaded. 'Take him out for a drink somewhere. Explain what happened and bring him back.'

'Sit down, sir, and Wally will explain what happened.' Larry offered Hyman the broken chair.

'Thank you, son. All right, tell me, Wally. But don't take too long. I've left Morrie in the bar.'

He listened to the chapter of accidents, which Larry wisely left Wally to describe, puffing on his cigar, and nodding every now and then.

'Well, that explains it, I suppose. I hope I can get Morrie to understand. He's staying up here tonight anyway before going on to Glasgow tomorrow to see a speciality act for the Golders Green pantomime. I think he's got a bird up there, meself.'

'All I ask is that you bring him back for the second house when my suit's cleaned up or I've brought my lounge suit from the digs.' Wally was wringing his hands as he spoke.

Tillson lurched into the room. He waved his hands in front of his face and coughed. 'Who's smoking bloody rope in here?' He peered drunkenly through the cigar smoke at Lou Hyman. 'Oh, it's you Hyman. You've got no right coming into a person's dressing-room and stinking the place out.'

'You can bloody well talk,' shouted Wally.

Unperturbed, the animal man crossed the room, fumbled with his flies and urinated in the sink.

'Turn the cold tap on, then. At least turn the cold tap on,' said Hyman from the depths of long experience. He leaned back in disgust and crossed his legs, careful of the crease in his trousers. The chair collapsed under him.

'Oh, deary me,' said Tillson, turning on the hot tap. 'It's not often you see an agent on his arse.'

Wally's prayers were answered when a still ruffled Hyman returned from the bar with the news that Green had condescended to stay for the second house.

'Cost me a few double whiskies, but he says he'll stay in the bar for the second half of this show and catch your act next house. Oh, my bleeding back!' Hyman rubbed himself. 'I ought to sue the management only Brotherton hasn't got enough money to make it worth while. Bloody theatre's a dead loss. Look at the bill this week—Julie Tempest right across the top. She hasn't been a box office draw for years. He hasn't got anything like enough acts this week, either. And the ones he has got aren't much cop—except for you, Wally. But then, I only put you in here to give you a bit of experience. And the lad from the army—what's his name again? Bower?—yers, well, he's a first-timer and he's only in as a favour to you, but Brotherton was glad to take him. Shows how bloody hard up he is.'

Larry came in. 'Jimmy says he thinks he's got rid of most of the stains but you'd better get your suit from the digs anyway. He'll have another go at it when he and George come off from their second spot. He'll work on your spots after he's done his own. That was his joke, not mine.'

'All right, thanks.' Wally was worried.

'Your own suit will be better than the thing you wore last time.' Hyman lit a fresh cigar and looked at Larry. 'Sorry, sonny. I know you did the boy here a favour and we appreciate it. Very nice of you, yers, very nice.' He inhaled deeply and prodded the air with his cigar. 'I'll be watching you tonight and if I like you I'll try and get you a booking somewhere.' The words floated out on a carpet of smoke.

'Preferably somewhere where there's a theatre,' said Larry.

'Of course, of course. Where else?'

'Thanks, oh master.' Larry bowed from the waist and backed out of the room, his hands pressed together under his chin in an oriental gesture of submission.

'Is he taking the piss or something?' Hyman didn't know what to make of this new generation of comics. He spent a lot of time looking for talent at the Nuffield Centre in Piccadilly, where young hopefuls from the services performed on the stage in the canteen for a plate of sandwiches and a cup of coffee. Last week he'd seen one young feller do an act with the back of a chair. Very clever, but would it go down with a provincial audience? That was the acid test. In young Wally he could see a potential Max Miller or a Trinder, a performer whose act the audience could catch on to straight away. If he handled him carefully there was a gold mine in this lad—he was a youngster in the old tradition.

He put his arm round Wally's shoulder. 'Go out there and kill 'em second house, son. I know you can do it—and what's more, I've told Morrie Green you can do it.'

'As long as I've got my suit I'll be fine.' Wally was feeling more confident.

'That's it, look smart. Always look smart.' Hyman shook his client's hand. 'Merde. That's good luck in French—merde.'

'Shit,' said Larry, re-entering.

'What? What?' Hyman turned quickly.

'That's what "merde" means in French. Shit.' Larry smiled politely.

'Yers, I see. Yers.' The agent gave him a suspicious look. 'Well, good luck in any language you like, Wally. Just remember to work well. There's a lot at stake.' He nodded briefly at Larry and puffed his way out.

'Look,' said Wally, 'there's no need to be bloody cheeky with Lou. He can get you a lot of work if he likes you.'

'I wasn't being cheeky, I was being polite. And if I were you I'd get off and get your other suit from the digs before Tillson gets back here. Armsworth's had a hell of a time with him just now. Nearly brought the tabs down on him. He's well pissed.'

186

Wally certainly didn't fancy another encounter with Tillson and was soon up and away. Larry was no more anxious to meet him either, so he followed Wally downstairs.

Tillson passed them on his way up but he was too far gone to notice. He clung to the stair rail for support and was mumbling incoherently to himself.

Larry went over to where Simba lay in his cage, his head against the bars. He looked up slowly at his friend and rumbled a greeting. Larry bent and tickled the animal behind the ear. 'You're not looking too well today, my forest-bred friend. No wonder—working with that drunken old sod.' He crooned to the lion for a while then straightened up and made for the corner. Jimmy and George were just finishing and Sammy and Arthur were preparing Julie Tempest's act. Her husband was patiently explaining the order of the slides to Sammy.

He smiled at Larry. 'Sorry Julie got so upset last night in front of everybody. She flares up like that sometimes, but it's soon over and after all, Lamarr *is* her act. All great artistes are allowed a little temperament now and again.'

'Great artiste!' thought Larry—he must be blind. Then he realized that it was precisely this delusion of Tommy's that enabled him to endure all the humiliations. He wondered what would happen when Tommy ceased to deceive himself.

Joe Armsworth watched the start of Julie Tempest's act and spoke to Larry, keeping his voice low. 'That bloody Tillson's really out of hand. By rights I ought not to let him work, but we're short of time as it is. I don't know what'll happen second house, especially with George Short feeling duff as well.' He looked at his time sheet. 'You were down two minutes early tonight and so was Wally—that's unusual for him, he's generally a few minutes over. You'd both better do your full time second performance or we'll have to have a thirty-minute interval and then the band'll get pissed. If it's not one thing it's another.'

Larry tiptoed away. He had no intention of being caught watching the stripper's act. There was no point in going up to the dressing-room where Tillson might be spoiling for a fight— the girls' room was out for obvious reasons, and he had no wish to intrude on Jimmy and George. Henri Lamarr, that's it. He'd have a chat with old 'Droppo'.

He knocked on the juggler's door and walked in without waiting for permission to enter. The first thing he saw was Henri's hairy behind, the muscles of which were flexing mightily. Around his waist was entwined a pair of legs whose owner seemed to be perched perilously over the sink. There was no doubt about what was going on, but in his confusion Larry pretended not to notice.

'I had no idea you were rehearsing,' he stammered, looking away.

'That's all right,' said Gwyneth. 'Close the door, love. I'm freezing by here.'

Larry shut the door quickly, his heart pounding with shock and embarrassment. By God, that woman gets into some queer positions, he thought. If it's not the stairs it's the sink. Must be very uncomfortable with those taps. Still, as he was finding out rapidly, variety was the spice of life. He decided he needed a stiff drink.

The second house began quietly enough. Larry, who had treated himself to a couple of large Scotches to numb his shock at seeing Henri Lamarr's unscheduled performance, waited for the girls' music to begin before coming down onto the stage. Wally had returned from the digs with his other suit and was practising funny expressions in the mirror; Jimmy was working on Wally's stage suit with salt and water, now and then looking anxiously across at George who dozed fitfully in his chair; Julie Tempest and Tommy were having a one-sided argument about Sunday's travelling arrangements; Henri and Gwyneth were renewing their old acquaintance after a brief time out for cramp; and in the darkness of Simba's cage Tillson lay flat on his back, snoring in drunken slumber. In one outstretched hand was a bottle of Scotch, the contents of which trickled slowly onto the floor of the cage forming a pool which Simba sniffed in tired curiosity. The fumes tickled his nose and he put his tongue experimentally into the liquid. The tingling sensation was pleasurable and he began to lap up the whisky with increasing enthusiasm. Ancient, primeval instincts stirred in his sluggish brain and his tail switched suddenly from side to side. He tried a snarl.

April and June had just started the last part of their routine and were trying to keep up with Dan, who had mentally left the orchestra pit and was now conducting the massed military bands at the Aldershot Tattoo in the greatest performance ever of 'Colonel Bogey'. His eyes closed in ecstasy as the magnificent sound flooded over him.

'He's gone again,' wheezed April to June, three beats behind the music and two behind her partner. She blinked the sweat away and scrutinized the stage for splinters. I haven't got any bloody tweezers, she thought, and instantly dismissed the idea of a splits finish.

The drummer came to their rescue. An arthritic knee—the result of years of trying to combine a day-time job as reader of gas meters in almost inaccessible cupboards with one that required constant use of the patella, twice nightly—finally rebelled. He stopped playing abruptly. Almost immediately the band followed suit and only the pianist, seizing the chance to do a solo piece, carried on. He swept up and down the keyboard, allowing the girls to finish their dance in some semblance of order. They left the stage to a good-natured reception from a nearly full house.

Dan, meanwhile, was still conducting his imaginary orchestra. The band, who would have taken their cue to start from the drummer, could not because he was doubled up in pain from his knee. They looked at each other blankly.

'Get out there quick,' hissed Joe Armsworth. 'Don't wait for your music. Dan's having one of his turns.' He pushed Larry onto the stage with a force that sent the comic reeling into the spotlight.

The audience began to laugh at his entrance and settled down contentedly, prepared for something unusual. Dan had suddenly regained control of himself and was looking sheepishly at his orchestra.

Larry recovered his balance and opened his mouth to speak.

At that moment Simba who had lapped up half a bottle of whisky from the floor, felt something happening to him. From deep within his belly a sound began to travel upwards towards his throat. Millions of years of evolution were in it; all the suffering of his wretched existence, the heritage of a long line of killers, and the pride of his ancestors were in it; and the voice of every lion that had ever been humiliated by man burst from him in one gigantic thunderous roar that spoke for them all.

On stage Larry, who had not yet managed to utter a word, put his hand to his open mouth and said 'Pardon.'

The roar from the audience was almost as great as the one that Simba had produced.

Meanwhile the lion, having asserted his right to be king of the animal world instantly abdicated. The sound had frightened him so much that for a second afterwards he cowered on the floor of his cage in fear at what he had brought forth. He looked around him for comfort. Tillson snored on, oblivious to what had happened. Simba decided he needed Larry and pushing open the door of his cage, which Tillson had forgotten to close, went in search of his friend.

'Bloody hell fire! What was that?' Joe Armsworth looked at Arthur who looked at Sammy.

'I didn't do it,' Sammy said defensively.

'Go and see if that lion's all right,' Joe ordered. 'I've never heard it do that before.'

Sammy went to look at the cage and on the way passed Simba, who, hearing Larry's voice on stage, was making in that direction. Wonder whose dog that is? he thought.

Larry had just eased into his act when Simba padded on from the side opposite Joe's corner.

'Ooh!' The audience drew its breath collectively and held it.

The young comic wondered what he had done for a moment, and then he saw the lion coming towards him. He felt no fear and at no time during what followed did it even occur to him that he might be in danger. To him, the lion was just an overgrown cat.

'Hello,' he said, breaking off his act. 'You're a long way from Trafalgar Square.' And he tickled his friend behind the ears.

'Aah!' The audience breathed out in relief. It was all right, it was all in the act. They laughed delightedly at their own unfounded fear and applauded this clever young man.

At the back of the stalls Morrie Green turned to Lou Hyman in admiration. 'Why, you sly old bugger, you! Now I know why you wanted me to stay for the second house. This lad's brilliant—what a great gimmick! A comedy lion act with no whip, no hoops and no cage. This could be what I'm looking for.'

Hyman took the cigar from his mouth and waved it. 'You know me, Morrie. Always something up my sleeve. He's one of my boys, of course. Got a great future.'

'Even the suit's right,' said Green enthusiastically. 'Not too smart. Gives him that gauche, helpless look which plays directly against the clever way he's handling the lion.'

'My idea, Morrie. My idea. He speaks French, too. That could be handy for working the continent later. He'd do well there.' Hyman already had an itinerary worked out for his new boy.

Larry was getting laughs with everything he did and Simba, glad to be with his friend, sat and watched, purring brokenly, his amber eyes half-closed against the light.

Larry ad-libbed the Cockcroft walk and turned to the lion for approbation. Simba fell over on to his back and waved his legs in the air for his belly to be scratched. The audience yelled with laughter.

'Want to go to sleep, eh? All right, I'll sing you a Welsh lullaby.' He sat down alongside the beast and cradled Simba's massive head in his lap. He began to sing softly, unaccompanied.

Backstage, Joe was in a dilemma. Sammy had rushed over with the news of the open cage, but by that time the stage manager could see what had happened. His training told him that he should bring down the safety curtain to protect the patrons from the escaped lion; yet he could see that Larry had everything under control and any signs of panic might upset things.

He decided to go along with what Larry was doing and hope that when the curtains came across at the end of the act the comic would take the lion back to its cage.

Both wings were full with stage hands and performers. Wally, hearing unexpected laughs coming up the stairs at the start of Larry's act, was first down. He bit his nails nervously as he watched his old mate captivate the public he so wanted to claim as his own. It's a put-up job, he thought savagely. He's been working secretly on this all the week, making friends with the bloody lion every day.

April and June watched with mixed feelings. His ex-fiancée was sneakingly proud of him, in spite of what he had done to her. June gazed expressionlessly at the scene, drumming her fingers thoughtfully on her thighs as she did so.

Jimmy and George felt almost paternal, or at least parental, towards the boy as he worked. George had insisted on coming down to see what was happening, brushing aside Jimmy's protestations.

'If by some miracle we could have had a son, I'd like to imagine that would have been our boy.' Jimmy squeezed George's hand as he said it, real tears in his eyes.

Henri, who was next to go on, cuddled an excited Gwyneth on the opposite to prompt side. He was unaware that Julie Tempest, potentially a far greater danger than Simba would ever be, was observing him.

When Larry began to sing to the lion Joe Armsworth brought the lights on the stage down low, instructing the spotlight from the front to focus on the two figures and leave the rest of the stage dark. It would be easier to get the lion back to his cage if there were not too many lights to confuse it. The unconsciously dramatic effect of Joe's action heightened the poignancy of the scene. As Larry sang 'David of the White Rock' in his strong, sweet tenor, Simba closed his eyes and lay, listening quietly, his head between Larry's knees.

Gwyneth dabbed at her eyes with a handkerchief. 'If it bites him in that position he'll be singing soprano next week,' she whispered to Henri.

'The boy can sing, too.' Morrie Green was very impressed. 'Of course, the lion is the gimmick.'

'He's a natural, that lion, always knew he had a sense of humour.' The agent wondered what had happened backstage. Wally had never told him about the lion working with Larry and he knew that it belonged to Tillson. Whatever had gone wrong, nothing could alter the fact that the boy could be a sensation in London with this act. He'd have to find something else for Wally—perhaps panto in Plymouth. If Morrie liked him better this house he might be able to fix up both clients. He sighed happily and looked back at the stage.

Larry finished his song, the spotlight went out and the sound of the curtains creaking across was clearly heard before a thunderous burst of applause came from the audience.

'Slowly, slowly with those tabs. Don't make any bloody noise and clear the stage as quickly as you can.' Joe gave his instructions in a calm voice. Everybody obeyed without fuss, leaving the stage empty as Larry rose slowly from his sitting position and rubbed Simba's mane gently. 'Come on, old son, let's get you back to your dressing-room.'

The lion grunted affectionately and followed him to the cage. It had been an exciting time but enough was enough and he sank gratefully onto the floor beside a gradually awakening Tillson.

'By bloody hell, your breath's bad, lass,' he said. His hand wandered drunkenly over Simba's flanks. 'And you never even bothered to take your coat off.'

'Well done, lad.' Joe slapped Larry on the back.

The applause had gone on long enough for Larry to return and take a curtain.

'Thanks, Joe.' Larry was curiously calm now it was all over. He had enjoyed the experience and knew now that given a chance he could handle an audience with the best of them.

The lion's entry into his act had been an accident, but in real show business tradition he had made a success out of it.

Before he could accept the congratulations of the others, Lou Hyman came and took him hurriedly to one side.

'Very good indeed. Yers. Very good. I didn't know you did a lion act. I was impressed, sonny. Very impressed.' His cigar waved expansively in the air.

'Just a minute,' Armsworth said, tapping the agent on the shoulder. 'No smoking on the stage, if you don't mind.'

'All right, all right. Let's go up to your dressing-room.' He took Larry's arm and guided him towards the stairs.

Wally stood beside the stage manager and watched them disappear. His agent had ignored him completely.

'Bleeding liberty,' he said angrily. 'He's done this on purpose.

'Done what?' Joe Armsworth could see the envy and frustration in Wally's face, but he didn't know what the young man was insinuating.

'The lion—all that bit. He's been working on that all the week. Tillson must be in on it, too.'

'Don't be a berk. You can take it from me he had no idea what was going to happen. Could have been a nasty bloody moment, that—a wild animal loose on stage. He handled the situation very well, I thought.'

'That thing's not dangerous. It couldn't eat its way out of a paper bag, mate, and you know it.'

'It took a bit of doing, whatever you say. Now go on and get ready for your act. If you're all that good you can do just as well yourself.' Deliberately turning his back, Joe returned to his corner.

Wally thought for a moment and walked to the cage. The stage lighting was dimmed for Henri Lamarr's finale and he could just make out the shape of the lion. If he can do it, so can I, he thought.

'Come on, Simba boy,' he called, putting a tentative finger through the bars.

Tillson bit it hard. 'That'll teach you to play around with my animal. Now get me out of here.'

194

Hyman was pacing up and down in the dressing-room, outlining plans for Larry's career and preparing a rosy future for them both. The younger man listened to the web of words being spun around him, and in spite of his natural caution allowed himself to be carried along by the enthusiasm Hyman was generating. He ventured an idea of his own.

'We could do a film version of Androcles and the Lion.'

'Andy who?'

'Androcles—the Greek who took the thorn out of a lion's paw.'

Hyman considered the possibility and then shook his head.

'Sorry, son. I can't see a film about a Greek vet being big box office.' He resumed his pacing and planning.

'What if Tillson refuses to play ball?' asked Larry, slipping easily into Hyman's jargon.

'He's *got* to go along with us. After tonight he's finished in the business anyway. We'll buy the lion off him and that's that. I'll get somebody from a circus to look after it and all you've got to do is go on and be as funny as you were tonight.'

'Do you mind if I come into my own room?' Wally was coldly angry. His finger throbbed where Tillson had bitten it, and when he had collected his suit from Jimmy Long he found that some of the blood-stains were still visible. He had dressed in the female impersonators' room and had come up to get his hat.

'Do your best now, this time,' said his agent. 'Do as well as this young feller and you've got it made. Morrie's still out there. He's coming round to see this boy—and you, of course— in the interval.'

'Thank you.' Wally was icily polite. He rammed his trilby on and turned the brim up in the front.

'I've been thinking.' Hyman looked critically at his client. 'Perhaps you're a bit too smart. Maybe you should look a bit more like Larry here.' He tried to remember the word Morrie Green had used. 'Grosh.'

'Gauche?' assisted Larry.

'That's it, yers. Grauche. Marvellous to have the gift of languages, innit? Well, good luck.'

'Merde,' said Larry.

'Shit!' snarled Wally in reply, and left the room.

'You're finished!' Joe Armsworth had Tillson by the collar. 'D'you hear me, you drunken sod? Finished!' He shook the man again and let him go. 'Look after young Winston's act for me, Arthur, I'm going to get this bastard slung off the premises.'

Now that the danger was past Joe allowed his anger to spill over—he hadn't realized until Tillson bit Wally's finger that he'd been asleep in the cage. Grabbing Tillson again he half dragged him to the stage door. The fight had gone out of the other man by this time.

'Lemme get me clothes.' Tillson's foul breath nauseated Joe.

'Go on, then, get 'em. But you'd better leave this theatre after that. You can collect your flea-bitten lion in the morning.'

For once Tillson had no answer as he shambled away. He knew that this was the last time he would set foot in any theatre. Nobody would ever book him again. He had worked only sporadically for the past year because his drinking made him more and more of a risk to theatre managements. It was time to pack the bloody game in. The lion was costing him money to feed every week and he was only just getting by on his occasional salary.

He was a ripe victim for Hyman when he swayed into the room for his clothes, and as he accepted the agent's offer of two hundred and fifty pounds for the lion and the cage Larry looked away from the defeat in Tillson's eyes.

Tillson snuffled as he folded the cheque awkwardly and thrust it deep into his trouser pocket. 'That's it, then. All over. Bloody life's finished.' He went to sit down.

'Not there,' Larry said quickly. 'That's the broken one.'

'Come on, come on. Get your clothes and go. We've got business to discuss.' Hyman was impatient to be rid of the man and his smell.

'I'm going, don't worry.' He started picking up his clothes from the various places in the room where he had dropped them. Larry went to assist him.

196

'I can bleedin' manage without your help. Only been in the business a bloody week. Gerroff.' He gathered his stuff together and stood up swaying, the clothes a creased bundle in his arms. 'You've stolen a man's livelihood from him. A lot of good may it do the both of yer.' He summoned up his energy, blew a wet raspberry and shuffled out of show business.

Hyman put a handkerchief to his nose. 'Dirty, smelly individual. Anyway, we've got the lion—you've got an act, and between us we can clean up a lot of money.' He rubbed his hands together.

'Yes, I suppose we can,' Larry said.

'I'd better see how Wally's doing. Morrie may fancy him for something.'

When he rejoined the producer where he stood at the back of the stalls, he was relieved to find that he was laughing at Wally's act.

'He's working better this house,' said Green. 'If I hadn't seen the other lad's act I might consider him for the West End show.'

'Yers. He's a good boy, but he hasn't got the class of the other one. There's a lot to be said for these new army comics. Y'know, I saw one last week do an act with the back of a chair. Very funny.'

'Indeed?' Morrie Green's attention returned to Wally's performance and Hyman was shrewd enough not to interrupt. He motioned to an usherette and asked where Lovegrove was. He kept cigars in his office.

'He went home early tonight. He saw the second house in and went home. It was about half past eight—when the girls came on to start the second show.' She knew all right because she was fresh to the job, and young, with a plump bottom on which a purple bruise was already forming from the manager's pinch. I only started working here last night, too, she thought. If this is show business I don't think I like it.

When Wally had finished, Morrie Green applauded heartily. 'Nice performer as you said, Lou, but I think it's Gower I want. Take me backstage to meet him.'

They went through the pass door at the side of the proscenium arch.

'I'd like to take Mr. Green here to see young Larry Gower,' said Hyman importantly to Joe Armsworth.

'Hello, Morrie.' Joe held out his hand to the producer. 'Long time no see, as they say.'

'Good heavens—old Joe Armsworth!' Green shook his hand delightedly. 'It's a few years since we worked together.' He turned to Hyman. 'We toured with *The Desert Song*, when I was company manager. He could have made a fortune if he'd come down to the West End when I did. Best stage carpenter and property master I've worked with.'

'No regrets, old son. I'm happy on my own little patch. Mind you—one more night like tonight and I'm taking up a milk round.'

'What happened?' Green was interested.

'Didn't you notice? By the bloody centre, we had some goings on back here. Tillson—the lion act man—got pissed and let his animal loose. It was only young Gower's presence of mind saved the day.'

'You mean the lion coming on wasn't planned?' Morrie was incredulous. 'I was told it was all part of the act.'

'Yers, yers. Well, it will be in future. Come and see my boy.' Flustered, Hyman shepherded the producer towards the dressing-room.

'You *are* a crafty bugger.' Green was clearly annoyed.

'I've arranged it. It's all fixed. Tillson's been fired and I've bought the lion.' He opened the door of the dressing-room. 'Here he is—oh, and Wally Winston too.'

The two comics, who had been sitting in silence before Hyman entered, stood up as he introduced the tall, elegant producer.

He shook hands with both of them and congratulated them on their performances.

'A very professional performance,' he said, addressing Wally. 'Made me laugh a lot, and that takes a bit of doing as Lou'll tell you.'

198

'That's right. He's seen 'em all, Morrie has.'

'Thanks, Mr Green.' Wally was suddenly flushed with excitement. The prospect of a West End show seemed to be still on the cards, then. He'd worked as never before, this house, and he'd gone big.

'As for you young Larry, I'd like to have a talk with you if I may. Do you mind, Wally?'

Larry's heart rose as his friend's sank. He was too elated to feel sympathy for Wally who seemed stunned as he left, closing the door slowly behind him.

Morrie perched himself on the corner table and swung one long leg as he considered the lad before him. Lou Hyman looked around for a chair and then, remembering the last time, decided to stand.

'I have to say that what you did tonight was very clever, and, I suppose, very brave. Until my old friend Joe Armsworth told me just now, I thought your act was rehearsed.'

'But I told you, Morrie. I've bought the lion. The boy can do it again. That wasn't just a fluke. It's in him. It's there.' Hyman thumped himself on the chest. 'Oh! I mustn't do that. It's me heart.'

'The whole point is this—as you know, I'm preparing a new West End production and I'm looking for a fresh face to be second comic. Now, if you can reproduce the act I've seen tonight *every* night, then I think you're my boy.'

'Ha, ha! He's my boy, too.' Hyman remembered suddenly that he had no contract with Larry. He'd have to sign him up quickly.

'In view of the fact that I consider this a very important decision to make, for your sake as well as mine, I propose to stop over until tomorrow night to see how you handle things under normal circumstances. Fair enough?'

Larry nodded. It was fair and he knew that he could do it again.

'The awkward entry you made without the play-on music and the lion's roar which you turned into a supposed burp— all that was pure accident, was it?'

Larry nodded again.

'Now that was the perfect kind of entrance for the new show I intend to produce. It was unexpected and the shock element of the lion coming on would be just the job for jaded West End palates. Could you do all that again?' Morrie raised his eyebrows.

'I'm pretty sure I could—except for the lion's roar. I don't think I could guarantee that.'

'Leave that to me,' said Lou Hyman, wondering where he could get hold of an electric prod.

'We won't discuss money at this stage. Let's leave all the sordid details until we've had another look at the act. Anyway, that's Lou's province.'

'That's right. You can leave all that to me.' Lou Hyman was in quickly. Should get a good figure for the act, he thought. I'll give the boy so much and keep back something every week to pay for the lion. Then there's commission, of course. He did some rapid mental arithmetic and smiled.

'Come on, Lou, let's leave the lad alone. He's had quite a time tonight. We'll go back to the hotel and have a bite to eat. Tell you what—we'll meet at lunchtime tomorrow, say twelve thirty here at the theatre and we can have another natter over a drink.'

Morrie Green swung his legs from the table and stood up. 'That's it, then.' He shook hands with Larry. 'See you tomorrow.'

Hyman followed him out of the room, then turned back to Larry and gave a thumbs-up sign.

Larry could hardly believe it. Hyman's talk of the West End big time—even continental tours when things got back to normal—had seemed unreal, but after talking to the down-to-earth producer the impossible was suddenly and miraculously possible. He sat down quickly before his legs gave out. It was the broken chair, but it held together. Everything was going his way at last.

Someone tapped on the door. He opened it and found April standing there.

'I'd just like to say that I thought you were very brave tonight and very funny.'

'Thank you.' Larry was relieved but wary.

'That's all.' She shrugged her plump shoulders and slapped her hands on her sides. Her breasts heaved as she breathed a deep throaty sigh. It's like watching someone doing P.T., thought Larry.

'Let bygones be bygones,' he said cautiously.

'Should auld acquaintance be forgot,' murmured April, moving closer.

'Lang may your lum reek.' He felt foolish.

She was closing in. 'You'll take the high road and I'll take the low road,' she whispered suggestively, reaching out a hand to touch the front of his trousers. 'How's the Loch Ness monster?'

'Shh! You'll wake him,' he said, firmly closing the door on her.

April banged hard on it. 'Our Bill will wake it up with his boot tomorrow,' she shouted angrily and clattered away, coughing and spluttering with rage.

'Phew!' said Larry and sat down heavily. This time the chair collapsed. He wondered if he was pushing his luck a bit. Then he brightened—perhaps I could set Simba on Bill, he thought.

He waited for a moment or two before cautiously putting his head round the door. No one was about and he turned the corner of the landing, smiling to himself.

Gwyneth rushed up to him, her eyes wide with fear. 'That woman's gone mad, boy.'

Julie Tempest came into sight carrying one of Henri's clubs. She was undressed for her act and as she crept menacingly up the stairs Larry was reminded of Dorothy Lamour as a South Seas Amazon, only there was now rather more on view.

'Now, now,' he said feebly.

'I caught her with my man.' Julie was hissing like a snake as she advanced.

'Who, Tommy?' Larry thought it prudent to pretend not to

know what was going on. Behind him Gwyneth cowered, trembling.

'He's not a *man*.' She spat out the words.

Tommy appeared at the foot of the steps with the Reverend Philpotts and Ivor behind him. They all stood looking up in silence.

Julie made a sudden rush for Gwyneth who darted from behind the cover of Larry's back. As the stripper raised the club, Larry shouted in alarm. Philpotts leapt up the steps and putting an arm lock on her, plucked the weapon from Julie's hand. He brought the struggling woman gently but firmly down to where Tommy and Ivor were standing.

'She belongs to you, I believe,' he said politely to Tommy.

'I'm afraid she does.' Tommy's face was grim.

'Then take her.'

Julie stood defiantly before her husband. Suddenly, he struck her with his open hand, once, twice, three times across the face. Her mouth opened wide with astonishment and outrage, but before she could speak Tommy had grabbed her wrist, dragged her into their room and slammed the door.

'I have the feeling that he should have done that a long time ago,' remarked Philpotts calmly. He looked at Ivor. Gwyneth peeped over Larry's shoulder at her bantam spouse who appeared to be about to make a momentous decision.

A groan made them all turn round.

Henri Lamarr was staggering dazedly up the stairs from his dressing-room, blood streaming from a wound in his head. 'She hit me with the club.'

'Poor boy,' exclaimed Gwyneth, going to him. 'He's a martyr to those clubs.'

Ivor's shoulders sagged. His moment had passed. 'Come on back to the Dragon, love. There's nobody looking after the saloon bar and the place is packed.'

The vicar looked at Ivor and shook his head sadly. He had brought the publican to the theatre after Ivor had gone to the vicarage in search of his wife. Philpotts guessed that they would find her here. It was time, he felt, that Gwyneth began to behave.

'I'll be with you now as soon as I've seen to this boy's head. Let's get it under the tap, Henri bach.' She took him back into his room and shut the door.

Ivor hesitated a split second, then opened it. He remained standing against it while Gwyneth attended to Lamarr's wound.

Philpotts smiled slowly at Larry. 'At least it's a start,' he said gently. 'As one door closes another opens.'

Armsworth came tearing up the stairs. 'What the hell's going on? Beg pardon, Vicar. Long and Short are nearly finished and there's no lion act now Tillson's gone.' He banged on Julie's door as he spoke.

'She's coming now.' Tommy's voice came authoritatively from the room.

'Well, tell her to get a move on.' The stage manager dashed off down to his corner.

Tommy came out of the dressing-room. He went into Lamarr's room, took a sheet of paper from his pocket and tore it in half, saying 'There's your contract. You're on your own now.' He shouted 'Get a move on' to Julie and descended the stairs.

'Let's go before she comes out. It wouldn't be right.' The vicar nudged Larry and they followed Tommy down.

Larry politely declined Philpotts's invitation to supper at the vicarage. He wanted time to savour the taste of success and he walked back to the digs slowly, thinking of what he would do when he got to London. How he would give his parents a trip up to the Big City to see him performing in a proper theatre. He'd write tomorrow and tell them all his news. I'll be a bloody star, he thought, a great big bloody star. Of course, old Simba'd get his share of the credit. Hell! I forgot to say good night to the old feller. Don't suppose he'll mind, really, he's only an animal after all.

As he approached the digs he felt less elated and more apprehensive. Ma Rogers would probably have put his suitcase outside the door after his parting remark to her that morning. Even if he was allowed in there'd be little friendly conversation from his fellow performers. He wondered if Wally had got back and how he was feeling now that his big chance had gone down the drain. April would have nothing to do with him—and June never had.

Only Old Man Rogers and the cat would give him any kind of welcome.

He turned off the main street into Windmill Terrace, uncertain what to do. There was a small Ford outside the house and a light shone in the window of the room across the passage from his own. That must be the parlour that no one's allowed to set foot in, he thought. Wonder who the hell's here? He wavered and then, screwing up his courage, he rang the bell.

Mrs. Rogers opened the door to him. Larry braced himself for the imminent tirade.

'Come on in, young Larry,' she said in a refined voice. 'We have a visitor from the Press to see you. My, my, you *have* caused some excitement.' She was obviously speaking for the benefit of someone in the other room. Larry followed her, dumbstruck, into the parlour.

An earnest young man of about his own age, wearing spectacles and an army officer's greatcoat with the insignia of rank freshly removed, stood up as he came in. He transferred the tiny glass of red liquid he was holding to his left hand, and extended his right to Larry.

'Tim Corfield—I'm from the local rag,' he said in an accent which matched the coat he wore. 'The theatre people told me I could find you here.'

'Do sit down, Larry,' urged Ma Rogers, indicating the peacock blue moquette double of the armchair from which the reporter had risen. 'I've been telling Mr. Corfield here about the stars we've had staying with us over the years. In all that time this is the first occasion we've been visited by the newspapers—although my husband and I had our share of publicity when we trod the boards ourselves, of course.' She threw her head back and gave a neighing laugh which rattled the bottle of Empire port wine and its two attendant glasses where they stood on a lace-covered table near the window. The room stank of moth balls and a quick glance around reminded Larry of similar parlours in the terraced houses of his native South Wales, only used for weddings, funerals and the withdrawal of endowment policies.

'A little glass of port for you, Larry?' Ma Rogers tripped across the room with the grace of a hippopotamus and poured him a thimbleful of tawny wine as though she were dispensing vintage champagne.

He took the glass from her. 'Thanks,' he said.

'I expect you need that after your tussle with the lion. Mr. Corfield has told me all about it.'

'Actually, I'd rather like *you* to tell me about it.' The reporter took out a notebook and placed in on his knees. He swallowed the residue in his tiny glass, handed it to Ma Rogers and whipped out a pencil. 'Now then, shoot,' he said, leaning forward.

The landlady stood holding the glass, aware that she had been dismissed. Still she lingered, the hairs in her wart waving like antennae, as though they, too, were searching for a reason to stay.

'Fee, fi, foh, fum!' remarked Larry significantly.

Ma Rogers teetered on her heels with shock. The mantle of gentility fell from her as she glared balefully at him. He looked back at her blandly

'I know when I'm not wanted.' She recovered enough to smile hideously at Corfield and flounced out.

'That's a sort of joke between us,' explained Larry with a grin.

'We must get on, I'm afraid.' The reporter looked importantly at his watch. 'The nationals may use the story and they'll want it quickly if it's to make the first edition.'

There was something about the way he spoke that made Larry suspect that he was new to journalism. As he gave his version of the incident, trying to make light of it without being too self-deprecating, he had to wait several times for Corfield's pencil to catch up with him.

When he had finished, Larry asked the reporter how long

he had been on the job. The young man blushed as he put away his book and pencil.

'Well actually, old chap, this is my first week. I was only demobbed a month ago.'

'I know how you feel.' Larry warmed to this young man who, like himself, was just at the start of his career. 'This is my first week as a comedian.'

He saw Corfield to his car, opening the door for him. A thought struck him. 'By the way, d'you know who wrote the review of our show this week?'

The ex-officer waited until he had started the engine before replying.

'I did.' He revved up and drove off fast.

'Bastard!' shouted Larry after him.

Jack Rogers served him his supper and sat down in the chair opposite, eager to hear about the lion incident. Once again Larry told the story, embellishing the details on the way and making more of it than he had done to the reporter. He also told the old man about his meeting with the producer and the offer which had been made to him, something which he had kept from Corfield.

'Morrie Green, eh?' Rogers whistled through his gums in admiration. 'Wally told us last night he was coming to see *his* act. Now he's out and you're in. Funny old business, this.'

Larry asked where Wally was. He had heard the girls come in when he was talking to the reporter, but he had seen no sign of his fellow comedian.

'He came home before you and went straight to bed. Looked pretty fed up with things. He wouldn't even have any of me steak and kidney pie.'

Larry looked guiltily at his own empty plate.

'April's not eating tonight either. I had a lot of trouble getting that meat from the butcher, too—had to fiddle with the ration books.'

April must be very upset if she's off her food, thought Larry.

The kitchen door opened and June sauntered in, wearing a

dressing-gown. She gave Larry a little smile before addressing Jack Rogers. 'April said she's changed her mind and can she have something to eat in her room?'

'It's against regulations, but I'll take her supper up to her myself. Might be my lucky night.' Jack winked hugely at Larry and prepared a tray for the sorrowing but obviously hungry April.

'I'll help myself.' June moved to the stove and put a small portion of steak and kidney pie on a plate. She came back to the table and sat next to Larry, who was surprised by her friendliness.

'I'll just nip up with this,' said Rogers, taking the tray out through the door.

June toyed with a piece of kidney and gave her neighbour a long look through half-lidded eyes. 'Morrie Green offered you the West End show tonight, I gather.' Her husky voice with its deliberately subdued Northern accent sent little shivers up Larry's spine.

'It's ninety-nine per cent certain, but he's staying over until first house tomorrow night to make absolutely sure that I'm right for the show. Lou Hyman seems to think that it's definitely on.' Larry essayed a modest smile.

'Of course you'll be doing the bit with the lion that you did tonight, won't you? I thought you were awfully brave.' June put down her knife and fork and looked straight into his eyes as she said it.

'Oh—it was nothing.' He swept a hand across the table in a gesture of dismissal and knocked the bottle of H.P. sauce into her lap. Fortunately it had the top on and June let it lie where it fell, making no attempt to move it.

'So sorry,' Larry stammered and made a grab for the bottle. As his fingers closed over it he was aware of the flesh of her thighs under the thin fabric of her dressing-gown. He swallowed hard and put the bottle back on the table.

'Thanks.' She made him feel as if he had just saved her from falling over a cliff.

'If you do get into that West End production you might put a word in for little me. I'm thinking of leaving the act and becoming a showgirl.' Her tone was casual but there was no disguising the ambition in it.

'You should stand a good chance,' said Larry, without the least idea but feeling he was required to say so.

'Wally promised that he would talk to Morrie Green about me, but now it looks as if he won't be able to.' June allowed a tiny frown to settle on her serene forehead for a second.

Larry gallantly chased it away. 'There's no problem. *I'll* do that for you. You see, I'm having a few drinks with him at lunchtime tomorrow.'

'That's very kind of you.' June leaned over and kissed him lightly on the cheek, giving him a good look at her breasts as her dressing-gown fell open.

Larry shot up from the table as Jack Rogers reappeared with April's supper tray. 'I sat there while she ate it,' said the old man. 'It only took her three and a half minutes. What an appetite!' He shook his head in wonder.

'Better get to bed.' Larry faked a huge yawn. Much as he fancied June, she was after all Wally's girl, and he'd done enough damage to the poor bloke's happiness for one day, however unintentionally.

' 'Night.' June smiled sweetly up at him.

'Good night, Larry,' called Jack, clearing up the stove.

'See you in the morning,' said June.

It was precisely three o'clock in the morning when she came to him. She scratched softly on his door with her fingernails.

He got up and went to open it cautiously, expecting to find April. She never bloody gives up, he thought sleepily.

June stood there in her nightie. 'I thought I'd better give you my address before I forget. Then you can let me know if anything comes up.'

Larry gulped and looked down at the front of his pyjama trousers.

'I can give you an answer now,' he whispered. 'Come in, you can save me a stamp.'

The door closed quietly on them.

Saturday

Today, said Larry to himself as he stretched lazily, today is my big day and last night was my big night.

He allowed his mind to wander over the unexpected bonus he had received, and was not very proud of himself for sleeping with Wally's girl. Still, 'to the victor belong the spoils', he thought, determined not to let any cloud of conscience shadow the bright sun of his success.

He arose and dressed. It was eight o'clock and no one was about upstairs when he used the bathroom. There was still no sound by the time he finished his ablutions, and he had managed to get his breakfast over before anyone else came down. Jack Rogers chatted gaily over the tea cups and Larry was content just to sit and listen without having to contribute much to the conversation. When he heard footsteps on the stairs he hurriedly excused himself and bumped into Wally in the doorway.

His army pal-turned-rival looked haggard in the sunlight which streamed through the kitchen window. Larry's natural compassion was stirred.

'You don't look too good, old mate.' He attempted to revive the easy companionship they had shared.

'There's nothing wrong with me that a contract for the West End couldn't fix.' There was no trace of humour in Wally's voice.

'Sorry about that, Wally, but it was none of my doing. I didn't let the lion out.'

'I'm not so bloody sure, mate. You took a lot of trouble to make friends with the thing during the week.'

'Don't be so daft, Wally. Why should I want to do that?'

'Because you're crafty, that's why. You probably arranged with Tillson to throw that meat all over my suit last night, too.'

'It's no bloody use talking to you if that's what you think. You're just a bad loser and that's all there is to it.' Larry pushed Wally aside angrily and went out through the front door.

June came down for breakfast just after Larry had made his exit. She sat down and began buttering a piece of toast. There were dark circles under her eyes.

'Did I hear you and Larry arguing just now?' she asked Wally.

'Yes. He's a wily bugger, that one. There's more to him than meets the eye.'

'There certainly is,' said June contentedly and bit into the toast.

The crisp sunny morning and the prospects for the rest of the day soon dispelled Larry's anger. He decided on a brisk walk up the main street and as he passed a newsagent's shop he remembered his interview with the reporter.

'That'll be tuppence,' said the newsagent handing him the *Daily Express* and the *Daily Mirror*.

He had certainly not made the headlines. The trouble in Greece claimed those in both papers. There was nothing at all in the *Mirror* and it was only after diligent searching through every column of every page of the *Express* that he finally found a three-line paragraph tucked away near the racing results.

'Lion loose' was the heading. 'Last night during a variety show at the Royalty, a Yorkshire Theatre, a lion escaped from its cage. There was no panic and it was soon captured.'

That was it—no name, no mention of his part in the affair at all. He crumpled the paper and threw it on the ground in disgust.

Overhead the sun disappeared behind a bank of clouds.

Larry arrived at the theatre at twelve fifteen soaked to the skin. In his angry departure from the digs he had forgotten his coat and when the sun went in he regretted his haste. It became very cold and he had tried to while away the time in a cheerless café where he ordered a cup of tea which, when it eventually arrived, matched the temperature outside. Never mind, old son, he told himself, it'll be caviar at the Ritz soon. His spirits had risen as he pictured how his life-style was going to change. Now, despite being caught in the shower on his way from the café, he was happy as he asked the stage door-keeper for his key.

'You'd better go and see Joe Armsworth before you do anything. He said to send you along to him as soon as you came in.'

Larry whistled his way down under the stage and knocked on the stage manager's door.

'The door's open,' called Joe. 'Come in. I'm afraid I've got some bad news for you.'

The young comedian's heart missed a couple of beats. 'It's not my mother, is it? She was fine when I heard from her this week.' His face was white with anxiety.

'No, no, it's nothing like that. Let's go upstairs.'

Larry followed him up onto the stage; his knees felt weak. Joe stopped in front of Simba's cage.

'Take a look, lad. The poor old bugger's had it. Last night's excitement must have been too much for him.'

Larry knelt down by the bars and peered in. The lion lay on his side, stiff in death. The amber eyes, half-open, stared sightlessly at him. He reached through and stroked the tangled mane, coarse and sawdust-covered beneath his fingers.

'I didn't even have the decency to stop by and say good night to him,' he said quietly. He had seen death many times in battle, sudden, violent and messy, and had become almost callous at the sight, feeling only relief that it was someone else and not him. Yet he was curiously affected by the flea-bitten form stretched out before him, stripped of any dignity it might have possessed, a husk of skin and protruding bones. If there was a heaven for lions he hoped that his old friend was there now, majestic and proud, stalking a herd of Tillsons through an eternal green jungle.

He stood up. 'When did he die?' he asked.

'The cleaners found him like that when they came in this

morning. He must have gone sometime in the night.' Joe looked into the cage and smiled. 'Still, he had a great night to finish on.'

The full implications of Simba's death began to hit Larry. There would be no contract for the West End now, surely. No big time. No continental tours. The dream world he had built up in his mind collapsed like a pack of cards and he put his hand to his head and groaned.

'Hello! Hello!' Hyman advanced towards them, his cigar forming the centrepiece of a beaming smile.

'Oh no!' said Larry and groaned afresh.

'Put that bloody cigar out,' said the stage manager sternly. 'On second thoughts, you'd better take a big puff to steady your nerves and then have a look at this.' He pointed to the cage.

'What do you mean?' Hyman sensed trouble from the look of Larry's face. He came forward and peered into the cage.

'Is it sick? I'll get the best vet up from London for him. That Greek feller—what's 'is name? You mentioned him, Larry.' He waved his cigar frantically.

'Too late, he's dead.' Armsworth took the wet Havana from the agent's suddenly limp fingers. 'I'll put this out for you.'

'Dead? He can't be. I bought him, he's mine.' It was inconceivable that an animal he had paid two hundred and fifty pounds for only the previous night could have played such a dirty trick. He shook the bars of the cage in a sudden frenzy. 'Get up!' he shouted hysterically.

'Don't be an idiot. It's not Resurrection Day—and anyway, you're no Gabriel.' Morrie Green, smart in a grey overcoat and black Homburg, flicked Hyman's shoulder with his glove to make him move aside and looked down at the lion's body.

'Poor old chap,' he said. He turned to Larry who was already coming to terms with the situation. 'And you, too. This calls for a drink. Let's go to the pub and talk things over.'

Hyman slowly released his hands from the bars. 'What am I going to do with a dead lion act?' He spread his arms in supplication and looked up into the unfeeling flies.

'It's obvious that everything has changed now that Simba's

gone.' Morrie Green handed the glum, still damp Larry a large Scotch.

Hyman took his brandy and mournfully swirled it round, looking into the glass as though he might find the solution to his problem there.

The producer paid for the drinks and sipped his Martini. 'Cheers,' he said.

Larry raised his drink in acknowledgement and Lou Hyman lifted his and downed the contents quickly.

'Look, Morrie,' he said, putting the empty glass on the bar. 'We can get another lion. Get a feller to train it—'

'Be sensible, Lou. You'd never get another animal as docile as that one. They're aways so unpredictable. You know that. It was the way it looked at Larry when he was working, the affection, the rapport between the two of them. You could never reproduce that with another lion. It was a once-in-a-lifetime combination. I'm sure you'll agree, Larry.'

Larry was leaning against the bar listening in silence to the requiem for his dead hopes. 'That's true, Mr. Green. It's no use pretending it could happen again.'

'How about doing the same act with a dog? A big dog. An Alsatian, or a St. Bernard, even?' The agent was thinking fast, trying desperately to salvage something from the wreck. 'I know—a Great Dane! They look a bit like lions. Put a false mane on it and turn the stage lights down a bit—they'd never know the difference.'

'I'm no good with dogs at all,' said Larry, shaking his head. 'I can handle cats OK but dogs don't seem to like me.'

'Lou, you're talking nonsense. We agreed that the lion was the gimmick I wanted. With all due respect to the boy here, no lion—no deal.'

'What about Wally, then?' Hyman had almost forgotten his other client. 'You liked him very much the second time, you said so yourself. You were laughing at him.'

Morrie rubbed the side of his nose slowly. 'I've been giving him some thought, as a matter of fact. He went very well last night, didn't he? It might be worth while staying on to see him again tonight. Excuse us for a minute, Larry.' The producer smiled briefly and turned away to talk to Hyman.

Larry drank the remainder of his Scotch and left the pub.

In the theatre Joe Armsworth and Lovegrove were having a battle royal. The theatre manager, who had left early on Friday, had remained unaware of the evening's events until the next morning when Fred Brotherton rang him at home.

'What the hell's going on there? Why didn't you inform me that a lion was loose? If I hadn't been looking for the result of the three thirty at Ripon I wouldn't have known what was happening in me own bloody theatre,' Brotherton had bawled.

Lovegrove had been shaken at first, but then he realized that he now had Armsworth exactly where he wanted him.

'I'm afraid I was not told myself, Mr. Brotherton. It was my early night, as you know. Friday has always been my early night. The stage manager is at fault. It was his responsibility to let me know immediately.'

After more conversation with the owner, Lovegrove had left for the theatre with a song in his heart. He had gone backstage to find Joe Armsworth, armed with Brotherton's angry instructions to fire him if he had no satisfactory explanation.

They now faced each other in Joe's cubby-hole. The stage manager was losing his temper.

'I've already told you that there was no bloody point in calling you. Nobody was in any danger—that lion couldn't have harmed a fly.'

'Mr Brotherton thinks differently. He's had the police on to him asking why they weren't sent for.' Lovegrove was quivering with the sense of power Brotherton's authority had given him. 'They said a very nasty situation could have developed if the audience had panicked, and there should have been men standing by.'

The stage manager was well aware that his proper duty was to call the police in such circumstances, but he had taken a gamble on Larry being able to handle the lion.

'Young Gower had the animal in complete control all the time he was on.' Joe knew that his explanation sounded thin.

'How did it get out in the first place? You're supposed to see that every precaution is taken back here to protect the public. You've always run everything your way backstage and now you've over-reached yourself.' Lovegrove danced in triumph, his shoes squeaking as he hopped from foot to foot. 'You're fired! Mr. Brotherton said I could do it if you had no reasonable explanation.' He was almost in tears with sheer joy. 'And you haven't. You're fired!'

'And you're coming with me, you nasty old devil!' Joe reached into his desk and drew out the two letters that Larry had received. He waved them at Lovegrove.

'I work for your brother-in-law now and again—making coffins. Carpentry's always been my trade and I can make a few extra quid that way in me spare time. I remember when he was getting them anonymous letters accusing him of flogging brass handles and other accessories after cremations. He was a very worried man at the time and he had every reason to be.' Joe winked at Lovegrove, who had gone rigid. 'Still, it wasn't very nice for him and we were all glad when they stopped. He never said who it was, but when I heard about the letters some of the artistes were getting here, I began to have me suspicions. I could never prove anything though, because all the letters were torn up on the spot, or you took them for "investigation".'

Lovegrove's mouth dropped open and his face turned a greenish colour.

'However, young Gower showed me the couple he got. It was simple to get hold of one of the letters your brother-in-law received. He thought one of us who worked for him might be responsible and he kept a letter in his office to compare with our handwriting. I managed to get hold of it yesterday.'

Joe took a folded piece of paper from his inside pocket and shook it in Lovegrove's face. 'Remember it? It's in the same writing as these.' He picked up the other two letters. 'We don't have to say any more, do we? Brotherton wouldn't like to think that his house manager is perverted, any more than he'd like to think his stage manager is guilty of a slight dereliction of duty, now would he?'

Joe put the letters away in his desk and locked it. He turned to face the shaking Lovegrove. 'In chess terms, I think you can call it checkmate, mate. You tell Brotherton that you're quite satisfied with my explanation and I'll just forget about these little notes.'

Lovegrove nodded dumbly, and as he walked away the squeaking of his shoes sounded muffled in defeat.

When he had gone Joe Armsworth opened the desk and took out the folded piece of paper. He unfolded it and chuckled. I'm bloody glad he didn't ask to see it, he thought. Still, all the rest was true.

He sat down at the desk with the paper before him and took out a stub of pencil from his waistcoat pocket. 'Let's try and work out a new running order for the second half, in case George is off,' he said out loud to himself and began writing on the blank page.

Larry walked back to the digs heedless of the rain which soaked his suit. Jack Rogers opened the door to him.

'They're all out,' he said. 'Even the missus, thank God.' He looked at Larry. 'Let me dry those damp things for you by the fire. Had some bad news, have you?'

He clucked sympathetically as Larry told him what had happened. The comedian sat listlessly on a chair in his under-clothes as the old man put his suit to dry on a clothes-horse in front of the fire. He refused the offer of food, and when his clothes were reasonably dry he went to his room to put them on. When he had closed the door he changed his mind about dress-ing and instead crept under the eiderdown and fell asleep.

He awoke at half past four unrefreshed by his sleep, dressed, and packed his case, tying it with the rope.

Jack Rogers was dozing by the fire when he went into the kitchen to pay his bill, the cat purring in his lap. He yawned and got to his feet.

'Sorry to see you go, son. Must have been a good experience

216

for you this week. You had your bit of glory last night—that don't happen too often to somebody who's only just started in the business.' He gave Larry his change and returned his ration book. 'You've missed the wife. Don't suppose that'll worry you, though. Buck up, mate, things could be worse, you've still got your health and strength.

Larry sneezed violently.

'Anyway, look after yourself. I'll follow your career, don't worry.' They were at the front door and Rogers opened it for Larry. 'If I was you, though, I'd try a spot of juggling in the act. People like a bit of juggling, y'know.' He waved briefly and shut the door.

Larry turned up his collar against the rain, and lifting his suitcase, left Windmill Terrace for the last time.

'More bloody trouble,' gloated the stage door-keeper. 'George Thingummy—you know, the little pouf—he's been taken to hospital.'

'Oh dear,' said Larry, his numbed senses beginning to come alive again. 'How is he?'

'Pretty bad, they say. The other pouf will tell you—he's up in his room.'

Larry put his suitcase in his own dressing-room, which was empty, then went down and tapped on Jimmy's door.

'Come in.' Jimmy's voice was choked. He was sitting in the chair in his ordinary clothes, a handkerchief in his hand. He had obviously been crying.

'Sorry to hear about George. How is he?' Larry asked.

'Not terribly well, I'm afraid.' Jimmy tried to keep his voice steady. 'He hasn't been too good all week, as you know.' He cleared his throat with an effort. 'Well, last night he was in terrible pain and he wouldn't let me get a doctor. Then this morning when he began bringing up blood I had to send for one. He came and took one look at him and rushed him into hospital straight away. Of course, I went in the ambulance with him and I stayed until they took him into the operating theatre. They told me there was nothing I could do, so I came along here.' He stood up and moved restlessly around the room. 'Apparently a piece of shrapnel was left in him and it's been gradually working its way into his lower bowel. Anyway, they're going to try to remove it, but they don't give him more than a fifty-fifty chance of surviving the operation.'

He broke down completely and began sobbing on Larry's shoulder. For a moment the comedian stood in embarrassed indecision, then, compassionately, he took the older man in his arms and comforted him.

Jimmy slowly gained control over himself and stood back. He wiped his eyes and blew his nose hard. 'Thank you. I'm glad that you were here. I'm fine now, honestly. They need me to do something in the show tonight. I worked with Tommy— Julie's husband—years ago in revue, so we'll revive some of the old stuff for the spot in the first half, and I'll do a solo in the second. Would you ask Joe Armsworth to come up and see me?'

He began taking off his coat. 'The show must go on, dear, as they say in the pictures,' he said with a trace of his old mockery. 'Otherwise we don't get paid.'

Wally was in the dressing-room when Larry returned from Jimmy's errand. Lou Hyman was with him, giving him instructions about how he should work.

'This is your big chance, boy, I'm telling you. Morrie's already half sold on you—all you have to do is go out there and—'

'Look smart,' interrupted Larry, stabbing an imaginary cigar in the air. '*Always* look smart.'

'Cheeky young bastard,' snorted Hyman. 'You cost me two hundred and fifty nicker for a dead lion and a cage.'

'Leave him alone, Lou.' Wally was sparkling again. 'It wasn't his fault the lion died.' He grasped Larry's arm. 'Sorry I was so narky last night, me old amico. You know how it is.'

I do, thought Larry, oh I do.

He managed a weak 'That's OK' and began to get ready for his act. Behind him Lou Hyman was working on his boy like a trainer on a champion boxer, telling him how he should time his gags.

218

'Wait for the laugh, Wal. Wait for the laugh.'

Wally was looking at himself in the mirror as he groomed his hair with his silver brush.

June clattered in and gave Wally a big hug. 'If I don't see you before you go on, good luck for the act.'

Wally hugged her in return—holding her carefully so that she wouldn't stain the suit with her make-up.

'If Morrie Green takes me on for the West End I'll insist he takes you, too.' Wally winked over her shoulder at Hyman.

'Of course he will,' said the agent, winking back.

'Thanks.' June kissed him and left without even a glance in Larry's direction.

'That's not a bad idea, though—can she sing? I've got an idea for a scene.' Hyman was suddenly inspired. 'If she can sing "I'm only a bird in a gilded cage", I could persuade Morrie to have her brought on in this cage—you know, the one I've got downstairs. I could have it painted gold and a feller in a leopard skin could pull it on.'

'Why not a lion skin?' said Larry. 'You've got one of those downstairs, too.' He blew one of Tillson's raspberries and felt better as he went downstairs.

Tommy was talking to Joe in the corner, explaining what he and Jimmy meant to do for their act.

'I can get into George's drag OK. We're about the same size. Don't worry about music, it's all patter anyway.' He seemed a different person since he had given Julie her come-uppance the previous night. At least some good has come from the week, Larry thought as he went on.

Morrie Green watched his act from the back of the stalls and saw Larry's inexperience more clearly now that the lion was not with him. There was a lot of promise there, he could see that, and he had a good singing voice. He made a mental note to keep an eye on the lad. Perhaps in a few years' time he might be worth a place in one of his productions.

He had no doubt about Wally's act. From the moment he came on he had the audience in the palm of his hand.

'Look at him. Listen to those laughs.' Hyman kept nudging as he watched.

'All right, Lou, I give in. He's the one for the show. Let's you and me talk business in the bar.'

Hyman clapped him on the back. 'What did I tell you when we came up in the train yesterday? He's the lad you're looking for, I said.'

'Shut up, Hyman, you make me bloody sick sometimes.' The producer was suddenly angry.

'What did I say? What did I say?' asked the agent querulously as he followed him to the bar.

Larry wandered around backstage after his act. He watched in the wings while Tommy and Jimmy did their spot.

'There's a bloody trouper for yer,' said Joe Armsworth. 'You've got to forget your troubles when you're on there.'

'What if you're a dancer and you've got a double rupture?'

'Ah, then you've got your hands full,' replied the manager.

Elwyn Thomas was waiting for Larry at the stage door in the interval.

'I haven't got much time. I'm off to a parents' night at the school. Can't wait to see what Cockcroft's father looks like, indeed.'

He handed Larry a large envelope. 'There's some music in there, like I promised. And also a script I've written with you in mind. If you like it, let me know. My address is inside the envelope. I've also put some addresses and phone numbers of some friends of mine in London. One of them's a BBC producer —very junior, mind, but he might help to get you an audition. They're doing lots of shows for the services—might be something in one of them for you. That's why I've written the script as for radio, you see. If you use it on the wireless there's a bill inside, too! Anyway, good luck, boyo. Been great seeing you.'

The schoolteacher gripped his hand, saluted, about-turned smartly and went.

Larry read through the script with increasing excitement. It was crisp and funny and he could see himself delivering it. He decided there and then that he would take the train down to London that night. He could stay at the Victory Services Club or the YMCA, visit some agents, phone the BBC bloke and try his luck. He had some money left in his post office savings book, and there was his salary to come tonight.

'What time are the London trains?' he asked the stage door-keeper. The one-armed man consulted the time-table on the wall beside him.

'There's one at ten fifteen, change at Crewe.'

'Thanks,' said Larry and bounded up the stairs.

He went in to see Jimmy and ask if he had any more news about George. He could see from his smile that things were better.

'He's out of the operating theatre and the ward sister told me on the phone just now that she thinks he'll be all right. They've put him on the danger list, but she said not to be too worried about that.'

'Thank God for that, then.' Larry was happy for this tall man who had been so kind to him since he came to the theatre. 'I'll say goodbye now, because I'm getting the ten fifteen train down to London tonight. I've got a few addresses and phone numbers of agents, so I'll have a go at finding some work.'

'You'll find it, dear. Don't expect too much at first. You were lucky last night to have tasted success so soon—even if it didn't last long. Learn what you can from the old pros like me and George, but do things your way. Because that's what matters in the long run—originality.' He took Larry's hand. 'I bet you were afraid I was going to kiss you goodbye.'

Larry laughed. 'You're not my type—too bloody tall.'

He met Henri Lamarr in the passage and said farewell to him. The Frenchman was sporting a plaster on his head.

'Au revoir, old Welsh friend. Things are working out well for me now. I have finished with Julie Tempest and they will let me do my muscle act tonight in the second house so that Jimmy can go to the hospital to see George.' 'No more clubs soon.'

'Give my love to Gwyneth,' said Larry.

'She is not at the pub today. She and Ivor, they go down to South Wales for a holiday, they tell me. What a woman, eh?' Henri dug Larry in the ribs.

'Does a lot of housework,' said Larry, leaving. 'Always slaving over the sink or working on the stairs.'

Lamarr's laugh followed him up to his room, which was empty, though traces of Hyman's cigar remained.

He hadn't changed out of his stage suit, so he had only to freshen up his make-up. When he'd done this he put the grease-paint in his case, wrapped in newspaper. Mind the suit, he thought. Mustn't get grease-paint on the suit when I pack it.

Lovegrove came in with the pay packets. He put Larry's money on the table.

'Fifteen pounds, less ten per cent commission, that's thirteen pound ten. Sign here.' He produced a piece of paper and a pencil.

'Would you like it in capitals, the way you write to me?' Joe had told him about their row.

'Just sign the bloody thing,' snarled Lovegrove.

Larry signed with a flourish. 'There.'

The manager picked up the receipt and stuffed it in his pocket. He started to say something but saw the glint in Larry's eyes and thought better of it. Larry shut the door on him quickly, knowing that he might hit the man if he lingered.

He suddenly remembered Bill—April's brother—who was supposed to be turning up to hit *him*. Mama mia! The music for the end of Julie's act came wafting unmelodiously up the stairs. That meant first house was over. If he could only survive until the end of his spot in the second performance, he would be out of the theatre in a flash and into the station.

The stage would be the safest place to hang about. He nipped down the stairs and whiled away the time talking to Arthur and Sammy. Quarter of an hour to go, he thought, looking at the clock in Joe's corner.

He ventured into the hallway by the stage door. 'Anybody been in asking for me?' he called.

The stage door-keeper shook his head.

Larry whistled tunelessly and went back on stage. Joe was preparing the set for the last show.

'Sorry it's nearly over, son?'

'Yes and no,' said Larry. 'I'm glad I've had the experience, but I'm not sorry it's nearly over. I want to go away and think about things—and look for more work at the same time, of course.'

'You'll make it, lad. You've got it there, but, as I said, it's rough yet. Polish it and work on it.'

'I'll do that, Joe. Thanks for being so bloody patient with me.'

'That's me job, Larry. I like seeing youngsters get on, provided they're willing to take advice. You'll need your band parts before you go. I'll get Sammy to collect them from Dan after your act and leave 'em at the stage door.'

Larry thanked him. He heard the sound of the girls' tap shoes coming down the steps and melted into the shadows.

Leave well alone, old son, he said to himself. He'd no wish to become involved in saying goodbye to either of them. June wouldn't want to know now that his West End chance had gone, and April might take it as a sign of weakness.

He watched them limber up for their act and smiled. At least two of his performances this week had been well received.

'Away you go,' said Armsworth when his turn came, and Larry went out confidently to face his last audience of the week.

They were good to him and he worked well as a result, playing them along, making them wait for the laugh and punching it home when it came.

Joe shook his hand when he came off. 'That's your best this week—except for last night with the lion.'

'Thanks again, Joe. I'm off to catch the train as soon as I've changed.'

'Call in when you're passing,' said Joe. 'If not, don't come back until you're top of the bill. Go on—get your train.' He turned away and gave Henri Lamarr's lighting cue.

'There's a parcel been left here for you while you was on,' said the one-armed door-keeper. 'The vicar left it for you.' He handed Larry a carrier bag and a note.

'Nobody else been asking for me?' asked Larry anxiously.

'No,' replied the other man, going back to his newspaper.

'Thank God for that,' Larry breathed. He took the note and left the carrier bag with the door-man. He would pick it up or the way out.

He read the note from the vicar. It enclosed the ACU form and wished him well in the future. 'I'm glad you have become disentangled from your clinging vine. Perhaps in future you will think twice before tampering with a lady's affections—that's a joke, of course. "Happy is the man that findeth wisdom and the man that getteth understanding"—Prov. Chapter 3 verse 13. P.S. Betty thought you'd like some Welsh cakes.'

He put the letter and the ACU form away and though about the message. This was no time for soul-searching, though Retribution might be around the corner.

The dressing-room was full of Hyman's cigar smoke. Both he and Morrie Green were too busy talking to Wally about hi part in the new show to take any notice of Larry's entrance. He took his case and folded his street clothes into it. His coat would cover his stage suit.

' 'Bye, Wal,' he called.

Wally looked up from his conversation and waved. 'Good luck, mate,' he said.

Green nodded pleasantly. Hyman went on talking.

Larry shut the door for the last time and went into the passage. A huge man in police uniform was rounding th corner. He was broader even than Lamarr, and Larry had no doubt who he was.

'I'm looking for a Barry Bower,' said the giant.

Larry thought quickly. 'He's in there,' he said. 'You can' miss him, he's a little fat feller smoking a cigar.'

'Thanks,' said Bill grimly.

Larry shot down the stairs with his suitcase, grabbed th carrier bag of food and his band parts from the stage door keeper and ran into the rainy night.

Outside he began to laugh. He did a little Cockcroft wal and headed quickly for the station.

224